Nobody Has To Know

By

Frank Nappi

ALSO BY FRANK NAPPI

ECHOES FROM THE INFANTRY
THE LEGEND OF MICKEY TUSSLER
SOPHOMORE CAMPAIGN

To learn more about Author Frank Nappi
www.franknappi.com

This is a work of fiction. All of the characters, organizations, and events portrayed within are either the product of the author's imagination or are used fictitiously.

Praise for Nobody Has to Know

"A haunting, briskly-paced page turner that explores the darkest recesses of the human psyche while propelling the reader through an intricate series of hair-raising twists and turns. Nobody Has to Know is a masterfully written tale that is expertly told. Frank Nappi knows how to entertain the reader from start to finish."

- Nelson DeMille, #1 New York Times Bestselling Author

"Nappi's prose tells a beautifully chaotic story of love and lust, suspense and madness - some of the greatest elements of truly powerful, absolutely moving drama."

- Christy Tillery French, author of *The Bodyguard series*

"A powerful, page-turning thriller that will leave readers riveted and wanting more."

– Armand Mastroianni, producer/director of *A Dark Plan*

"Frank Nappi is a master wordsmith of many genres. Hugely successful with his first three novels, he now takes the plunge into the dark literary waters with Nobody Has to Know... everything a thriller should be."

- Susan Alcott Jardine, author *THE CHANNEL: Stories From L.A.*

"From award winning author Frank Nappi comes a roller-coaster ride into the anarchy of a personal inferno... A nightmarish and terrifying tale. *Nobody Has To Know* is a bewitching thriller that will keep you guessing until the final act!"

- Barbara Watkins, author of award-winning *Hollowing Screams*

"One doesn't simply read a Frank Nappi story, one lives and breathes it. In this gripping tale of a teacher's forbidden obsession, Nappi's artful language catapults the reader into his story as few writers can. This nationally-acclaimed author keeps pulling out surprises and pulling us in."

 - Betty Dravis & Chase Von, co-authors of *Dream Reachers*

ONE

Cam knew he should not have encouraged her -- should have never pursued her. It was the first thing he was told before he took the job. It wasn't so much an admonition as it was a statement of fact.

"Remember, you can be friendly with these kids, but you are not their friend," his mentor, a seasoned veteran of twenty nine years, warned. "Especially the girls. That's just trouble waiting to happen."

Cam shrugged it off. He had heard that warning before. Besides, he had no interest in teenage girls, especially the ones sitting in his classroom.

"No problem there John," he had explained at the time. "I have it covered. I have no time for any of that. I'm involved already. College sweetheart. It's cool. Really. We've been together for years."

"Is that right?" John commented. "Then what's the deal? I mean, twenty five isn't old friend, but seems to me you should have taken it to the next level by now."

Cam flushed and stood more awkwardly now. John marveled at his protégé's attempt to free himself from the moment's grasp.

"I don't know," Cam replied. "Why does everyone ask me that? I really don't know. I guess the timing has never been quite right." He paused briefly, gleaning some obscure meaning behind the raised eyebrows of his friend and mentor, then continued to speak, like an actor who had just been cued from offstage.

"But that should change soon. Hayley and I will probably be engaged by Christmas."

Cam should have remembered John Volpe's words. He should have listened to logic, and tucked away those feelings. He should have done a lot of things, like remembered his master's thesis – the one that explored La Femme Fatale. He knew all the names. The sirens of Greek Mythology. Mata Hari. Memo Paris. Daisy Buchanan and Mattie Silver. And of course there was Nabokov's Lolita. She was the one he remembered most. "All of them," he had written, "are so very beautiful, so alluring, yet deadly – life draining vampires who possess the power to transfix the opposite sex with their feminine wiles, leaving these spellbound males weak, vulnerable and ultimately barren." He should have remembered. He should have considered how much he loved teaching and his genuine affection for everyone at Hillcrest High School. He tried. But all he could see was her. For some reason, all he could think about was her long dark hair, and what it would be like to touch it – to let the soft strands cascade across his own body. And the wet shine of her lips. My God, what would it be like to feel those as well? To press his to hers. She was so beautiful, so exquisite, so young.

So many times, during their little chats before and after class, he stared into her blue eyes, marbled with gray flecks, and was lit by her electric smile, all the while wondering how it was that this universe managed to give birth to such a perfect creature. She *was* perfect. She was just as Nabokov had described his Lolita -- the nymphet, a mystical, magical, sweet smelling creature budding with sexuality, ripening on life's vine, right before his very eyes. Yes, the forbidden fruit. Oh how she tortured him. The curve of her mouth; her slender waist and fully formed hips, both attenuators to the rhapsody of her walk; her sweet smell and the softness of her tan skin. Everything about her called to him desperately. It was a familiarly paralyzing feeling. The girl was also familiar. He could recall, as a kid, humid summer evenings with his friends, racing around on camp lawns under a gray sky that had just begun to soften into the pitch of night. Freeze tag was the game most often played. Some complained it was a bit juvenile, but there were all sorts of variations, including a wrinkle that included their favorite alcoholic drink of choice.

The rules of the game were basic: once touched, you could not move. You remained frozen in place, sometimes drinking to excess, until someone freed you from your current state. He could still remember waiting, silent and still, for what seemed sometimes to be an eternity. It was uncomfortable. Cam's knees would ache and his arms would burn. It was interminable. He was always tempted to transgress, to flex his muscles under the cover of the deepening night. He never did. Even though he *could* move, he never did, for the spirit of and passion for the game always trumped logic and reason.

He played it all the time, with Maleigha. She was his first love. It was the summer before he began high school when he met her. She had just turned fourteen, and was visiting her cousin, who happened to be his next door neighbor. He was slightly older and they had spent that entire summer together, swimming and riding bikes. He often thought, even now, how odd it was how they seemed to click instantly. She came from a Latin American family that lived in a trailer in New Jersey. She was a singer, and a lover of jazz music. He was just a kid from Long Island who loved the Mets. Their cultures and upbringing differed greatly as well. Yet somehow, none of it mattered. It was part of the magic.

The days that summer were filled with innocent fun with a group of others. They sat around many afternoons listening to their favorite tracks from *Rage Against the Machine* and *The Smashing Pumpkins* while playing Super Mario 64 on his Nintendo. When they tired of that, the world outside offered more frivolity, including whiffle ball, Marco Polo, tag, and man hunt. They were rarely at a loss for entertainment. Those were good days. But night time was really special. At night, it was all about Maleigha.

Often, Cam would take her for walks through the nature preserve not too far from his house. She loved the sound of the crickets, and the gentle trickle of the shallow waterway that snaked its way through the underbrush. It was there they would hold hands and talk about the summer and the beach and about their feelings for each other.

"This is very different from where I come from," she said, marveling at the moon through the treetops. "I really love it here."

"Is Long Island really that different from New Jersey?" he asked.

She looked at him with bubbling amazement.

"Yeah, just a little," she answered, shaking her head playfully.

"Well, it's not that far," he said. "Maybe your family can move here."

She never looked so sad.

"I don't think so Cam."

"Well, you never know," he continued. "Besides, you can always visit, right?"

She was thinking of her mother, and the last thing she said to her before Maleigha left.

"Have good time at Carla's, behave yourself Maleigha, you hear? No trouble, okay? But by time you get back, we be all set to leave for Ecuador. No worries mi hija. It be fine."

It will be fine, her mother kept saying. Somehow, Maleigha just could not see how moving to the other end of the earth would ever be fine. Not now. Not ever.

"Sure Cam," she said through glassy eyes. "I can visit."

He thought of Maleigha often. It was eleven years since he had last seen her, and he was now a twenty-five-year-old man with a beautiful fiancée and a promising career. Time had altered many things for Cam, but Maleigha remained a part of him. And although life had offered him a promising path to follow, other thoughts were now surfacing as well, like how this new nymphet of his, Nikki, knew very well, on some level, just how enticing she was. That's why her sweaters fell the way they did across her round breasts, and why her clothes left very little unknown about just how shapely she was. It was the same reason why she twirled her hair when she laughed and why she giggled flirtatiously every time she said hello to him in the hallway. She was no child. No way. And he was no longer a man in control, but a tortured soul, slave to her essence, lost always in beautiful, woeful distraction.

There were moments when it was almost more than he could bear. When she touched his arm playfully, or blinked her eyes in that coquettish way of hers, it rendered him in agony. His heart would rebel feverishly, and his reality would divide instantly into two sectors – the ecstasy felt from the passing of electricity through that touch or flirtation and the devastation of a world that simply forbade any further advance. Those fires of love, or perhaps lust, burned wildly in the chasm between hemispheres and transformed quickly into waves of passionate thought. What would it be like, he wondered, to press his body up against hers? Just once. To feel, with all his being, her tight, silky skin next to his. It was a desire that ruled his soul.

Even so, he should have known better. Although only seven years separated the two, it should never have gone any further. It should have ended with those harmless flirtations, like their conversations about things they both loved, like the Mets and

Kanye West, and the way he always saved her a piece of his Orbit gum or the many visits he made to Carvel, where she worked part time, just because he was "in the neighborhood."

"You again?" she said laughing. "This is the third time this week. You sure must love ice cream."

"What can I say Nikki," he answered. "I'm addicted."

Yes, he should have recognized the signs and just walked away. But he didn't. Somewhere, deep within the darkest chambers of his soul, lurked the feeling that he had to have her – that his body would not survive in her absence. It was an uncompromising pang. Not even John's advice and knowledge of all that he could lose were enough to extricate him from the blissful imaginings and real life longings. No. It did not matter. Nothing else mattered. Not any more. His world had been turned upside down in an instant, and he had reached the point of no return.

TWO

Cameron Baldridge and Hayley Lofton met while attending Queens College. When he first saw her, he was scared to talk to her. She was incredibly beautiful. Way out of his league. The kind of girl you fantasize about while you are with the one you have. He noticed her long, sandy hair and smooth, tan skin the minute she stepped into Lucky's Tavern. She noticed him too. Even though her glance was only vaguely in his direction, he could sense her interest. And Christ, he was ready. He was just coming off a long, stormy relationship with Lynn, a girl he had dated for most of high school.

They had been together since the day she sat next to him in Mr. Frattalone's Italian class Sophomore year. He had only just begun to function without Maleigha. They were only fifteen years old. But she was so cute. She had long, dirty blonde hair that she always wore pulled back. And her face was perfect, soft and smooth, like one of those porcelain dolls some women collect and display in a china closet. He was so scared of her. What would he say to a girl like this? How could he ever get her attention? He sat in that class for months, pining for her in silent desperation. Poor kid. He was certain he would never get his chance. But when Frattalone moved her seat next to his because Richie Oberson was shooting spit balls in her hair, everything changed. Good old Richie. He had done for Cam what Cam just could not do for himself.

He could always count on some sort of playful exchange with her during class. The borrowing of a pen. Commiseration over exams and homework. The mutual rolling of the eyes when Frattalone told one of his corny jokes. It was all part of this glorious, pubescent dance. And even though he was usually stammering over his words and awkward as hell, he was on his way.

It wasn't long before things really took off. They were good together, and it was perfect while it lasted. The park. Von Leesen's Confectioners. The movies. It just worked. They were totally in sync. But, like all things free and easy, it did not last. As time went on, it became evident that they were really *nothing* alike.

11

She was vacant, and incapable of anything that fell beyond her own immediate needs. I guess that's true of all teenagers, but this was more than just the usual narcissism. He should have seen that. But he missed Maleigha. So it went on. They were together at graduation. Then it was the prom, and the tearful signing of the yearbook. Even after school was officially over, they still could not free themselves of each other.

The relationship lingered. And the two of them slowly drifted in different directions. He refused to see it. He did ask her repeatedly what was wrong, but never got an answer. That should have been enough. They laughed a lot less. She always found an excuse for them not to be together. He just couldn't see it at the time. Maybe he just didn't want to. He had invested three years of love and sacrifice and intimacy into the vision that they would always be together. He had everything planned in his mind, foolish as it was. Engagement. Marriage. Children. Lynn was a part of it all. It wasn't until *she* raised the issue that he began to see.

"Something is wrong, Cameron," she said one afternoon. They had just ordered lunch. She was twisting the ends of her hair, and gazing off at some distant point.

"Jesus Christ Lynn. What is going on?" he insisted.

I don't know," she said. "Things have just gotten old with us. There's no fire anymore. I know I should want to be with you. You're smart, attractive, and all that. But I just don't. I don't want you to take this the wrong way Cam, but you're just not the sort of guy who keeps butterflies in a girl's stomach. I'm sorry. You're just too nice – too safe. I love you, I do, but just not that way."

His heart sank. She was the first girl he had opened up his heart to since Maleigha. Her words were like daggers.

"I can change that," he pleaded. "Let me try. It can be different. We can be different. I know we can. I still love you Lynn."

He inched closer to her, swallowing one of her hands with both of his. He squeezed tightly, but she would not look at him.

"The important thing is that we still love each other," he continued. "We can work out all the rest. We still love each other, right Lynn?"

They must have sat there a good half hour, without saying anything else to each other. Then she finally spoke again. Uttered the true song of the cowardly. As they sat in that corner booth, wrestling with their strained relations, she hit him with it.

"You know, it's nothing you did Cam. Really. I shouldn't have said what I said. It's not like that. It's not you. It's me."

He could not believe it. Weeks of waiting for something definitive. A tangible target at which he could direct his anger and frustration. And this is what she offered.

"What the fuck does that mean?" he thundered.

She got all embarrassed. Clenched her teeth and moved her eyes in the direction of the other tables around them. Everyone was staring. He didn't care. But she hated that sort of thing. Everything always had to appear just so with Lynn. Even if it wasn't. That was all part of her façade and part of her deficiency as a person.

"I don't give a shit who's looking," he mouthed to her. "This is bullshit."

It was all just too much for her to handle. Her emotional constipation would not allow for anything further to transpire. So she slid her jacket over her shoulders and just left. That moment marked the beginning of the end. Her touch grew increasingly cold and she became distant and reticent. He tried. Begged her to just talk to him. She claimed, again, that she just didn't know what was wrong. That it was some ineffable presence making her feel this way. That maybe it would pass. She was a liar. And he was a willing victim. He convinced himself that maybe it *was* nothing. It was textbook. Classic denial. He spent the last two months of their time together trying desperately to keep the moribund dream alive, unaware that sadly, it was already behind him.

Lynn had already moved on. She was involved with someone she met at the library, where she worked part time -- some pedantic jackass she continued to see behind his back while he remained faithful to the vision. Cam didn't matter much to her. Truth is, he never really did. That's what hurt him the most. He realized later on that the only thing they ever had in common was that they both loved the same person. Lynn's self-absorption and disregard for his feelings precluded any hint of honesty; she did what worked best for her, seeing both Cam and this other guy for weeks, despite his heartfelt pleas for an explanation as to why things had gone so wrong. It would have gone on a lot longer if

Cam's romantic vision had not yielded to the tiny glimmer of reality which came by way of a friend's observation.

"Wake up Cameron. She's banging someone else."

It was a bitter pill to swallow. He recalled her words.

I love you, but just not that way.

Nothing was ever the same after that. And when he heard about her infidelity, this time from her lying lips, a part of him was lost forever.

"It just happened," she finally admitted later on. "What can I say? He makes me feel alive."

"What do you mean?" he questioned her desperately. "What does that mean?"

She had nothing to say. She just sat there, locked safely inside her vault of emotion. He couldn't believe what he was hearing. It was like a scene out of a movie. He could see words coming out of her mouth, but he could not really hear them. The sound of her voice was all distorted. He couldn't breathe. His mouth went dry and he could feel the back of his neck, damp with perspiration. He just sat there, like a baby, his eyes welling with tears. He did not know what to say. He looked around the room. Everything seemed different to him. He just wanted to die right there.

"Well?" she finally mumbled, growing impatient. "What now?"

"What?" he said.

"What now? What are we supposed to do now?"

She was a heartless bitch.

So Hayley came to Cam like sunshine after a long, cold rain. She was warm, sensitive and genuine, everything he imagined Lynn to be but was not. It wasn't long before a new vision replaced the old and life for Cameron Baldridge was wonderful once more.

The night they met was special -- one of those moments in time that just seemed to transcend everything else. It was perfection. He tried to play it cool, which was no easy task for a guy who got flustered by Victoria's Secret catalogues, drinking his beer while pretending to check the score of the baseball game on the television screen behind the bar. He watched the Mets retire the Reds in order, then casually turned to face her direction. He wanted so desperately to be indifferent. Cavalier. The way Brad

Pitt would look. Carefree. Confident. He wanted to be that guy that Lynn said he never could be. There's nothing worse than looking desperate. But he spent too much time worrying about his image. By the time he had mustered up the courage, and was ready to finally make his move, she was gone. Disappeared in the crowd. He exhaled the overwhelming disappointment into the top of his Heineken bottle, creating a droning hum that matched the hollow feeling he sported inside. What was he thinking? You don't get second chances with hot girls.

He was certain that he had blown his opportunity, and was already preparing for another evening of drinking and enjoying one of those catalogues, when all of a sudden he saw Hayley slither gracefully through the mob of drinkers and emerge once again from the smoky crowd, her shapely form poured into a white T-shirt and faded jeans. She walked over to the bar where he was sitting and took the seat next to him.

"You know you have something on your face," she said smiling.

Before he could respond to her playful salutation, she moistened her thumb with her lips and gently massaged the tiny smudge from his cheek.

"There. That's better."

"Is there anything else that I should know about"? he asked sheepishly.

"No," she answered, stepping away from him for a second. "Everything else looks pretty good from here."

They both smiled. Something exciting was kindled between them during this flirtatious exchange.

They spent the rest of the night together walking the path along the Shore Parkway, watching as the undulating ripples of the water in Gravesend Bay passed swiftly under the Verrazano Bridge and gently swallowed the lighted silhouettes of the buildings off in the distance, only to release them and swallow them again and again. It was the best he had felt in a long time. He felt like he was over Lynn, for sure. It was great, although in the darkest recesses of his mind lingered thoughts of Maleigha. She was always there. Still, after all he had been through, these moments with Hayley still felt good.

"So, I can't believe you go to Queens also," she said. "I haven't seen you around."

"Yeah," he answered. "I guess it's a big campus."

"What classes are you taking?" she asked. "I mean, have you declared a major yet?"

"English," he said, laughing out loud. "I take a lot of English classes. I'm not sure what exactly I'm going to do with that, but I'm thinking about teaching. I really like kids."

She was smiling. They walked a little more before she spoke again.

"That's cute," she said.

"What is?"

"You teaching. I can almost picture that. You in your classroom. All the girls fawning over you." She placed her hand over her mouth to conceal her laughter.

"Cute? That seems *cute* to you? Bummer. Not exactly what I was going for."

He bent down to pick up a rock, then cast it into the night. Only a distant splash signaled its final resting place.

"What about you?" he said. "What do you want to do Hayley?"

"Business," she told him. "It's sort of like the whole English thing with you. I've always been interested in business. I want to make money. Lots of money. I think I get that from my dad."

He was staring at her, smiling. She smelled like the lilacs that bloomed each spring in his parents' backyard.

"What? What are you looking at?" she asked, uncomfortable under his watchful eyes.

"Well, I was just thinking about something."

"Yeah?"

"I was thinking that if we were working for the same company, and you came into my office wearing that shirt and those jeans, I'd be fired on the spot for inappropriate workplace behavior."

She smiled back.

"That's what you think, huh?" she responded playfully, tugging at his shirt sleeve. "What makes you so sure I'd complain?"

Before long, they discovered that the two of them shared many of the same interests: good Italian food, baseball, the beach in the fall. They were both recovering from bad relationships and were not actively seeking another. They were two people who just wanted to feel good again. Things *were* good, but he was haunted by Lynn's words; he carried them around with him, like they were some sort of prophecy he was destined to fulfill.

You're just not that type of guy.

He hated her for that. He knew that proving her wrong would forever be his quest.

Cam and Hayley were good almost instantly. They shared everything. Their dreams, their fears, and their pasts. She was particularly open with him, something she had never been with anyone.

"On my sixteenth birthday," she explained, "my family had plans to have dinner at Luigi's, my favorite restaurant. It's all I really wanted. Well, that and a Prada bag. But my real gift was supposed to be dinner with my family." Hayley went on to describe how her parents' marriage was failing, and that this birthday dinner was supposed to mark the beginning of something new. The reservation was for six thirty. Mr. Lofton was supposed to catch a five forty train out of Penn Station and then meet them there. "He never showed Cam. He just left us there, waiting."

Hayley revealed to him how the painful memory had haunted her ever since, especially during the days that preceded her birthday each year. That horrible image of the whole family just standing awkwardly in the restaurant lobby for over two hours, trying desperately to ignore the grim reality that the man for whom they waited was not coming.

"Don't worry sweetheart," her mom kept saying. "Something must have happened. He'll be here." She could barely hear a word her mother said. Her palms lay flat on the glass, her face in between, hopeful that at any moment, she would see her dad's navy blue Mercedes pull into the lot. But each minute that passed was a painful harbinger of a world that was beginning to crumble. At eight forty five, she peeled herself away from the window.

"Hayley," her mother said. "Honey? Come on. It's time. He's not coming dear. I'm sorry. So sorry."

The girl was broken.

"This is so humiliating," she cried. "I feel like such an ass. Look at me."

"It's okay honey," her mother said. "It's not your fault. It's not. And don't worry about what anyone else is going to think or say. Nobody has to know."

Hayley was filled with such sadness. Such awful resignation. She never answered. Just walked slowly toward the door, and left her corsage of sixteen tiny pink roses withering in the lobby ash tray.

And it just got worse. She was awakened in the wee hours of the morning by the tumultuous winds of discord generated by a man who stumbled through the front door, reeking of Jack Daniels and cigarette smoke and by the cries of a woman who had finally reached her limit.

"How could you?" her mother kept screaming. "Of all nights. How could you?" He was in no mood for questions. The inebriation had rendered him tired, irritable and unbalanced. He just sat there, rubbing his forehead, blinking his eyes erratically. But she pressed on, empowered by the liberation that comes from the articulation of words held dormant for far too long.

"Answer me, you son of a bitch! Don't you dare just sit there," she cried, grabbing his shoulder and rousing him from his stupor. He looked at her quizzically. Then, after wringing his hands momentarily, the demon of the disease reared its ugly head, launching him into a harangue about bitchiness and ungratefulness and her failure to understand him and the pressure he felt.

"You stupid bitch!" he thundered. "This is how you repay me for all I've done for you? Who the fuck do you think you are? Huh? Look at you. You think-"

"That's it! I'm through with it. I have had enough of your drunken outbursts. You will not talk to me this way. Do you hear? I do not deserve this. You are horrible. You are a horrible, little man. Just get your stuff and-"

Hayley heard the slap from behind her door and the subsequent crashing of her mother's defeated body into the sofa table. The sounds of broken glass and empty promises and the uncontrollable sobbing of one who had struggled for years against an opponent far more formidable brought her from her bedroom.

She needed to be with them. To try and understand what was happening. What she saw, instead, was the undeniable reality of a dying vision that followed her father out the door for the last time.

"So what happened to your dad?" he asked her.

"Never saw him again after that night."

"And your mom?"

"She remarried a year and a half later," she told him. "Things there have never really been the same either. I mean, we moved on, but the fear of him returning was always there." She paused, trying to rid herself of the lump that had formed in her throat. "We always thought how much better off we would have been had he just died. It's the only way it's ever over. And, not to sound crazy or morbid or anything, but I really thought about it. You know, making it happen. I actually hate him enough to kill him. Isn't that sick? This is what his betrayal has done to me."

"Look Hayley, maybe it's just that-"

"Sometimes, I think I should have. I do. As crazy as that sounds, it's the only way you are ever really free."

His eyes narrowed and he shuddered, just for a moment, at the resignation floating in her eyes. He thought of asking her more about what she had shared, but did not bother. He was smitten. Her vulnerability captivated him. It was part of her appeal. He could help her, he thought – really make her his. But he was hesitant at first, about being *that* guy – the one who was just too nice. So he was guarded for several weeks, suppressing his natural inclinations until he could no longer betray who he really was.

"I've got some great plans for us tonight," he told her on the evening of their two month anniversary. "Wear something nice."

She was completely overwhelmed. Nobody had ever really bothered with her. All of Cam's attention was wonderful but totally foreign.

"Luigi's?" she asked tearfully as they pulled up to the restaurant. "You remembered that?" He smiled, and wiped her tears with his hand.

"Of course I did."

She was so touched, but managed to hold herself together. On more than one occasion, she felt herself losing her grip, as the painful memories collided with what she knew, just knew, was a wonderful future. She had almost made it through the entire dinner when one of the waiters brought over a beautiful floral arrangement, made up of a variety of fresh cut flowers and baby's breath accented throughout with the careful placement of sixteen pink carnations.

"I know it's a few years late," he whispered to her. "But every girl needs to be sweet sixteen."

She broke down and wept like a little girl.

There were many moments like that early on. He could make her laugh and forget about the things that bothered her. Like the time she slammed her brand new Mustang convertible into the back of a pickup truck on the Cross Island Parkway. She was devastated. He showed up later that day with a rental car coupon, two gallons of her favorite ice cream, a bag full of her favorite toppings, and a giant bowl with two spoons.

"Just what the doctor ordered," he announced smugly. She collapsed into his arms and cried once more.

"Thank you Cam. You are so good to me," she told him later on. "Where would I be without you?"

Then there was that awful day one summer, when she found her cat, Pringles, on the side of the road. The sun was just coming up over the horizon, and she was marveling at the brilliant splashes of red and orange stretched across the morning sky. She was out for her morning run, had just turned the corner by her apartment when she discovered him in a crumpled heap. He wasn't more than a year old when it happened. He still remembered the hysterical phone call.

"Cam he's dead," she cried. "Pringles was hit by a car last night."

"Stay where you are Hay," he told her. "I'll be right there."

He rushed right over, and held her while she sobbed. Then he helped her bury the orange and white tabby in the yard, and stayed with her the rest of that day.

The next few months were rough for her; she had such deep attachments. She found it hard to concentrate at work, and seemed to bust out into tears with just the slightest provocation. He was beginning to think that she would never get over it when he found a way to resurrect that smile.

"Where are we going?" she asked.

He was playfully cryptic.

"You'll see," he told her.

They spent an entire afternoon at the North Shore Animal Shelter, where together, they picked out a beautiful Norwegian Forest cat that had just come in. She fell in love the minute she saw him.

"He's perfect Cam," she said. "I love him. Thank you so much."

"I'm glad Hay," he said. "It's the least I could do."

She hugged and kissed him, thanked him about twenty five more times, then gave him just one more thing to do.

"I want you to name him," she explained, laughing for the first time in weeks.

"Obviously, I'm no good at that."

It did not take him long.

"Othello," he said confidently, "after my favorite Shakespearean play."

Their past was filled with all sorts of tender moments, but time had somehow changed all of that. His ability to mitigate the damage that her past had caused suffered in the wake of their recent struggles. He could no longer perform the same magic. He wasn't even sure if he wanted to. She was bitter and irrational and always angry. He was growing fearful and could never seem to find the right words to say.

"Why are you always at that damn school Cameron?" she asked. I mean, really. Gymnastics meets. Football and soccer games. Concerts. Why do you have to go to *all* of them?"

He stared at her, his mouth slightly distorted.

"What about you Hay? Huh? All those late nights at the office. All those 'eleventh hour' deadlines? And what about all of the fucking work you bring home? Huh? When was the last time you fed the cat, or bought groceries? Are you kidding me? Your job is the problem here. Not mine."

Her face hardened. Words flowed now, abrupt and harsh.

"Oh please. That is a bunch of bullshit and you know it. *My* job is a problem? Please Cameron. Don't even go there. We're talking about two different things here. I have multi-million dollar accounts I am responsible for. I have no choice. It's not like I am babysitting, or playing games with some teenagers who probably don't even give a shit whether you are there or not."

"Fuck you Hayley. Okay? Fuck you. Is that what you think I do all day? Babysit? The kids like me. What can I say? It's nice for them, that their teacher cares. You might not be able to measure it, like your fucking flow charts and profit margins, but it matters. It matters a lot."

She just looked at him with a peculiar loathing. Her mouth moved once or twice, as if she was going to say something, but nothing came. Then, after a short time, she uttered the words he had been secretly dreading all along.

"Things with us seem a little off Cameron. You know, tired. I don't know. Maybe it's time for a break. Maybe we've been together too long. I don't know if I feel the same way. About you, and us."

It was uncanny the way that same wave of nausea he was stricken with years ago rose up and greeted him. Yes, it was hauntingly familiar, except this time, it was accompanied by another emotion – anger. He hated Lynn all over again, as if they had just broken up. And now he hated Hayley too.

"Hey whatever," he said, desperate not to give her any satisfaction.

And then later on that night, something inside Cameron Baldridge snapped. It was as if the internal barrier that separates the two worlds we all house -- the world in which we live and the one in which our wildest fantasies are allowed to run unchecked – had allowed a tiny piece of one to infiltrate the other. It was an odd sensation – frightening, yet curiously exciting. All at once, he was thinking of things he had never really considered before. It was then that Cam decided to explore things with *her* – his young, ebullient admirer who had crept into his consciousness at every turn. Temptation, he considered, was just a moment, an explosion of danger and risk that sent blood and adrenaline and tiny sparks of reckless abandon rushing through his veins, electrifying every nerve in his body. Suddenly he was a kid again, whisked away by the exhilaration of his first game at Shea Stadium and the thrill of all the roller coaster rides he took at Six Flags. For that moment, it didn't matter that he had a girlfriend with whom he shared a home. It was of little consequence.

This recklessness hit him hard in the face, made him realize that perhaps all he had always worried about was pointless. Maybe the apartment, the talk of marriage, the family commitments didn't mean a thing. For the moment, it was a liberating thought. He had always been judicious with his emotions. Yeah, that was him. True blue Cameron. Old reliable. The moniker made him sick. He began to consider that part of the reason love was always shitting on him was because he was so nice all the time. He was thinking differently now. He was pushing himself, daring his sensibilities to take an uncharacteristic leap.

He pulled his phone from his pocket and scrolled through his contacts list. He was outside of himself, watching the action from a safe distance, as if he were seated in a movie theater, impervious to the inherent danger of what might come next. Perhaps it was because he had been waiting for this to happen. Somehow, he knew something like this was coming -- that it would happen to him, one way or another. It had to be. Things with Hayley had been in this silent state of decline for too long. It was always on his mind, trailed him like an apparition whispering the reminders of discontent in his ear. Now it was all different. He was not going to be the same old Cam. Sure, it seemed new to him. This rush of autonomy and self-gratification. But even though he was experiencing it for the first time, there was an inexplicable comfort of which he himself was only now just aware.

He began asking himself questions. He wondered if this moment was the right moment or if he had just misread the signs of the past few weeks out of sheer stupidity or desperation. Maybe Hayley was right. What if the kids really did not care about him? What if Nikki was just being nice to him, and had no real feelings for him at all? The thinking quieted the recklessness and the moment was over. He put the phone away. But he couldn't forget, mostly because he did not want to. He simply tucked the feeling away neatly in one of the private recesses of his mind; there it would have to stay. But having finally been exposed to the light; it had begun to take on a life of its own. Sure, he pushed it aside. But he was uncomfortably aware knowing that it was there, just waiting to be summoned, should he ever be tempted again.

THREE

Am I really falling for this girl? Cam wondered. He laughed at the absurdity. If he was, and by his own estimation it certainly seemed that way, it would explain his spiraling thoughts and erratic behavior. He was definitely unmoored. Each time he saw her, or they spoke, the impression lasted that much longer than the time before, as though she had somehow found entrance into his most private chambers and stamped his soul with her angelic likeness. Why did he have to be her teacher? What a cruel irony. That, above all else, preyed upon him. What would people say? He knew the answer, and even so, he was tempted -- truly frightened by what he had begun to consider. It was only when he was away from her for a while, and he could focus on his professional obligation and Hayley without interruption, that the impure thoughts floating in his imagination yielded to the prickly reality, bursting like a salvo of soap bubbles just above his head.

The next couple of days with Hayley were better; they talked a little, and agreed to work on things. It still wasn't great, but it made him feel better, like he was in control again. He still found everything about Nikki utterly intoxicating, but knowing Hayley was there for him, and that they were perhaps moving toward something real and permanent took the edge off. He was happy, even relieved, that Hayley had unknowingly made his life a lot easier. He was feeling especially good about the Friday night they had just spent together. It was her idea. Drinks at O'Briens, followed by a nice dinner at Gramercy Tavern on 42nd street, then on to the WaMu Theater at Madison Square Garden, where they had third row seats for Van Morrison, one of Hayley's favorite artists.

They drifted through the bright lights of the city hand in hand like two moths, halting their travels only to enjoy all of the pre-determined stops, and some impromptu ones as well. Dinner was wonderful. So was the Gelato they shared on their walk back uptown. Cam even agreed to do a little window shopping, and actually enjoyed himself.

"You have certainly shown me a good time Mr. Baldridge," she said, wrapping both her arms around him as they strolled. "I am so happy. And you know what kind of mood Van Morrison puts me in. Tonight just may be your lucky night."

They rode the train home in relative silence, each of them entranced by the inimitable vocals still playing in their heads. He sat with his back up against the window, and she lie limp in between his legs, her head propped up against his chest, drifting in and out of sleep until their stop was called.

When they arrived home, Cam was eager to put the finishing touches on what was a perfect evening. He caught her from behind in the bathroom, as she was beginning to remove her eye makeup and contact lenses.

"You look especially good tonight Hay," he said, reaching around her back and placing his hands across her breasts. "You really are amazing Hay." He continued to whisper loving overtures in her ear as he kissed her neck and pressed up against her.

"Thanks Cameron, she said, wriggling free from his grasp and turning to face him. "I had a great time tonight, but I'm a little tired. Maybe we can try in the morning, okay?"

He was both confused and offended. Everything had been perfect. What more could she want?

"What's wrong Hay?" he asked. "Did I do something?"

Her mood changed instantly.

"Why do you always think there has to be something wrong?" she snapped back. "Stop analyzing everything all the time. Aren't I allowed to be tired Cameron?"

His desire faded, but the frustration remained. *Unbelievable*, he thought. He was right back where he had been before.

"Sure Hayley, you can be tired, or bitchy, or anything else that you want to be," he said. "Why should tonight be any different?"

He felt the same frustration a few weeks later, while sitting with her at GrillFire. They had just eaten dinner and were working on dessert when the contents of his stomach began swirling in a violent dance of sorts.

"I've got a lot to do this weekend," Hayley said. She was staring at the periwinkle tablecloth, tracing the floral patterns with the tip of her finger. "I have a hair appointment tomorrow morning, my car needs an oil change, I need to finish up that merchandising report before I leave for England, and I still have not found a dress for Alicia's party."

Cam just sat, eyes distant, as he stirred his coffee.

"What about you?" she asked. "What do you have to do?"

"Nothing much," he replied. "The usual stuff. Papers to grade. I have to make a test. Football on Sunday. That's about it."

She sat with odd anticipation, as if they were about to have their picture taken.

"That's good," she said, reaching across the table to grab his hand. "Just make sure you leave some time to pick up a suit jacket for next weekend."

The words were far more acerbic than they should have been.

"Next weekend?" he repeated.

"Uh, Alicia's party? Remember? We are leaving for Ithaca Friday night."

His face was now contorted, severe and twisted, like he had just put a slice of lemon in his mouth.

"You're kidding Cameron, right?" she asked. "You do remember us talking about this, right?"

"Well, I remember *you* talking about it, but I never agreed to go. She's *your* college friend Hay. I don't even know her."

"But you know *me* Cam. And I want you there. *You* should want to be there with me. Isn't that what we do for each other?"

She huffed loudly and folded her arms across her heaving chest.

"It's just a stupid thirtieth birthday party," he said. "I'll just be in the way. Besides, I have to be at school this Saturday night. You know it's Battle of the Bands Hay. I'm working."

"Since when Cameron?" she screamed. "When did this happen?"

"It's been on the calendar for weeks Hay. Why the attitude? I'm not giving you shit for taking off to England for your job. But we all know that *your* job is more important. Certainly more important than us."

"Yeah?"

"So, what about all your talk about 'what we do for each other'? Please. We have not even touched each other in days. You could not be more distant. Is this your idea of moving forward?"

Not another word was spoken. Hayley left for Ithaca and attended Alicia's party by herself. It was a wonderful event, and she was happy to have the time to spend with Alicia and many of her other college friends. In fact, she had just about decided, on the long ride home, that she would forgive Cam – maybe even apologize to him for being so irrational. Somehow it just never got that far.

"What the fuck is this?" she wailed. She was holding his jacket. The pockets were turned inside out, and her free hand contained the damning piece of evidence.

"It's not like it seems Hay," he pleaded. "I did not plan it."
"Oh, okay," she mocked. "So you just happened to come across a ticket to the Rangers/Islanders – even though the game has been sold out for weeks?"

Cam grabbed the jacket from her hand and tossed it on a chair.

"Someone at school had an extra ticket. It's no big deal."

She shook as though from an unexpected chill. Fear of vulnerability took possession of her.

"Really? No big deal? How nice. I suppose missing 'work' was no big deal either? What happened to the big show at school?"

He did not answer her. His mind just continued to spin in large, sweeping circles. They argued the rest of the week – fought like two cobras exchanging shots of venom -- so when he left the house alone that next weekend, he felt justified – did not feel the least bit of remorse for turning over in his thoughts everything about Nikki.

He could hear her voice, soft and vulnerable. He envisioned the two of them sitting closely, shoulders touching, and the curve of her face. The sweet scent of her was strong in his nose. He could swear it was on his hands. On his clothes. He placed two fingers to his lips and ruminated over what she could be thinking. What she could be feeling. How would he ever know?

He must have removed his phone from his pocket and put it back at least a dozen times before finally texting her from his car. They had exchanged cell phone numbers weeks ago, when she was having trouble with a paper he had assigned.

"I might need some extra help on this Mr. B," she said that morning after class, with entrancing softness.

He couldn't help but smile.

"Well, I don't do this for just anyone. And you need to keep it on the 'D.L.' as you guys say. You can always call me if you need something. I'd be happy to help you out."

She was at home, in her room, when she got his text.

Hey, how's that paper coming?

He sat in his car, phone in hand, his heart racing, his thoughts scattered in a queasy scramble. Would she answer? And if she did, what would he say next? It didn't take very long for him to feel foolish. What was he doing? This was stupid. He felt a loathing now for Hayley, more than before, and for everything else, especially himself. How had it come to this? He was just about to get out of the car, and go back inside, when his hand shook from the vibration of his phone.

Hey Mr. B. What's up? I am sitting here now with my paper. How'd you know? Are you stalking me? LOL. It really sucks.

He smiled. His thumb was sweaty.

Don't work too hard, he texted. *Remember, I will help you anytime if you want.*

She was quick to respond.

Can I call you?

He smiled again. He felt good. Alive. He could play this part. Maybe this wasn't so bad after all.

Sure. Call me now. I am free for a while.

Their conversation was just as it always was – light, playful, suggestive. Yet it was different somehow. There was an element of tenderness there, something ineffable and remote that belied the true purpose of the call.

"Are you okay Nikki," he asked while playing with the radio dials on the dash. "You sound a little upset or something?"

She sighed.

"No, I'm not upset. Not really anyway. It's just my mother. She's driving me crazy. She's such a bitch sometimes."

"Are you sure? You don't sound so convincing. Is it school?"

"No," she said. Not exactly. It's really everything. She's just in one of her moods. I need to get out of here."

"I understand that. I am having a little trouble of my own at home."

"Really? That must suck. I hope it's not too bad."

He thought about telling her everything, right then and there. Things like how his relationship with Hayley had grown stale, predictable, and now contentious. And how they just could not get on the same page. He also thought about telling her about this feeling he was having – and that he could not stop thinking about her – dreaming of her.

"Ah, you don't want to hear about my problems," he said.

"Sure I do. I do. Really. I'm just surprised to hear you say that anything's wrong. You always seem so happy at school."

He laughed. "I am happy at school Nikki. It's the only place I *am* happy. It's really who I am. I love being a teacher."

"Well, you are really good at it," she said.

"Thanks Nikki," he said. "And thank you for being you. You really are sort of one of the reasons why school is so pleasant."

"Aw, thanks Mr. B. That's really sweet. I feel the same way about you."

He was pleased at the way the discourse was evolving.

"Yeah, we do seem to have a lot in common, right? You are a lot more mature than most of the other kids at Hillcrest."

"Uh, yeah," she said. "That's why I have like no friends. Everyone here is so shallow and into their designer shit. And who's best friend's with who, and whose boyfriend is flirting with who. It's just too much drama for me."

"Yeah, I get it," he said. Makes sense. But I have to say. And I hope you don't think this is creepy or anything. But I am amazed that *you* do not have a boyfriend. I mean, you are great Nikki. You're smart, pretty, fun to talk to. When I was in high school, there were no girls like you around. I think the guys here are all nuts not to have noticed."

There was a pause, and for a moment, all that was audible over the phone was a feint hum. He was nervous again.

"Hey, I'm sorry Nikki," he said desperately. "I shouldn't have. I didn't mean to -"

"No, no, it's fine," she insisted. "Really. I was just thinking that we have the same problem Mr. B." She laughed. "There are no boys at Hillcrest who are like you."

There was silence again, as if both of them were weighing the same possibility.

"Can I tell you something?" she asked.

"Sure."

"This may sound sort of stupid, but I feel different when I talk to you. Not in a bad way. It's good. It is. You know. Happy. Excited. I guess sort of like – now don't laugh – like I have butterflies in my stomach."

He could not hold his smile.

"I know what you mean Nikki," he said. "I do."

There was a brief silence.

"Uh, I don't want you to think I am weird or anything like that, but do you think we could meet Mr. B? You know, just for a little while, to talk about my paper?"

He was surprised. He had not expected those words to come so quickly or even at all. "Yeah, I think we could do that. But I - "

"It's okay if you can't. It's cool. I know you have things to do and all."

"No, no Nikki. It's fine. I mean it. It's just that I wouldn't want people to talk. You know, if they saw us together. I mean, we were all told that we are not allowed to tutor our own students. Get too close and all. Board policy or something like that."

"That really sucks. I guess I get it and all. But it's stupid."

"Hey, I'm serious here," he said with great urgency. "I *really* do want to see you. I do Nikki. More than you know."

She waited a minute before answering.

"I think I know Mr. B."

Nothing else was said for several seconds. The two of them just listened to each other's breathing on either end.

"So what are we supposed to do now?" she finally asked, wanting very much to bring the issue to some closure.

"I don't know Nikki," he said. "I just don't know. This has never happened to me before."

"Well, that's good to hear," she answered, laughing nervously.

They talked some more about their situation, and possible ways around the obvious obstacles, but could not arrive at any solution that seemed feasible.

"Well hey, there's always school, right?" she said. "Maybe we can meet after class on Monday or something."

His heart stalled, the steady beat replaced by a faint, timorous despair.

"Yeah, we could do that. But I'm not sure how smart that would be."

"Why?' she asked. "I thought you were okay with this?"

He thought of all the work he had done the last few years, and how he had really come to cherish his position at Hillcrest as "good old Mr. B." He loved those kids and the way teaching made him feel. The thought of losing all of that made him gasp.

"I don't know Nikki," he said. "It's very complicated. That's all."

"Ok," she said. "No big deal. I get it. I will take whatever you can give. But if for some reason we should just happen to run into each other somewhere – say at Penn Station or someplace like that -- who could really say something? Right? I mean, lots of people go through Penn Station every day."

"I guess so," he said, sighing. "You know what? It's a funny thing. I was thinking that I was going to do some shopping in the city today. I'll probably be at Penn around noon. I love the Dunkin' Donuts there. The coffee just tastes better. Maybe I'll run into you or something."

"I guess I could see that happening," he replied. "I just might be passing by that very spot later today, around the same time."

She laughed.

"Are you sure you're not bi-polar or something?"

"Come on Nikki, you know that this is not-"

"I know. It's cool. Seeing you would be awesome. If you're there, and you see me, make sure you stop and say hello. If not, no big deal."

Cam had just enough time to run home and shower. When he came in, he was greeted by a pile of dirty clothes on the couch. He called for Hayley, but heard nothing in reply. Then he saw the note.

Had to go to the office. Feed Othello and take these to the dry cleaner. I did it last time.

He rolled his eyes. He felt once more the sting of his interminable situation.

That day was particularly warm. The train was crowded and he was sweating more than he would have liked. His knees felt weak and timorous and his breathing was labored. As the train sped toward Manhattan, the colliding of worlds in Cam's head continued to enervate his present resolve and burgeoning panic prompted him to leave his seat on several occasions. Stops at Valley Stream, Jamaica, Kew Gardens and Woodside seemed like opportune moments to flee the train and put an end to this insanity; he was close enough to the exit to feel the warm air outside once the doors opened, but he sat back down each time and decided to stay. He spent much of the remaining ride thinking about Nikki, how he was shocked and alarmed, yet somehow touched, that she had offered to him her emotion – so quickly and so naked and true. It unnerved him, made him question repeatedly the sensibility of such a situation. But it also made him crave her even more. The paradox was mastering.

Penn Station was crowded. The smell of coffee and baked bread grew stronger as Cam leaned oddly against the side of a trash receptacle, as if he were trying to balance himself while thumbing perfunctorily through a Christian Right pamphlet he had been given just moments before. He stood there, pretending to be relaxed, his eyes vacillating between the apocalyptic visions delineated in his reading material and the surging crowd washing across the station floor. He was uncomfortably warm. Random thoughts floated through his consciousness, a stream of separate bubbles that presented themselves individually for a fleeting second, then burst just as fast, vexing him momentarily before giving way to the next bubble in the fizzing progression.

There were so many things to consider. Did he really want to risk his reputation and career for a few minutes of ecstasy? The longer he considered it, the more he realized how stupid it all was. He should have gotten off the train. Even though he was miserable at home, Hayley was still on his mind. What would she do if she ever found out? He wondered briefly if he had been fair to her about her job and some of the other issues they fought about, and if things with the two of them were really as bad as it seemed. He also thought of everyone at Hillcrest. He loved his colleagues. And those kids. They made him feel special – like he mattered. And despite Hayley's claim that his efforts really did not matter all that much, they loved him too. This dormant sensibility rose to the surface and collided with the thrilling discomfort he was feeling. The possibility of losing everything, especially his reputation, was a suffocating prospect.

The longer he stood there, the more he realized how absurd this whole thing was. Risking everything this way, just for a taste of that sweet nectar of youth? It was crazy. He was feeling very foolish again, and probably would have left right then and there had she not emerged from the crowd when she did. She was not like the other girls. One word from her, and he was lost again in the communion of passion and adventure. All of his prior concerns abated, and he was, once again, lit by the intoxicating notion that had previously possessed him.

"Mr. B. Hey Mr. B. Over here."

She was breathtaking. Standing there, before him, she looked so much older. Maybe it was the way she had done her makeup. Or the fact that he had never seen her outside of school. Whatever it was, he was dazzled by her beauty, her untamed sexuality. Her hair seemed softer than ever. He loved when she wore it that way – long curls that fell gently over her shoulders. She always wore just the right thing as well. Today was no different. He loved the way she looked. Gray, V-neck sweater dress and knee high suede boots. How could he have ever considered leaving?

"Hey Nikki." He swallowed hard. "Well, this is certainly a pleasant surprise," he said, touching her on the shoulder briefly before stepping quietly around her. "If you didn't get one of these," he continued, holding up the pamphlet before depositing it in the trash, "don't worry. You didn't miss anything."

She smiled.

"I have no interest in that anyway," she said, wetting her lips with a quick pass of her tongue. "I'm just here for the coffee."

He wanted to smile but could not.

"Hey, you okay?" she asked.

"Yeah, why?"

"You don't look so good." She saw he was struggling. "If you want to just -"

"No, no," he said quickly, as if the terseness of his reply would somehow make it real. "I'm fine. Really. Just a little concerned about – well, you know."

They continued to banter as they walked without purpose up and out onto Seventh Avenue. He was amazed at how at ease he was with her, despite the conflict raging inside of him.

Once outside, Cam was also taken by the city he had known for years. He had walked this path a thousand times, yet it was all different somehow, as if he were a foreigner from some remote land, a traveler making his first visit to the Big Apple. Somehow, there was more energy, the frenetic pace not so much an indictment of a world in chaotic flux as it was a testimony to others who were feeling the same inebriation with life. It was glorious. The universe, at that very moment, seemed brimming with endless possibility.

"So, where we headed?" Nikki asked. "I brought my paper. It's in my bag."

In the uncertain light slanting between the massive buildings, his brow furrowed a bit when he realized he had never gotten that far in his head.

"I don't really know," he answered. "I guess it depends on what you want to do."

"Well, it might seem weird if we were just walking around the city and all. You know, like you said before. That wouldn't look good. We should probably go somewhere."

"I agree," he said, his attention diverted momentarily by a scruffy, weathered man with one leg, a self-appointed city evangelist preaching about Jesus and the forgiveness of sinners.

"I figure it might be best to just hop a cab to someplace private," he went on. "You know someplace quiet. Where we can talk. And, since we *are* discussing the Transcendentalists in class Ms. Dillinger, what better place is there than Central Park."

Cam smiled in a semi-desperate attempt to mitigate the possible distance between them.

"Okay," Nikki said. "You're the teacher. Central Park it is. But promise me one thing?"

"What's that?" he answered.

She was staring at an elderly Asian man, who was sitting behind a tiny table on which rested a series of brushes and an assortment of paints. Just behind him were photos of his work; a collage of faces, arms and legs, all adorned with the mark of his talent.

"I love Anime," she said. "On the way back, we have to stop. And we both have to get one. Promise?"

What could he do but smile.

Cam's forehead was beaded with sweat and he was content now to just carry his jacket. They walked through Central Park, and for a long time said nothing to each other. It was not an awkward silence, the kind that makes your mouth dry and beads of sweat form in the palms of your hands. It was a comfortable quiet, just two people trying to find their way through a similar fog. They watched as the joggers and roller bladers negotiated the winding paths that cut artfully through the myriad trees that were all but barren now. There were things that each of them needed to say, things that rattled around inside their heads like marbles in a tin can. Yet they were content to say nothing; the need for articulation acquiesced to the peacefulness created by the celebration in the park of the last few days of life, a last dance before the shroud of winter fell across the dying landscape.

They came to a bend in the path. To the right was a dirt trail, twisting down to a group of saplings that stood impatiently like a group of skinny school children waiting at a bus stop. Where the trees began, the ground dipped down, a modest incline on which hundreds of brownish leaves, remnants of the summer past, rattled in the crisp breeze that had suddenly blown across their faces. Their feet, steady but anxious, disrupted nature's choreography, crunching and grinding the crispy carpet until the air filled with thin flecks of brown, a cyclone of confetti that twisted and turned in the air before them.

Deeper in the park, just beyond the first gray stone wall they saw, the narrow trail widened, giving way to an open area with a sculpture in the center. There were several people there, tourists he thought, snapping photographs. They frowned at each other, and opted for a different path, one less traveled; they walked closely without touching, chatting about only topics which were safe and easy, until they came to rest on a rotting log that was out of the park's main flow. It was blissful agony, being that close to her. He was smitten by the fragrant shimmer of her hair and the sparkle in her eyes.

"So Nikki," he began, rubbing his hands on his jeans. "Should we talk about that essay now? I mean, the deadline is coming up."

"Yeah, I guess so," she said unconvincingly.

He hesitated before speaking again. "Well, if you want, we can hold off on that," he said. "I mean, if there is something else on your mind."

"It's kind of hard to explain," she said desperately, her hazy longing becoming more distinct with every word she spoke. "I guess it's home. I feel so alone most of the time. Like nobody gives a shit about me. Like nobody gets me." Her eyes welled with tears. She paused a second and collected herself. "Everyone's always bitching at me," she continued. "Nothing's ever good enough. I can't stand it anymore. You're the only one who seems to understand. It's easy with you."

Her thoughts were funny to him. He wanted to tell her that he felt the same way about her too. And to express to her somehow that he thought, without question, that the vacant corners in both their lives could be filled by what was transpiring between them. But his tongue grew thick and the words would not come. He settled for something more innocuous.

"It's okay Nikki. I get it. Believe me. You've got a lot going on. It's not easy. Sometimes this unpleasantness just creeps up on you, and you don't see it coming. I know. It's bad sometimes. I feel that way too." He paused just long enough to express some of what he was really feeling. "Hey, but it's all good," he said, gently sliding the hair from her eyes with his finger. "I have a special place for you."

They sat close together, two stars in a vast and changing galaxy, united inexplicably by the same emptiness. He placed his hand on top of hers, but neither one could look at the other for some time. They both just stared out in front of them. She felt a warm sensation rush over her. He had articulated the very thing that she had been trying to identify herself. That's one thing she loved about him. He always seemed to know what she was thinking, feeling. He always knew just what to say. He felt the sensation too, as if somehow, when he touched her, her blood had mixed with his. Yes, it was an intense feeling, one that was soothing and exhilarating yet somehow embarrassing and shameful.

Their feet were restless and loud in the leaves below. It was awkward. He felt as though he should say something, something else to mitigate the clumsiness spawned by his previous words. *I have a special place for you?* What a jerk. Why did he have to say that? Where was he to go from there? What was he going to say now? He thought, perhaps, that he would just wait, silently, wait until something cute or insightful came to him.

He pulled his hand away slowly, and placed it on top of his other in his lap. Still nothing. He tortured himself with his lack of something else to say. Something to move things forward. He was blank. He thought now that perhaps he would take the easy way out; wait for her, follow her lead. It seemed so immature, so cowardly but he did not know what else to do. He was afraid he had made her uncomfortable. Freaked her out. That's the last thing he wanted. Oh, the agony. He had come this far – had all but consecrated his fantasy and all of his wildest dreams, only to stall now. That made him feel even worse. He stared out beyond the trees at the sinking sun, knowing that daylight was waning, and his time with her was running out. Maybe it was all for the best. This was foolish anyway.

"Okay Nikki," he finally blurted out, turning to face her once again. "How about that paper of yours?"

She looked at him, as though emotionally stranded, and took back his hand. Her touch was electrifying. His heart felt like it would burst. Her eyes were deeper now than he had ever seen, wells of deep blue longing and passion. She blushed shyly, yet continued to move closer to him. He could smell her breath now, young and sweet. His brain was spinning. She was the most lovely, bewitching creature he had ever seen, and her spell had now rendered him full of lust and desire He stroked her cheek with his finger, then brought it gently to her lips. She sighed softly. They were aware of each other now like never before, startled briefly by their own unconscious thoughts. The magic of the moment pulsed on.

"You know, we should not be doing this," he said. "I could really get in a lot of trouble."

She nodded, her eyes now just partially open. He leaned his head in toward hers. She followed his lead, and under a twilight sky now tinged with streaks of red and purple, his entrance into this reckless, rapturous new world was complete.

He caught the 6:47 home. Sitting on the train, thoughts of her remained with him. They assaulted him, surrounded him with a kind of golden haze through which the faces all around looked distant and spectral. Once or twice he closed his eyes, certain that when he opened them once more, everything would regain its focus, present itself the way it always had. But the sound of the wheels grinding along the tracks was hypnotic, and soon he was lost even deeper in a world both dreamlike and elusive.

He could still smell her, still taste her. The kiss they shared was perfect. Soft and tender, with just the right hint of untamed desire. He could feel her body awakening beneath her clothes, a hatching passion that matched his own longing for her. It was electric. Pure energy. What would he do with that feeling now?

He thought that he might be able to just forget about her, go home and pretend like everything was just as it had been when he left earlier that day. Maybe lose himself in a television show, or perhaps some laundry or something. He didn't care. Something, anything to restore the balance. He even entertained the idea of taking Hayley out somewhere. He told her that morning, before he left, that perhaps they would go out to eat or watch a movie. It seemed like a good idea at the time. Yes, it may have been a rationalization, a tacit bargain for an afternoon of infidelity. But it got him out of the house. Now, as he silenced his cell phone and buried it deep in his pocket, he wished he had those words back.

He decided that time was the one thing that could help him. Time, and perhaps alcohol. Lots of alcohol. He would go to Johnny's Tavern, have a few, then head home to face the music. However, two beers turned into six, and one hour became three.

When he got home, Hayley was in the bathroom. He sat on the edge of their bed, listening to the distinct sounds of her before bed ritual. She was never more fastidious than when she was in front of the mirror. Exfoliating scrub. Clarifying lotion. Moisturizing gel. Disinfecting solution for her contact lenses. He listened as she removed each bottle, applied the contents, then placed them back in the medicine cabinet. Agitated by the predictability of the routine, he got up and stood by the door, waiting in the dim light. He was thinking about Nikki and how nice the afternoon had been. He could hardly believe it had passed. It made him smile. Then the door opened abruptly, and a sharp wedge of light flashed across his face.

"Thanks for calling," she said, and slipped by him without another word.

Once in the bathroom, he was slow and deliberate. There was no urgency. He tried to remember exactly how long they had been living together but his mind was elsewhere. He felt a little jittery. Like he needed to reach out to her. Right now. The sound of running water was perfect cover. He opened the sink faucet, sat down on the edge of the tub, and took out his phone. There was a message.

Thanks. It was fun. See you Monday.

Somehow, her words, distant as they were, made it all real to him. Yes, he was in this now. The fantasy was no more. It really did happen. And it was glorious. His fingers worked feverishly to return the sentiment.

Yes, it was fun. Really. But let's be careful. See you then.

Once both the inbox and sent messages had been cleared, he closed his eyes and sighed. Then he cupped his hands and let the warm water spill across his face. He thought again about that kiss, just hours before, and how it had ignited inside of him a fire that he had not felt in forever. Her tongue inside his mouth, his in hers. It was warm, and soft, and rocked him so that he felt as though their union had summoned the stars and the earth and everything else in the universe, and that everything around him was somehow feeling the wonder and perfection that filled his soul. It was ecstasy, a blind passion that buoyed his spirit until he opened his eyes and looked in the mirror at his own reflection. It was not what he expected. *What the fuck are you doing?* he thought to himself. This can never work. It's complete insanity. He moved to the toilet, and let his head slowly hit the wall in front of him. Then with myriad thoughts hammering away at his temples, he emptied the contents of his stomach with one violent heave.

When he came out, Hayley was already in bed. She was curled in a ball, her back toward him. He could tell she wasn't asleep yet from the heavy, irregular breaths she released every few seconds. He closed the light on his nightstand immediately. It was just easier in the dark. If she was going to say something to him, he didn't want to have to look at her. He stripped down to his T-shirt and boxers and slid carefully next to her. He could smell her lotion, that familiar, antiseptic scent. The sheets were cold and spawned a rash of goose bumps across his arms and legs. He traced the thin path of light from the moon outside their window.

He imagined how great it would be if he could somehow ride that beam of light outside, like a magic carpet, all the way across town to Nikki's. He couldn't help it. He wondered if she were awake in her room, looking at the same light. He thought about what it would be like watching it next to her. He tried like hell to lose himself in the fantasy. What would she be wearing? Was her skin as soft as it looked? The possibilities were delicious. He felt a swelling against his thigh. They were beautiful thoughts - - beautiful, liberating thoughts. He was certain he would be able to fall asleep, secure in the daydream. But somehow, despite the breathless images that filled his head, his focus always returned to his reality, and how he would manage to navigate these dangerous waters.

What was next? And could he trust her? He had never thought of that before. There were so many things to consider now. What if her parents found out? Or if someone had seen them? Surely, that would be the end. So many questions, and he had no answers. So, he did not sleep. Not a wink. His soul chained by the daunting ghost of so many questions unanswered.

FOUR

Young Cameron Baldridge was hired to teach English at Hillcrest High School when he was twenty two. It did not take long for his youthful exuberance, sense of humor, good looks and animation in the classroom to make him one of most popular teachers at the Queens high school. The young teacher had it all; muscular build, wavy blond hair and searing green eyes that made all the girls giggle every time he passed one of them in the hall.

He was the new guy, the teacher who made learning different and fun. He played Lil Wayne downloads when they were analyzing *The Catcher in the Rye,* showed a YouTube video explaining the slave trade explored in *Uncle Tom's Cabin,* and brought in a shopping bag filled with crazy props in order to make the sword fight in *Macbeth* come alive. His classroom was bristling with life. He was magnetic, the sort of teacher to whom the kids just flocked. The membership of the school newspaper tripled after Cam took over as advisor. He organized car washes and candy sales, all of which took in record donations, single handedly resurrected a moribund student government and turned it into a legitimate Student Council, packed his classroom every other Tuesday and Thursday night for Regents review, and even got Jonathan Keppler, a kid whose hatred for reading was rivaled only by his abhorrence of school in general, to read and finish *The Legend of Mickey Tussler* in only two days, just because Cam suggested it.

"Hey, Baldridge," one of the older teachers in his department barked on the way out of school after a faculty meeting. "How come so many of *my* kids are going to *you* for extra help? What kind of brainwashing are you performing in that classroom of yours?"

His charm was unparalleled, and had really blossomed in the short time he was at Hillcrest. He had a way with all the kids, as the saying goes. The academic bunch -- the nerdy, straight A type -- found him intelligent and engaging. The popular kids thought he was 'mad chill' and the quiet, disaffected misfits gravitated to him, drawn in by his warmth and protective mien.

41

"Now, based on some of the things I've been hearing, I believe that a few of you seem to think my friend Chris's glasses make him look silly. Is that right?"

Cam was standing next to the over- weight boy's desk, tapping his copy of *American Poetry* into his open palm while panning the faces of the rest of the students. He had requested one morning that Chris stay after class and asked the much maligned boy if he wanted him to try and help. The boy stood at Cam's desk, scratching nervously at the backs of his hands with dirty fingernails.

"Would you really, Mr. B?" he asked. "Do you think it will help? I know the other kids are just teasing, but I do get sick of it sometimes."

Cam took the boy aside, and explained some things that he could do himself to mitigate a little of the negative attention – ways of navigating the social jet stream of high school. Then he sent him off to his next class.

"Just leave the rest to me Chris," he said before the boy left the room. "I know exactly what to do."

The class had just settled in when Cam began to unfurl his plan. "I wonder," he said with some deliberation, if you feel the same way about me. Huh? Do you think *I* look foolish too?" he continued, walking up and down each row of desks with furrowed brow. "Anyone?"

The boy sat quietly while his teacher championed his cause. No one else knew what to say either. It was certainly awkward. They all just sort of stared at each other. It was probably just one of those rhetorical questions, most of them thought, the kind designed to make you think. No hands necessary. Yet there he stood, pacing the room, insisting on an answer.

"Well, does anyone want to share his or her thoughts?" he said, circulating around the room. "Hmm? Come on. Look at me. Do I look foolish to any of you?"

The discomfort yielded momentarily to a murmur of nervous giggles and awkward stares until at last one adventurous soul dared to jump into the pool.

"Come on Mr. B, you know what everyone thinks of you."

The girl slumped a little in her seat, as if she had just expended all of her energy with her proclamation. The announcement went relatively unnoticed, except for another student sitting directly behind her – a heavily made up girl with blonde curly hair that had been vigorously straightened and pulled to the side in a ponytail that hung ornamentally on only one of the shoulders of her sweater – a red and white one with a chenille "H" emblazoned on the front. Except for the bulging rack of Juicy Couture garments she owned, that sweater was her favorite thing to wear.

"No Melanie, we all know what *you* think of *him*."

Everyone snickered at Samantha Brocking's sarcasm, the way everyone does when one of the most popular girls in school says something, and for a brief while anyway, there was an awkward, looming silence.

"Easy Sammy," Cam gently chided. "There's no need to get your pom poms all twisted up."

Samantha was his greatest challenge from day one. She was unlike any other student he had had in his brief tenure at Hillcrest. She said all sorts of outrageous things, created all kinds of controversy in class, and unnerved him with a stare that was both purposeful and penetrating.

"So, Mr. B, where do you hang out on the weekends?" she asked after class on just the second day of school.

"Uh, I don't know," he replied. "Here and there I guess."

"Do you ever go to bars, or clubs?"

"No, I'm not really the club type," he said. "Besides, how would you know anything about that, uh-"

"Sammy. Sammy Brocking."

"Sammy, right. Sorry. How would you even get in places like that Sammy? You're only seventeen."

She giggled and shook her head with playful incredulity.

"Fake I.D.," she said, pretending to hold up the card. "Don't tell me you never heard of such a thing. Wanna see?"

A disquieting eeriness crept over him. He took a step back away from the desk and began packing his things.

"You should be careful with that," he warned, sliding a couple of folders into his bag. "Sounds like trouble."

"I can take care of myself," she said. "Always have."

"Well, all the same," he said, with one eye on her and the other in the direction of the door, "you should probably-"

"Ever date a student Mr. B.?" she asked, circling the desk with careful deliberation.

"Excuse me?"

"Aw, I'm just playing. But come on, it's not that strange. What are you, twenty three, twenty four? Why would that be so weird?"

His nerves gathered and bubbled in his throat, so that when he opened his mouth again to speak, the explosion was instantaneous.

"Come on now Sammy," he laughed awkwardly. "Date a student? No, I don't do that. I can't do that. None of us can. That would be very inappropriate."

She was just getting started. He could see the bizarre ruminations flickering behind her eyes, a wicked fire that was doused by the fortuitous ringing of the bell.

"Well, there's the bell," he said curtly. "Gotta go."

"Well, it happens," she said, backing up just far enough to let him through. "Just saying."

Then there was Melanie Randolph. She was the textbook attention seeker, and no match for someone as confident and moody as Samantha. Melanie was a brilliant, straight A student with absolutely no social life. She just did not fit in with the other girls at school. Her mousey hair, thick glasses, and lanky body only made matters worse. She was a military brat most of her early life, jumping from state to state, never making any sort of permanent friendships. It's all she really wanted – to be part of the cool crowd. The only thing she had, though, was an impeccable academic record, something her father, who had many contacts at most of the Ivy League schools around the country, was always telling her.

"Daddy, I am tired of always studying," she often complained.

The girl longed for some attention outside the academic arena. She watched the other girls, and wished secretly for acceptance into their world. She would have traded every A she has ever received on her report card for just one invitation to a sweet sixteen or keg party.

"Studying is your ticket Melanie," he always reminded her. "I mean, look at yourself. You're not in line for any beauty contests. That may seem a bit harsh, but I'm telling you for your own good. Brains is all you have to offer."

"But that's just it daddy," she protested. "I'm not that smart. I'm not. I only get the grades I get because it's all I do. And I am getting-"

"Nonsense," he reprimanded. "You are smart, you hear? Ivy League smart. And it's nobody's business how much time you spend studying."

Melanie got along with all of her teachers, and most certainly preferred the company of adults – especially Cam. He was her favorite. She often lingered after class, to ask a question or to make a comment about his shirt, or about the lesson. He was good to her, even patient to a fault. She occupied many of his free periods, just talking to him. She would prattle on about her cello, or a song she just heard or the new boots she was planning on buying. It did not matter much really. It was clear that all she really wanted was the company. But even Cam was tiring of her presumptuousness. Things had seemed to escalate recently, particularly after the other girls began riding Melanie about her 'crush' on good old Mr. B. Any other kid would have backed off instantly. Not Melanie. She was odd that way. The more she was pushed, the harder she pushed back.

"Okay, Okay class," Cam said, trying to direct the class' focus back to the issue at hand after they had finally finished snickering over Samantha's remark about Melanie's not so subtle affinity for Mr. B. "Settle down. Let's remember what we said earlier this year about respect for each other. And about answering questions in class. And, uh, seems to me that nobody has answered the one I just asked. And when nobody answers a question, you know what happens."

They all groaned, and stared at him with painful anticipation. They knew his methods well by now. He would not be denied in his classroom. If a question was on the floor, and an answer had yet to surface, everything would cease until the matter was resolved. And they all knew the safest approach in situations like these was to meet the challenge head on – look directly at the man, for if your eyes wandered and you tried to look busy, as if taking notes or searching for a misplaced paper, or if you were just not paying attention at all, he was sure to call on you first. They all got it. But sometimes, the spirit of the challenge was just too much to resist.

"Mr. Jacobs," Cam announced demonstratively, zeroing in on the often distant, long haired skater kid who sat in the last seat of the last row by the window. "I would love to know what you think. Tell me, do I look foolish to you? Do I look like – now what's the word I heard some of you using yesterday – a loser? Would you describe me that way?"

Tommy Jacobs took his hand off his head, pulled the white chord from his hidden ear and smiled. "Oh, snap Mr. B. You're good. How'd you know?"

Everyone laughed.

"Well, can you help us Tommy? Am I a loser?"

"Come on Mr. B," Tommy pleaded. "You know the deal. You're mad cool. Everyone here knows you're the bomb."

Cam smiled. Tommy's comment was just what he wanted, the cue for his calculated lesson in humanity.

"Well, that is certainly true," he said, laughing out loud at the absurdity of his own pretentiousness. "But, be that as it may, there's a lot of things that you guys do *not* know about me."

He reached into his bag, fumbled through a folder for a second, then pulled out a photograph of a young boy – perhaps thirteen or fourteen – and held it up to the class. The kid was awkwardly fat, a clumsy teen with blotchy skin, cropped hair, braces and thick dark glasses.

"Anyone care to guess who this is?" he asked, as he slowly made his way back to Chris's desk. "Anyone?"

A discordant murmur surfaced and rose steadily among the class as everyone strained in their seats to get a closer look.

"No way Mr. B.," someone finally screamed from the back of the room. "Don't even tell us that was *you*."

He laughed. Then it grew oddly quiet, his demonstration having engendered a sort of breathless attention from his now captive audience.

"John F. Kennedy High School," he began. Freshman year. The red and green striped shirt was a birthday present from my Aunt Marcy."

He talked a little while longer about his difficulty fitting in with the popular crowd, mostly because of what he called his "high school handicaps" -- braces, glasses, a portly body and an egregious lack of fashion sense. The room remained silently charged, the air amplified by the poignancy of his reminiscences.

"So when did it all change for you Mr. B.?" another student asked.

"That's not really the issue here Blaine," he instructed. "All you guys really need to know is that it did. It *did* change. And you should think about that before you go around labeling people. Think about that – and the rifle –wielding madman from *Billy Madison.* You know, the one with the lipstick and list of people to kill from high school?"

They all laughed, even Chris, and everyone was feeling better until an untimely comment killed the moment.

"That's right Mr. B.," Melanie announced. "I agree. That's an excellent point. I think -"

A chorus of groans rose quickly to a crescendo, and Cam was right back to damage control.

"Okay then, if there are no more questions or comments, I think we will proceed with our analysis of poetic devices. I have something I think you guys are going to like."

"What about your funky picture, Mr. B.?" Tommy interrupted. "Can we just please throw it out? It's killing us!"

They all laughed again.

"Yes, please, throw it out," another pleaded.

Cam paced methodically in front of the room, seemingly afflicted by an impassioned regard for this ghost from his past.

"Not only am I *not* going to throw it away, I am going to tack it up on the front bulletin board here, as a reminder to all of you that life is not decided in the halls of high school, by a few who have deemed themselves more worthy than others."

After class, Nikki stayed back, waiting patiently behind a few students, including Samantha and Melanie, for a chance to speak to her teacher. That's how it all started. He remembered how surprised he was when she approached him. She was very quiet in class, rarely spoke at all in fact, and never initiated any sort of conversation with him. He had noticed from the very first day how striking she was, but never gave it a second thought until that day.

"I really loved class today," she said. "Jay Z's 'Empire State of Mind' was a great idea. I never learned poetry through music."

"Thanks Nikki," he said. "I try."

"It was awesome. Really. I never thought I'd ever be listening to Rap in class," she continued. "Especially after last year, with Mrs. Polchinski. I think she would have had a stroke if she heard what was going on in here today."

He was smiling in such a way as to suggest he knew something that she had not yet discovered.

"Why? It's not that much of a stretch," he said. "A lot of music, including Rap, is very poetic. Come on. Even Mrs. Polchinski would have a tough time arguing with 'concrete jungle where dreams are made of.' I mean, it's not exactly Emily Dickinson, but that's good stuff Nikki."

She smiled. She stood in front of him quietly, her books pressed tightly to her chest, possessed by thoughts known only to her.

"Is something else on your mind?" he asked.

She set her books down and smoothed the sides of her blouse.

"Well, no, not really. I just really like what you did today for Chris," she said, placing both hands on his desk while hunching her shoulders slightly forward so that her hair dangled playfully in the air. "It was really very nice."

His eyes, now firmly affixed to hers, made him uncomfortable.

"Thanks Nikki," he answered, careful to fix his gaze elsewhere. "Chris is a good kid. He deserves better than what's been happening in here. Some of you guys are brutal."

She flipped her hair off her shoulders and raised her eyebrows.

"Yeah, and you would know about that first hand, right?" she asked, winking at him.

Her eyes were much bluer than he had ever noticed before. He leaned back and folded his arms, trying to hear his scattered thoughts over the steady hammering of his heart.

"Now Miss Dillinger, are you suggesting that I told a lie in class today?"

For a moment, she was tempted to say something over the top – to explain to him that his earlier display, while clearly fabricated for a purpose, was the most endearing thing she had ever witnessed. It touched her somewhere remote. She was gushing with emotion. She wanted to tell him all about herself, how her life at home was miserable, and how her parents, especially her father, made her feel invisible. His heart was as hard and cold as the silver computer attaché he always had his nose in. But there was so much to tell. Too much. Where would she start so that he could understand her suffering?

"No, I'm not saying that," she said, lifting his Blackberry off the desk top. "It's cool." She flipped her hair again and giggled nervously. "My mother always told me that a lie is only a lie if the other person has a right to know the truth."

"Hmm, interesting idea," he said, lost in the shimmer of the flirty repartee. "I'll have to remember that."

"Yeah, you do that," she said smiling. "And while you're at it, you should also remember not to leave your phone out on your desk the way you always do." She looked curiously at the shiny black instrument in her hand, then placed it back on the desk. "Someone could get your number – and who knows what could happen."

FIVE

The conversations between Nikki and Cam grew far more frequent and personal in nature. There were still many nights when he lie awake, torturing himself over all he had to lose. But in talking to her, he was thunderstruck, discovering that he was indeed interesting and exciting. And that he could still feel good. He was all at once deflected from the doom and gloom that had been defining his days recently. Even the fear of losing his job seemed to pale with time. Maybe he did not have to settle. Maybe he did not have to be a regular Joe – the safe, predictable guy who had numbed himself to a world filled with excitement and opportunity. The longer he got away with it, the more invincible he felt.

"Do things ever get easier when you are an adult?" she once asked. He had just gotten finished making some phone calls to the parents of a few of his students when his phone went off.

"Do things ever get easier?" he repeated laughing.

"Yeah, you know. Once you are older, and in control of what you do."

"Easier? No, not easier. Different? Yes. But easier? No way. I have doubts sometimes too Nikki," he explained. "I feel sometimes like I have gotten stuck in things in my life just because it was comfortable and expected. I think I was duped by the safety of it all. You know, I stayed with my high school girlfriend even though it wasn't right just because I thought I should be with her forever. Then I met Hayley and the same is true. I've always been this way. I majored in English, and my parents were thrilled. 'Oh, it will be so nice to have a teacher in the family.' That's not what I decided. But, naturally, the next safe, logical thing was to teach – because what else would you do with an English degree? Right?"

Saying the words out loud made more him certain that pursuing this thing, whatever it was, was just what he needed.

"Well, I kinda know what you mean," she said. "Obviously, I don't understand all of that, but in my house, I am just expected to know what to do. Nobody really bothers too much with me. I'm sort of on my own."

"What about your brothers and sisters?" "Gone," she said. "All of them are grown up and out of the house. My oldest sister Karina is thirty two, Shari is twenty nine, and Lauren is twenty seven. I was obviously an oops."

He chuckled.

"Hey, don't say that. Come on now. How do you know that's the case?"

"Uh, how about they told me."

"Oh, come on Nikki. I'm sure they were kidding."

His understanding stalled. An eternity of minutes passed before he said something else.

"Well, what's the deal with your parents anyway?" he asked. "Were you guys ever close?"

"They're always busy," she explained. "My dad's an attorney at some big firm in the city, and my mom is a hospital administrator or something like that at Franklin General. They're never around. And when they are, they are always picking at me about something."

Every night, for several weeks, the two of them talked. She was becoming so much more than this young, beautiful object of his raw desire. She was, in many ways, this newly discovered life source, coursing through his body. Everything he had, and everything he saw, was sort of redefined now in terms of her. The feeling amazed him. It was as if he had swallowed a bolt of lightning, and the electricity was shooting out of every pore; every inch of his being was tingling, lit by the charge. There were e-mails, text messages, and phone conversations, all which occurred when Hayley was not around. They grew closer and closer with each exchange, and before long, the conversation turned to something far more urgent.

"So, what are we supposed to do now?" she finally asked him. "You know, about us?"

"Nothing," he said. "We are just friends. There is nothing wrong with that, right?"

He was surprised that she had been the one to finally articulate what both of them had been cultivating in this secret garden. He also thought that the smart thing, the logical thing, would be to just walk away, before it went any further. Before things got messy. But he was thinking about Hayley's constant carping and her recent habit of wearing sweatpants to bed. He shuddered. Worse than that was Nikki, and the way she was in his head, all the time. He just could not stop all the wonderful imaginings from coming. So many of these were basic curiosities. He pictured her in bed, and what she would be wearing, curled up under a soft, downy comforter. He saw her at the kitchen table, with her homework, and imagined her wet and soapy in the morning shower. He wanted to forget but couldn't. So instead of telling her that he was sorry for the way things had gotten out of hand, and ending it, he kept moving forward.

They saw each other more and more after that first "chance" encounter at Penn Station. It was like a drug in his system. He needed more and more to sustain the high. At first, it was enough just to sit with her, talk and feel her lips on his. Then he found himself wanting more. He *needed* more. He needed to touch her, to feel her body beneath his touch. His car became the place where the two of them first began pushing the limits of their forbidden passion.

They spent several hours one night, after the sun had dipped behind the dunes at Jones Beach and lit the sky with brilliant splashes of orange and purple, tearing at each other in the safety of the falling darkness. Their mouths, warm and ravenous, each took a turn devouring the other. She was soft and limber, and he was mesmerized by her beauty, drunk with the artistry of her shapely form lit faintly now by the dim fluorescence of the distant lights shining through the steamy windows.

"You are so beautiful Nikki," he whispered, freeing himself from the shadow of her embrace long enough to see into her eyes. "I can't get enough of you. I have thought about you for so long. You are the most beautiful girl I have ever known."

His confession was far more reckless than hers.

"I really like you too," she said, placing her hands flat against his chest.

He was lit now by the surging energy between them. In her eyes he now saw the possible finish to his dreams – she was his angel, there to whisk him away to paradise. His hands worked feverishly now. He could no longer wait. He wanted to be inside of her – to feel her heart on his. But her face was awash with fear and shyness; he could see she was struggling.

"What's wrong Nikki?" he asked, pulling away. "Did I do something? Say something?"

She frowned. Her eyes began to fill up.

"No, it's nothing like that. I want to. Really. But we need to stop. At least for now. It's too fast. It's going too fast. I've never done this before."

In the shimmer of the moonlight, they dressed themselves and sat quietly, her head resting silently on his shoulder. Cam kept his gaze off in the distance, focused on the car parked some two hundred yards in front of them. He couldn't think straight. Her scent, her leg stretched across his lap, her breath, still warm against his neck – it was all so distracting. What the hell was he supposed to say now?

He considered, once again, that perhaps he had expected too much – that this whole idea of he and Nikki as lovers was preposterous. The thought filled him with a tender dread. He squeezed her hand gently and kissed her forehead.

"You going to be okay?" he asked her.

"Yeah," she said. "I'm okay."

He watched as the headlights of the other car came to life, piercing the stillness of the dark. The vehicle inched forward, turned slightly to the left, then drove away. Cam followed the two hazy red tear drops as they faded off in the distance.

"What about you?" she probed. "Is everything okay with you?"

He fidgeted then pulled her to him; he did not want her to see the disappointment he was wearing on his heart.

"Me? Sure. Everything's fine. No worries."

"You're not mad or anything? You know, at me? For stopping?"

"Come on Nikki," he said, breaking their embrace just enough so that he could look at her directly. "There are no rules here. You know that. It's okay. We just have to take things one step at a time."

"I know, I know," she said frowning. "But this is all so hard. I really like you. I've never felt this way before about anyone. It's a little scary. Part of me wants to run and hide from the world, but another part of me wants to tell everyone about us. It just doesn't make any sense."

He chuckled. It was not the sort of laugh associated with pleasure and frivolity but more of a self-deprecating snicker.

"It doesn't have to make sense," he said, lifting her hand to his mouth and kissing her fingers. "These things rarely do." He paused before speaking again. "And just so you know, don't lose too much sleep about telling everyone. I'm okay with you not. "

She smiled.

They sat a little while longer, reclined now, looking through his moon-roof at the brilliant starlight, the two of them suspended in the mingled sensations of loneliness and belonging. She clung to him tightly, her eyes wide and teary. She was, somehow, more beautiful, more alluring now than ever before. Her desires, fears, and youthful illusions circled above her, forming a halo of uncertainty that spoke to him most tenderly. Sitting there, listening to her uneven breathing and feeling the unsteady hammering of her heart, he knew he had crossed a line; he also knew, despite everything else, that what had begun as lustful longing had turned into a most rapturous, unexpected love.

SIX

Cam flew through the next few weeks like a demon, possessed by her tender, dreamy glow. Her lips had definitely touched his soul, igniting something most urgent deep within him. The feeling continued to flow, like soft fibrillations, a faint, intermittent reverberation that pulsed through his veins like a warm current passing through a channel far too small. Seeing her the way he did made rapture out of the empty squares on the calendar and the idle minutes when they were apart. He was thrilled, living from one interlude to the next, but discovered, with only a feint tremor of concern, that it was not enough – time had fanned the flames of desire, so that he now wanted to possess her, all of her, and thought that he would not ever rest again until he did.

He was weary with this excitement, this fevered expectation, for although he was drunk with euphoria, and was reveling in its mystical power, he thought that what was happening to him must surely be discernible to others. Oh what a cruel trick. To feel this joy, this unbridled rush of energy, and have to worry about hiding it from the world! It made him consider again the chimerical nature of pursuing things any further. Despite the magical nature of it all, things had to stop.

Naturally, his first concern was concealing what was going on from the school community. He knew he did not want to lose Nikki, but he refused to lose his job. He was determined to have it all. So this thing with her, whatever it was, would have to wait. This would be a daunting task, for the one thing that frightened him most was the same thing that thrilled her like nothing else.

"Come on Nikki," he admonished her after she had lingered after class a third straight day. "This is no good. The other kids are going to start talking."

"They don't know anything," she replied, shrugging her shoulders before tilting her head playfully to the side.

"Not yet they don't. And I'd like to keep it that way. Besides, other kids need to see me Nikki. About assignments and things like that. Did you see Melanie's face today? She has been waiting to see me for days. And then there are other kids too. They need things too, and you're always here. Trust me, it's a problem."

Nikki, seized by a sudden wave of invincibility, leaned across Cam's desk.

"Melanie Randolph can go fuck herself," she whispered softly, toying with the contagion of his concern. She slid her hand across the desk, just far enough toward his so that the tips of their fingers touched. "And so can all the rest. They're just jealous. That's all. All those other girls really want is a little of what we both know is all mine."

There was something charming in her sentiment, but his smile yielded almost instantly to a vague apprehension.

"Just be careful Nikki," he said with more urgency. "A school building has eyes and ears lurking around every corner."

"It's no big deal. Really. Nobody knows."

"Well they might start to figure it out," he said. "And I cannot have that. In fact, I think it might be smart if we just left our meetings and conversations to here at school. Just until you graduate and we do not have to worry so much."

Her whole body sagged. "Really? Is that what you want?"

"Come on Nikki, you know what I am saying here. It's just best for now."

Cam had also grown mindful of Hayley, who ironically had become so much more attentive and agreeable ever since he had begun whatever this thing with Nikki was. It confused him. Perhaps his entrance into this secret world had somehow made him more appealing to her. The thought made him laugh to himself. It sort of made sense. He was no longer questioning her, and was far too occupied now to trouble her about her schedule, dinner, or for sex, although he was thinking that if he didn't have sex soon, he would simply burst. He could not be certain exactly why things had turned for the better, but whatever it was, she softened.

"I think we should talk Cam," she said "This fighting has gone on long enough."

She sighed deeply.

"We should settle this, especially before I leave for London. You do remember I have that convention, right?"

"Yes, I remember."

"Well, I think the eight days apart will do us good, but I want to be able to come home and not have to worry about things – so that we can just start repairing this mess of ours. Do you agree?"

Cam leaned to his side, clicked on the lamp on his nightstand, and studied her face. She looked old to him. The dark circles under her eyes and the severity of her hair, pulled tightly away from her face in a neat bun, assaulted him like never before.

"I think you are right," he said, as if offering up a prayer for the dying. "The eight days away from each other will do us a lot of good."

She said nothing. His words had barely reached her when he shut the light again, and their strained sensibilities finally surrendered to the pall of sleep.

Things in Nikki's house were not much better. She was fighting now more than ever with her parents. It was a misery. All the little things that had previously bothered her suddenly assumed a far more menacing presence, and she was no longer inclined to acquiesce to them. It was as if something had grabbed hold of her and was imploring her to take control of her body, her soul.

"Are you going to clean up your room anytime soon?" her mother said to her one afternoon after Nikki came through the door. "I am sick of looking at it."

"So close my door," she replied. "It's not like you're home all that much anyway."

"What kind of answer is that? Is that the way you speak to me now? What's with you Nicole? You don't talk anymore, you're always in your room. I can't even remember the last time I saw you with a book in your hand. And look at this place. It's a disaster. We don't hang up coats anymore, or put away dishes, or empty the recyclables. This place is a shithole. What the hell is the matter with you?"

"Just leave me alone, okay," she fired back. "If you guys would just leave me the fuck alone, I would be fine."

"Leave you alone? Is that what you said? First we're not around enough, now we are on top of you? Which is it? You're all over the place. Maybe we need another trip to Dr. Corgi. Maybe it's time to up the dosage of your Lexapro."

Her mother's remarks scorched her like an open flame.

"Fuck off," she said, eager to escape upstairs. "I am so done."

Nikki definitely felt different, as though she were seeing everything around her with another's eyes. The poignancy of this revelation vibrated deep inside her. She could no longer stand it there. It was intolerable. Actually, her mother was intolerable. And her father, as usual, was just not there. She sat down on her bed, then got up and paced around a while, then sat back down. She felt like her whole body was turning itself inside out, like her insides were stretching her skin, straining to burst free and escape somewhere. She could hear her mother downstairs, storming from room to room, cursing to herself as she cleaned up and put everything back in its rightful place. She hated her. She was such a control freak. Nikki could swear that the walls all around her had begun their steady march toward the center of the room. Surely, she would be crushed if she did not run.

Hey Mr. B. she texted. *U there?*

It took less than thirty seconds for the vibrating response to arrive.

Yes, what's up?

She looked around again – at the clothes strewn all across her floor, and the pile of college brochures her mother had left on her desk. Then, in the gentle light of her room, her eyes found the picture of her parents, and her throat tightened.

I'm ready, she wrote. *I am. Let's do it.*

He called her instantly. Her voice was off, and she was sort of scattered and out of breath.

"Hey, I know you said the other day that we were doing the right thing by not-"

"We are Nikki," he assured her. "It's best if we do not see each other again outside of school. I cannot think clearly when we are alone. We managed to escape so far. Let's be thankful. Like I said, maybe after graduation, when the risk and all the weirdness is gone, but for now, I think we need to let it be."

He could still hear her erratic breathing on the other end. It was loud and desperate and grew to an alarming crescendo when she began to cry.

"What's wrong?" he asked her. "Did something happen?"

"No, nothing really," she said through sobs. "Well, nothing that has not happened before. My mother is such a bitch. I can't take it. I really can't be here anymore."

"Come on Nikki, I'm sure it's not so bad. Did you try talking to her? I mean, can you try to work it out so that-"

"You don't understand. Can't we just see each other one more time," she asked. "Nobody will know. Just a drive or something. To talk. That's it. I really need to see you."

"I don't know Nikki," he said. "I don't think I am the one to help you. I think I have made everything worse. Besides, maybe someone your own age would understand better -- is better able to really help you deal with your mom and what's going on at home."

"I told you, seven years is not a big difference," she said. Really. Just think about it. When you are thirty five, I will be twenty eight. Now does that sound like something so bad?"

He felt oddly acquainted with the weakness he had for her. It bothered him, made him stop and consider again how this thing, whatever it was, could destroy him, although somehow at that moment he was not afraid of any punishment, and was for the most part calm.

"Nobody has to know anyway," she insisted. "Please. I really need you."

He felt everything inside of him pulling in opposite directions. He could not speak for several minutes.

"Just this once," he finally said. "I'll pick you up on the same corner as last time. Twenty minutes."

They drove to the beach again, parked exactly where they had before, and in the forgiving darkness that hung between them, talked about Nikki's life at home, and about school, and about everything else that flooded their minds.

"I just feel like I'm gonna explode," she said, sobbing. "I don't know where else to go."

"It's okay Nikki," he said, stroking her cheek gently. "Come closer. Put your head on my shoulder."

"This is the only time I feel right," she confessed, the tears continuing to stream down her face "And it can't be. Not now anyway. So what does that mean? Where does that leave me?"

"I understand," he said. "I do Nikki. I just don't know."

They sat silently for a while and just watched the clouds as they swept across the black sky. It felt good to be with her. No words. Just the tacit communion of something so incredibly wonderful. When they did speak, in between cleansing sighs, the exchanges were emotionally charged, suggestive sentiments that brought them closer and closer to the brink of what each of them slowly began to realize was the inevitable end. He held her close. She was so forlorn, so desperate. Her vulnerability called to him, stronger than before, creating exhilarating ripples that spilled across his sensibilities.

"Hey, look at me," he said, shifting his weight so that he could look directly into her eyes. "It's going to be okay. Don't worry."

She did not answer, but he heard what she was saying as she leaned in toward him, caught in the emotional rip tide. He stiffened at first, mindful of what he had promised himself, but her eyes were closed, and her lips were in front of his; he crumbled. And in the pale moonlight now seeping through the moon-roof, they kissed again.

She tasted even sweeter this time. All of his dark thoughts melted away as the two of them tore at each other, swept away by the painfully rapturous throbbing. The forbidden lovers devoured each other, their judgment eradicated by the fitful bursts of passion that had placed them on the precipice of the much imagined union. He thought that he should never again want anyone the way he wanted her, and that the wild promise possessed in her blue eyes was the sweetest thing he would ever know. But the sound of the waves crashing in the distance summoned thoughts of that summer with Maleigha, and he suddenly found, much to his amazement, that *he* was the one stopping things this time.

"I really want to Nikki,' he said. "God I do. But not this way. Let's go somewhere, when the time is right, and do this the right way. It just doesn't feel right like this. I don't want this to be dirty in any way."

Cam's world the next two days was cast in the glow of expectation. He had never felt so alive. So exultant. It was as if he were beyond everything else, that he had somehow harnessed all of the energy in the universe and swallowed it. He could hardly contain this fantastic carnival of thoughts. What were the odds of getting caught? But the mere thought of exposure halted his progression momentarily, until he recalled the ecstasy of their last encounter and was amazed by the message he sent to her:
Comfort Inn – Thursday 6:30...

Hayley's plane took off at 5:18. Cam kissed her goodbye and then drove back to town, where he stopped at a liquor store before heading over to the motel. He was filled with both excitement and alarm, fearful that at any moment she would call and say she had changed her mind. His foot weighed heavy on the accelerator, as if the speed at which he drove would somehow ensure her arrival.

He pulled into the parking lot at 6:10. He sat in his car, concealed by the mysterious shade of the emerging night, his face twisted by the same unrelenting dread. He was angry with himself for feeling anything but bliss. He fought against the impulse to drive away – the impulse that told him that what he was about to do was crazy. He dialed her number.

"I'm here," he said.

"Okay. I'm on my way right now," she explained.

"I had to wait for my mom to leave."

His breath was faint.

"Hey, are you okay?" she asked. "Is this still okay?"

He was still suffering from feverish turns, weighing one thought against another. He thought he should play it safe, and pull away before it was too late. But somehow, he could not rid his imagination of what was about to happen. The hold on his sensibility was just too formidable.

"Yeah, yeah. It's fine," he finally said. "Just use the money I gave you, and once you have the key, call me. I will come around and knock five times on the door."

It was a typical room, a small, dimly lit space with commercial carpet and vinyl papered walls. Nikki turned on a light and threw her coat on the bed. The bathroom was cramped and smelled appallingly sweet, like artificial flowers in those spray cans, but she lingered in front of the mirror anyway, just long enough to fix her hair and apply a fresh coat of lip gloss. Then she walked over to the door, stood there and dialed.

He was careful but quick. She hadn't even had time to think about what was about to happen when she heard him knocking. She undid the latch and let him in. The two of them stood awkwardly at first by the turned door, struggling a bit with the reality before them.

"What's wrong?" she asked, her voice full of dread and alarm.

"Oh, nothing," he said, shaking his head as though trying to wake himself from a dream.

"You look amazing."

She smiled and licked her lips. A heartbeat of silence fell between them before he placed the bag he was carrying on the floor, grabbed her around the waist and kissed her – harder and more passionately than ever before, his tongue frolicking with hers in a primal dance that touched both of them in every secret place imaginable. When the kiss was over, they remained by the door, his face close to hers and their hands intertwined, their hearts wrapped in the intensity of the moment.

"Nobody knows you're here, right?" he asked breathlessly.

She shook her head, but was thinking of yesterday, in the girl's locker room. She had just finished changing for gym class when Melanie snuck up behind her.

"Hi Nikki," she said smugly. "Nice shorts."

"Get lost Melanie," she responded. "You're so creepy."

The girl was just staring at Nikki, hatching something deep inside.

"Yeah, I bet you wish Mr. B. could see you in those," she continued.

"Too bad he can't stand you. Truth is, nobody can. You're stupid. You can't even see it."

Nikki rolled her eyes.

"Listen, you pathetic loser. Look at yourself. Why don't you turn around, walk away and go fuck yourself. We all know it's the only way you'll ever have something between those legs."

Melanie hated her. The truth was, she hated just about all the girls there.

"Oh, like you're getting anything," Melanie said.

"Just because you flirt with guys doesn't mean anyone wants anything to do with you."

"Is that what you think?"

"What I think, Nikki, is that you are making an ass out of yourself. Especially in English class. Really, I'm just looking out for you. You're not his type."

"Oh, and I suppose *you* are?" Nikki said.

"Yeah, I'm sure Mr. B. just gets all hard over the nerdy troll type."

She slammed her locker and turned to leave.

"You know I'm right Nikki," Melanie persisted. "That's why you're so upset."

Having tired of Melanie's bullshit, Nikki walked over and got right in Melanie's face. Then she reached into her pocket, and held her hand open. She touched a few buttons, smiled, and extended her hand in front of the girl. Melanie's ashen face glowed in the light of Nikki's phone.

"Who's upset now loser?" she said, as the stunned girl read incredulously. She was speechless.

Now hours later, standing there, in his arms, Nikki thought that perhaps she should tell him, but did not want to kill the moment.

"No, nobody knows," she reassured him. "It's cool." She seemed to linger over her last words.

"Are you okay Nikki? Is everything alright?"

He touched her cheek and placed his hands behind her neck and fanned her hair up and away from her skin.

"Yeah, I'm okay. Someone broke into my gym locker and took some of my shit. And I have such a friggin' headache. But it's all good. I took some of mom's migraine medication before I left. It'll pass."

He put the bag he was carrying on the tiny table at the foot of the bed and looked around. Something about the room bothered him, just seemed off. It was not what he expected. She interpreted his disappointment with a modicum of awareness.

"What about you?" she asked. "Are you okay? I mean, are you still okay with this?"

"Of course," he replied. "Yeah, everything's cool."

"What about your girlfriend? What did you tell her? She's not going to come barging in here and make a scene, is she?"

He shook his head no, and said nothing else for a few seconds. He was thinking about a few years back, about a former student named Kathleen Bennet. She was a beautiful girl with big blue eyes and a bewitching smile. It was only his first year at Hillcrest, and he was nervous and overly sensitive to anything that would place his career and reputation in jeopardy. His relationship with her was innocent. He had spent some time with her after school, in the library, helping her with her college essays. She was a brilliant math and science student, but her writing was fairly pedestrian. Her post high school plans included studies at one of the better universities, including several Ivy League schools. Consequently, Cam's assistance became crucial to the girl's future.

He could still recall that early spring morning, when Kathleen found him. He had just gotten up from behind a pile of essays he was grading when she came flying into his classroom, threw her arms around his neck, and began rambling breathlessly about the amazing thing that had just happened.

"Mr. B," she said, squeezing him tighter. He was a little uncomfortable. He tried to free himself from her fevered grasp before anyone else saw what was going on, but she would not release him.

"It's Cornell!" she went on, her body still pressed closely against his. "I did it! I got in. Can you believe it? I'm really going!"

When she had said all it was that she wanted to say, she pulled back, eager to read his expression. He was happy that she had finally done so, and even more grateful that nobody had seen.

"That is awesome Kathleen," he said, smiling. "What did I tell you? I was never worried at all. Come on, who's better than you?"

"Uh, you, that's who," she said. "Thank you so much. The admissions officer said that I was on the bubble, but after he read my essay, the decision was easy. Thank you so much."

She hugged him again before zooming off into the hallway to share her news with others. But before she left, she turned around one last time.

"Oh yeah, I almost forgot," she said. "I have something for you. I'll be back after ninth period."

He could remember being full of energy the rest of that day from the surging satisfaction over having helped the girl. He was feeling great, and just wanted to share it with the world.

"What's in the box?" Hayley asked later that night when she saw the token of appreciation Kathleen had dropped off for him sitting on the kitchen counter.

"Homemade chocolate chip cookies," he said smiling. "One of my students made them for me."

She popped off the cover of the clear plastic container and looked inside.

"Why?" she asked in a querulous voice.

"This is amazing Hay," he explained. "Remember the girl I was helping with her college essays? The one who was applying to all the good schools? She got in to Cornell. Can you believe it? She's the only one from Hillcrest so far this year."

"That's great Cameron," she said through tight lips. "You must be happy."

Her perfunctory reply irked him. The thrill of the moment was entirely lost.

"You know, you can be a little more enthusiastic Hay," he said. "It's not a multi-million dollar merger on Wall Street, but it is sort of a big deal."

She did not like him questioning her posture.

"Look, it's great that you helped her Cam, it is. But you should not be taking presents from students, especially students who happen to be eighteen year old pretty girls."

"Come on Hay, you're kidding, right?" he snapped back. "They're cookies."

"I don't care what it is," she ranted. "Do not do it again. One thing leads to another. These girls get crushes real easy. I bet some even fantasize about you Cam. You don't realize. And I don't like it. I'm telling you right now, I will not compete. If I can't trust you-"

Cam hated to see her this way -- so afraid and so threatened.

"Okay, Okay," he finally said, pulling her close to him so as to muffle her complaint. "I understand. I get it."

He held her for a few more seconds, kissed her face, and pledged his undying love for her. Her face finally softened, and she kissed him back. Then they parted ways, but not before she had the final word.

"I'm serious Cam. I can't do it any other way."

Looking at Nikki, he was so glad that Hayley was out of town. It made it so much easier.

"There's nothing to worry about Nikki," he finally replied. "She's on a business trip. Miles away. You do not have anything to worry about. Besides, she's not some kind of psycho."

His voice cracked a little; he didn't dare tell Nikki anything about Kathleen, or how the very next day, Hayley paid a visit to school -- showed up at his class, looking for the girl. She just stood outside his door until the bell rang, then slipped into his room before the class departed. When he questioned her later that day, she didn't even try to disguise her intention. She was very clear about what it was she was doing.

"I wanted to get a look at little miss cookie dough," she said. "And I wanted her to see me too, so that she knows you are involved."

From that moment on, Cam said very little about anything that happened at school.

With the night creeping outside the frosted windows, he cracked open the cap on a bottle of Absolut Raspberri. Then he dimmed the lights, filled two glasses and brought them over to the bed, where Nikki was sitting Indian style.

"Ever drink vodka?" he asked, handing her a glass.

"Well, most of us are more into beer," she mused, "but I'm sure I can manage."

They sat next to each other on the edge of the bed, sipping from their glasses and talking about the brilliance of their plan. She was perfect. Everything was perfect.

"I know I keep saying it, but you are just so damn beautiful," he said, taking the glass from her and placing both of them on the tiny desk top across from them. Then he slid his right hand behind her and up the back of her shirt. She closed her eyes and sighed softly. He whispered to her, something soft about the two of them and secret worlds, then placed his lips against her cheek, glowing white and angelic in the cabin of darkness. Her hands were restless. She found his face first, then his lap, and he felt her warmth as well as waves of titillation throughout his entire body.

"You are amazing Nikki," he whispered in her ear.

She looked down, embarrassed by his attention, then moved her other hand to meet his. Sitting there, fingers sweaty and intertwined, they both felt the full rush of energy that flowed between them. It was hot and fast. The moment was everything he had been dreaming of for weeks. The time, he thought, was finally right. He leaned in toward her, and in the peculiar shadows of the musty room, his lips found hers. She sighed again. It was just as heavenly as the other times they had kissed, only now, there were no questions left. No hesitation. There was only her tongue, and her taste, and her breath, soft and warm.

They fell back on the bed, their mouths still joined in glorious exploration. He could sense her entire body coming to life, ignited by his kiss, and she could feel him next to her, stiff and ready. His fingers found their way under her sweater and across her bra, then moved quickly inside her pants, where he pushed aside the lacy cloth beneath and began touching her softly, rhythmically. She responded wildly, pulling his shirt over his head. Her breathing was hard and erratic. She removed her own shirt next, helped him with his pants, and in the deliberate pantomime that seemed to usher in the mutual surrender that was washing across both of them, pulled him on top of herself.

He was gentle at first, each of his thrusts slow and even. He watched her the whole time, trying to read the effects of his efforts. He kissed her eyes and cheeks and her lips again, but her movements would not allow him to linger there. As the two of them melted more and more into each other, the union became more furious. He continued to dive deeper and deeper inside her, spurred on by the emerging reality that he had aroused her as much as she had him. They moved together, lost completely now in the flush of emotion. She was warm and wet and whimpered with pleasure. Nabokov's nymphet. He was so right. Her body was soft and tasted like berries or some celestial nectar. It made him shudder with delight. She was good, did not move like a girl who had never done this before.

He wanted to freeze the moment, to suspend himself indefinitely in the warmth of her presence, so he slowed his approach, trying desperately to last as long as he could. He quivered with the exertion of restraint, fighting against the formidable build up. It was like nothing else he had ever known. He thought he would just surrender to the rush, embrace the volcanic explosion of passion and savor what would follow, when he suddenly stopped. Everything inside of him seized, and all at once he was outside of his body, frowning on the face of all that was before him.

"What's the matter?" she asked. "Did I do something wrong? Is everything okay?"

He pulled away so that he could look at her clearly, all the while struggling with feelings that were seemingly beyond his strength.

"I can't Nikki," he said. "I just can't.

"Why?" she asked. He eyes began to leak.

"It doesn't feel right. I don't know what it is, but it's definitely there.

"But we love each other, right? I thought-"

"I don't know Nikki. I'm sorry. It's just that – I can't risk all of this. Hayley and my job and all. I love teaching. It's everything to me. I just can't-"

"It's okay," she said, grabbing his forearm and squeezing tightly.

He slid her hand off his arm and held it in between his own.

"I'm sorry Nikki. Maybe it will be different after June. But right now, I just can't."

She said nothing. His words wounded her deeply. He had never seen her face so broken. He was upset too, now possessed by the inexplicable sense of having been betrayed by suddenly finding himself. What had he done? He loathed this sudden attack of right versus wrong and derided himself even more when she began shaking her head sadly and crying.

"Please Nikki, no crying. Okay? I didn't mean you and me are not right," he explained desperately, grabbing her hand.

She was sitting quietly, her head slumped down to the floor. Her heart was banging away inside her chest and the tears just kept pouring from her face with such ferocity that he could scarcely conceive of how there could be any left.

"Believe me, you make me feel like I have not felt in a long time. I – I love you Nikki. And I want to be with you. I do. And we will. One day. You are everything to me. But I don't want things to start like this."

She could not speak. The sight of her crumbling before him bewildered him. He sat across from her, motionless, with his eyes now directed to the floor. His mouth was dry and he struggled himself with the threatening rush of tears. This truth which had risen to the surface overwhelmed his fading resiliency.

"Look," he said, lifting his eyes so that they were again fixed on her. "June is not that far off. That will give me time to end things with Hayley, the right way, and it will also allow us to be more free with each other. There is no law that I know of preventing an eighteen year old girl and a twenty-five-year-old guy who are in love from seeing each other."

He squeezed her hand tighter. He thought about the next few months – about the beautiful secret they shared and what lay before them. The aching in his groin reminded him that he wanted to be with her, right there, but somehow knowing that she would be waiting for him, and that the "dirtiness" of it all would no longer sully the splendor of what they shared was enough to get him through.

She sat for another minute or two silently. Her absence began to trouble him a little. He released her hand and, with the tips of his fingers, gently lifted her chin so that she was now facing him again. He felt a vague pain when he saw that all the color had drained from her cheeks and that her breaths were forced and erratic.

"Come on Nikki, you believe me now, don't you?" he asked.

She stifled a sigh and nodded; the tears just continued to roll down her face.

"Hey, it's okay Nikki," he said, brushing the errant strands of hair from her eyes. "Come on, where's my happy girl?"

She breathed in deeply, as though she could not get enough air, and offered what he ascertained to be the glimmer of a faint smile. Then her eyes rolled back in her head, and she began shaking uncontrollably -- a violent, spastic series of gesticulations that went on for several seconds until she lost consciousness.

"Hey, are you okay?" he asked, trying to rouse the girl.

The episode continued to unfold.

"Nikki, Nikki," he repeated now more frantically, tapping her face gently. "Can you hear me? Nikki?"

He ran his hand across her forehead and again tapped gently at her cheeks. She was drenched with perspiration. He ran to the bathroom, and came back with a damp cloth which he placed first on one side of her face, then the other.

"Nikki, Nikki," he implored. "Come on now. It's me. Come on Nikki."

He tried desperately to wake her, but she would not respond. With his head whirling, despite the mesmerizing gravity of the scene unfolding, he began blowing into her mouth and pumping feverishly on her chest.

"Nikki," he kept saying. "God Damnit Nikki, come on!"

But she did not move; she was lifeless. He repeated the same process, two or three more times, but there was no change.

"Oh no, oh God no," he said, moving away from her. She had no pulse. She was completely limp, her eyes and mouth still partially open.

He stood up, weak and shaken. He thought instantly of the Shakespearean dramas he taught, those tragic heroes with their tragic flaws, and knew, as if Shakespeare himself were whispering it in his ear, that he had just played out a pivotal act in his own twisted drama. His heart tightened with such loathing for himself that he gasped out loud for air.

"Fuck, oh fuck me!" he cried, his face drained of all its color. "This can't be happening. Not again. Please no. I can't do this again."

He was thinking of Maleigha. And the night that summer they had found their way to Gilgo Beach. She had finally told Cam that she was moving to Ecuador the next day. This was to be their final night together.

"I want you to be my first," she said to him, as they slipped secretly over weathered wood and wire fence stretched across the dunes. "I love you Cameron."

It was a perfect night. The sky was filled with glinting diamonds, and the air was sweet and cool. They stood on the sand, holding each other, Maleigha's long, dark curls spilling all over her bare skin.

"Where should we go?" he asked her. "I really don't know this beach well."

She ran her hands over his back and smiled.

"Let's swim first," she said, taking his hand and pulling him toward the surf. "It's so pretty."

They held each other as wave after wave crashed over them. Cam showed her how to ride the big ones, just beyond the breakers, and she laughed when an unexpected rip tide took his feet out and knocked him to the ground.

"I guess I'm not doing it right Cam," she teased. "I'm still standing."

He grabbed at her playfully, and they kissed. His whole body was tingling, his skin now a thin veil between the inner rush of blood and the cool salty water.

"Come on Maleigha. Let's go back and stretch out the blanket."

She wrapped her legs around his middle, and her arms around the back of his neck, and kissed him again.

"Go ahead Cam," she said. The moon's glow centered on the curve of her face. "Surprise me. I just want to ride a couple more. I'll be right there."

The blanket was soft against his skin. He was nervous now, waiting. What should he do? How should he act? She was to be his first as well. Sure, he had read all about sex in books, and seen his fair share of cable T.V. movies. But this was the real deal. None of that seemed to matter much now.

He looked down at himself, suddenly aware of his raw nakedness, and decided to throw his shirt across his lap as he looked out at the ocean, waiting for Maleigha's silhouette to emerge. He felt fourteen. Awkward and afraid. He was also sad. He was going to miss her. She was unlike any other girl he had ever met. Beautiful. Funny. He never got over her. Maybe if he had actually had her that night, felt her heartbeat on his, things might have been different. He might have moved on. But Maleigha never came back that night. He may have had a chance of getting over it if he had had the opportunity to say goodbye. To see her, to touch her, one last time. But they never found her body.

It was this same pain and void that Cam was feeling again, now, years later. Stiff with shame and terror, he backed away from Nikki's body slowly, a procession of grotesque images unfurling before him. Yes, it was the same feeling, only this time, it was worse. He felt threatened. He was scared. *What the fuck am I going to do now?* he thought to himself. He couldn't think. Sweat rose to his skin and he was beginning to feel nauseous; he knew the sickness would only worsen until he struck a blow against it.

He crossed the gap between sorrow and self-preservation quickly enough. With thoughts of CSI episodes littering his brain, he began wiping down everything he had touched, and threw all the objects of damnation – vodka bottle, his glass, and the condom wrapper – in a bag. Then, with tears streaming down his face, he covered her from the waist down with the twisted sheets and went over the entire room one last time.

Standing in the pale light, he struggled with the immediacy of the situation. His eyes scanned the room with feverish desperation. Had he remembered everything? Had he removed all traces of his presence? He surveyed the ugly face of his actions and wept openly. He counted his breaths, trying to mitigate the tightening of his chest, all the while lamenting why it had all happened. Why? How could it be? Why did he have to pursue her? Why didn't he have the strength and good sense to just say no? Why? Why couldn't he have just been with her that night in his car, and she still be alive? What sort of punishment was this? He had no answers, no insights, and no idea where this sordid chain of events would lead him once he slipped out of the room and into the night.

SEVEN

Hayley's plane touched down three days after the shocking news about Nikki's death hit the newspapers. He met her at the gate. She came through the tunnel carrying two bags filled with mementos from her trip and wearing a radiant smile. He was happy to see her too, truly. Almost relieved. He tried to return the smile, but most of him was clearly absent. He was haggard. His face was pasty and unshaven, his eyes vacant and dark.

"What on earth is wrong with you?" Hayley asked, dropping her bags before placing her hands on his cheeks. "What the hell happened?"

He was shaken as he whispered his response.

"It's one of my students," he said, swallowing hard. "She passed away a few days ago."

The words spilled from his lips with greater ease than he had anticipated. He had isolated himself and had remained silent since it happened, swollen with guilt and worry. Yet now, seeing Hayley, this tide of darkness flowed from his most remote regions into the vast reality before him, and suddenly, he was separated from it somewhat and feeling, at least for the moment, connected to the world once again.

"When you said on the phone that you had something terrible to tell me, I never imagined," she said. "That's awful."

He held her bags for her as they made their way through the airport with short, deliberate steps.

"What happened?" she continued. "How did she die?"

He wanted to tell her everything right there, to release his encumbered heart so that he could breathe again. He wanted to apologize to her, to cry in her arms and ask her for her help, and tell her that he never meant for any of this to happen. But his tongue was thick and his mouth dry. The words just would not come.

"It looks like a drug related thing," he said, his eyes narrow and fixed to the ground. "A bad mix of some things. I think the police are still investigating. So far they have no real information."

"Those poor parents," she said. "I can't even imagine. The funeral must have been a horror."

His mind drifted back instantly to the surreal moment. She looked so beautiful in her casket, dressed in an azure gown that matched the blue in her still eyes; she was as beautiful as she had been that night. She was still the most magnificent thing he had ever seen. But the cold, mahogany box that housed the fair nymphet poisoned the image. The incongruity rattled him. So did the haunting words of one of one of their earlier conversations.

It was a Friday night. He had just stepped out of Home Depot with a bag full of tape and spackle for a weekend project he was about to attempt when his phone rang. She had been crying.

"What's wrong Nikki?" he asked. Where are you?"

"I'm outside, down the block from my house," she told him. "I had another huge fight with my mother. I swear I just don't belong here anymore."

She went on to describe the argument, and her mother's ridiculous rules and conditions, and how she had really grown to hate all adults. They always made her feel weird. Like they knew she was mature enough for what she wanted, but would not admit it, for fear of losing control. They would use words like "precocious," and invoke expressions like "too big for her britches" and "not dry behind the ears yet." But the truth of the matter, at least as Nikki saw it, was that they were all threatened by her. All that is, except him.

"You're not like that Mr. B.," she went on. "You never were. I don't know, it's weird, but I am just so comfortable with you. It's all just so easy."

"I know what you mean Nikki," he said. "I don't even feel this way about most of the adults I am involved with."

He listened some more as he walked through the parking lot. It was a nice night, so when he arrived at the place where he had parked, he just placed the bag on the hood of his car and jumped up next to it.

"You want to hear something crazy?' she asked him.

"Sure Nikki," he said. "How bad could it be?"

"Well, I sort of believe in reincarnation," she explained. "Not like you come back as a lizard, or tree frog, or anything nutty like that. But I really think that people live more than one life. And that we're not supposed to remember the ones we have already lived. Only, sometimes, I think you do. At least a little part of it. You know what I'm saying?"

He laughed.

"You *do* remember that it was *you* who said this was crazy, right?"

She scolded him playfully, then continued.

"Come on, you know what I mean. It's like that whole déjà vu thing. That's no accident. You feel like you have experienced something before because you *have*."

"Okay Nikki," he said. "I admit it. "You win. This *is* crazy. What are you talking about?"

"You and me," she said. "It's no accident. I feel like we are both old souls, ones who knew each other in another life. Come on. How else would you explain it?"

He loved her innocence and enthusiasm.

"Yeah, I guess you are right," he admitted. "There is something awfully warm and familiar about all of this."

They talked for a little while longer, until he had to go. She told him that she should be getting back home as well. They made plans for their next conversation, exchanged warm good nights, and then she said something that now, weeks later, made the hair on the back of his neck stand straight up.

"I hope that this one is a good one," she said.

"What is Nikki?"

"This life," she said. "We're old souls, but we don't know *how* old. I believe that when you have finally completed your journey, you die. But nobody knows when that is."

He remembered telling her she had nothing to worry about.

"Well, I wouldn't lose too much sleep over that one," he said.

"As my grandmother used to say, I think you can still buy bananas."

"What?" she asked. He chuckled at her innocence and naïveté.

"Never mind."

She was in a much better mood now. Her voice was light and playful.

"Okay, I'm not sure exactly what bananas have to do with anything, but I'll take that as something good."

Standing near her casket, he desperately wished he could talk to her again. He was also disturbed by the noticeable absence of people. Where was everyone? He looked around at the sparse groupings of people milling around the room. It bothered him. A life should never end, he thought, without enough people taking notice. Thankfully some of the kids from class were there.

"This is rough Mr. B.," Melanie said as he took a seat in the front next to hers. "I know she was your favorite."

Cam made little protest over the comment.

"I love all you guys Melanie," he said tearfully.

He remembered how Melanie stayed by his side all evening, as if she were waiting for an opportune time to share something to him – something that would make him feel better. She was sweet that way, he thought.

"It was awful Hay," Cam continued to explain. "There was nobody there. Just a handful of relatives. She didn't have many friends either. A bunch of kids from class showed up. Most of them were really shaken up. One girl, Melanie, even made a small photo board that all the kids wrote messages on. She even made a little speech. It was odd, and awkward, but sort of touching."

"What about her parents Cam?" she asked. "Did you speak to them?"

"It was just awkward Hay," he said again. "Christ I was so uncomfortable. What do you say? I said something to one of her sisters. But her father wasn't even there. Imagine? It was the most awful thing I have ever experienced."

The afternoon was falling fast, a gray, numbing, wintry shroud punctuated by a creeping dampness that chilled their bones as they walked to his car. She told him a little about London, and about some of the things she had brought back, but he heard very little of it. Somehow, it was okay with her. She understood his mood, and decided that she had more important things to tell him anyway.

"Can we turn off the radio for a little while?" she asked.

"Oh, sure. Yeah, I guess so. I was – I just wanted to catch the news."

"Well, the news can wait. I think I can cheer you up a little Cam," she said, rubbing the back of his neck as he drove. A fleeting thought struck him.

"Cheer me up," he answered. "I doubt that."

"I was thinking, while I was away, that I have been really moody lately," she said. "You know, a little bitchy about things. And maybe unfair. I'm sorry."

He nodded.

"I just want you to know that I really am sorry, and that I really want to start over – for us to try and make this work. I want to tell you, right now, that I am making you my number one priority. No more dinners at the office, Saturday meetings, midnight conference calls. It's all going to change. And, I'm sort of hoping that you like the idea, and that you're into it. And that maybe you can work on some things as well. I think we can make this work."

He was straight and cold.

"Did you hear what I said Cam?" she asked.

"Yeah, yeah Hay. I heard you."

Her mouth morphed into an odd shape.

"Well, that's not exactly the response I was hoping for."

He touched her hand. It was warm, familiar. He liked everything she had said – especially the part about starting over. That's what he wanted, now more than ever. He wanted to begin right now, but wondered silently whether or not he could ever get there. He wanted to be good old reliable Cam again. Boring, vanilla, hum drum Cam.

"I hear what you're saying Hay," he said, full of twisted feelings. "I do. I would like the very same thing."

Despite ten straight days of roiling nightmares and pangs of guilt, Cam's spirits were buoyed by reports that the police were having trouble piecing things together. The toxicology report was conclusive – Nikki's heart was jolted into a fatal arrhythmia as a result of the lethal combination of her prescribed anti-depressant and the Imitrex she took from her mother's pill box. There were also traces of alcohol in her system. What the detectives still could not figure out was why she was there, and who was with her. It seemed that every avenue they pursued was a dead end. The motel clerk who signed Nikki in said that as far as he knew, she was alone. He never saw anyone else with her that night. There were no witnesses, and her parents could provide no substantial names of friends or acquaintances for investigators.

"Our daughter," they explained tearfully, "was sort of a loner. She really did not have any friends."

The announcement frustrated those in charge of the investigation.

"You realize that we have virtually nothing else to go on, right Mr. and Mrs. Dillinger?" they asked. "Are you sure you can't give us anything?"

"What can we say," the girl's father said. "Just do the best you can with what you have."

The few students the officers did manage to question had little to offer as well.

"I don't know much about her at all," was the common response.

"She sort of kept to herself. She was a little weird like that."

Each day that passed ended with the same frustration. There were just no leads. Even the attempt to access Nikki's cell phone records, something that they were certain would unlock the case, proved fruitless when the wireless carrier informed authorities that the record detailing Nikki's account activity during the past few months had been expunged prematurely, along with the records of thousands of other customers, due to a computer virus.

"We'll keep trying," the lead investigator announced, "but with not much to go on, this is going to be a rough one."

Cam was also pleased that Hayley had kept her word. Things were better. He did not know exactly why, nor did he care, but it felt like this restless longing and discontent that had plagued him for so long had finally been satisfied.

"What do you say we drive out east this weekend?" he asked her. "Get ourselves a room for the night, on the ocean. You know, like we used to. We should really get away."

She was already thinking about all the shops she wanted to visit, and where they would eat, and about the delightful possibility that she and Cam were finally ready to move things to the next level.

"That would be wonderful," she said. "I'll arrange for someone to feed Othello and make some calls today from work."

That Saturday was a perfect day for a drive. Blue skies, brilliant sun, and a gentle, temperate breeze that belied the usual severity of the season. She always loved to sit in the car on days like these. There was something about taking a drive. She opened the window and just let the cool morning air bathe her body as she watched the miles of wild flowers and Pitch Pines roll away just outside her door. It was soothing. Cam felt it too. Every mile they drove dulled the horrible images in his mind, made it all seem like it was just a bad dream, like nothing had ever happened at all. Maybe it was the hypnotic grind of rubber on asphalt or the whistle of the wind moving in and around the windows. Perhaps it was the smell of the morning grass or the way the first rays of the sunrise seemed to melt the road ahead. They didn't know. Whatever it was, they were both happier than they had been in quite some time.

Their first stop was Pindar Winery, where they spent a couple of hours curling through the sculpted gardens and exploring the rustic cellars while sampling all of the latest blends. They both were surprised to find the whole wine tasting process was really quite interesting, although the lecture they were sort of forced to listen to became a little tedious. It was a little more intense than they expected. Actually, they both felt like they were back in school. They stood around, sample cups in hand, while some middle-aged connoisseur with horn- rimmed glasses and a cardigan sweater pontificated about the "art of wine tasting," from the viewing to smelling and finally the tasting.

"You must chew the wine," he said in a peremptory tone, "allow it to spill across the palate. Then, before swallowing, aerate the wine in your mouth. Like so."

It was the most ridiculous sight they had ever seen. Something in particular struck Hayley so funny about this stuffy guy contorting his face and making all sorts of sounds as he demonstrated his technique for the entire group.

"Can you believe this guy?" she asked quietly, elbowing Cam in the side.

Then she crossed her eyes and made a puckering motion with her lips, thinking about how hilarious it would be if Professor Vineyard's dissertation was interrupted by a little of that sacred elixir rushing out of Cam's nose.

"Shut up Hay," he said through tight lips as his shoulders began to shake with comedic tremors.

They were both struggling to bury the laughter, like two kids in a church pew battling humorous thoughts under the watchful glare of our parents. She could feel her sides beginning to hurt from holding it in. When the effort not to explode became too much to handle, they both slipped away, off to the side, and laughed until tears rolled down their faces.

"Is this guy for real?" Cam laughed. "What a dork."

She could barely breathe from laughing so hard.

"You must chew the wine," she mimicked. "Ha, ha. This is unreal. What a piece of work!"

It had been so long since they laughed like that. It felt so good. Liberating. They ended up falling into each other and kissing, with some difficulty; both of their mouths were numb, dulled from all of the wine they had swirled in our mouths that afternoon. He was having another issue as well. He couldn't help but think of Nikki, and how her kiss was different.

"You know, I was thinking Hay," he finally said, lifting another paper cup to his lips. "Maybe we should talk about us. You know, our future."

He seemed to be considering something well beyond the sentiment while he said it. In the shadows of a stone stairwell, she listened to him and composed herself with the patience of an actress awaiting her cue. She was excited and scared, all at once. She was still not sure it would work. She wanted to believe him. But she was frightened to think of what she would do next if it were just another lie.

They arrived on the windswept sands of Gurney's Inn a few hours later. It was the first time they'd been back since their junior year. They unloaded their belongings in the room and with scarcely a thought of anything else, grabbed some light jackets and ran down to the beach. It was just as she remembered it. Soft dunes sprawling seaward, flanked by dancing patches of ornamental grasses; rolling waves that licked the water's edge and teased the gulls wrestling with the remnants of shellfish that had washed ashore; boats off in the distance, scraping the horizon. It was paradise. It wasn't long before they were walking, hands joined, while being serenaded by the rhythmic song of the Atlantic.

"Water, everywhere you look," she said. "The end of the island. And on the other side, Europe. It's absolutely incredible."

Cam gazed out at the whitecaps through the heavy air. "Not exactly Jones Beach, huh?" she continued.

"What do you mean?" he asked, his feet now still in the sand. There was a faint agony surfacing behind his eyes.

"Nothing. I just mean that this part of the island is far more beautiful," she explained. "You know, unspoiled."

He licked his lips and exhaled. "It *is* pretty," he agreed.

Then he pointed his finger in the other direction, at the houses that overlooked the beach from high atop a sandy embankment on the opposite side.

"That's what I really like," he said, pointing in that direction. "Which one would you want Hay?"

"Come on Cam," she said. "Can we talk about something serious?"

"Vacation, right Hay?" He rolled his eyes gently. "Come on now. Which house? You know, if we could afford it?"

"What are you, crazy?"

"No, what I am is the guy who just got a letter from Merrill Lynch. Remember the trust fund I told you about a while back – from my uncle?"

"Yes?" she answered, her face erupting into a smile.

"I just got the notice in the mail yesterday. It's come due."

"Really?" she said, her eyes flickering with excitement. "What are we talking about?"

"Well, it may not be enough to buy your dream house, but half a million bucks isn't a bad start."

The two walked some more, both of them feeling good.

"So, let's keep playing," he said. "Just in case. Which house would you want to live in?"

"I don't know Cam. What's the difference? You said it yourself. It can't happen."

"Come on," he insisted, jabbing her shoulder playfully. "Pick one."

Her eye stretched reluctantly across the shore line, then back again, and through the haze of smoke, despite obvious irritation, she surrendered.

"Okay," she finally said. "I'll take the big one over there -- with the greenhouse and pool."

She played along with him for a while. The mood was right. Eventually, they stopped walking and just stood, as they used to, looking at each other. She bent her face close to his and kissed him gently, laughing when she saw that the Vaseline she had rubbed on her lips had slipped onto his.

"Ooh, now that's very attractive, Mr. Baldridge," she teased, pointing at his mouth. "I don't know that I want to buy anything with you."

He laughed a little too. He was pleased with the little steps they had taken. This was the best they had been together in months. Perhaps he should have just embraced the moment, and left things the way they were. It did feel good to breathe again. But he had other ideas that were weighing heavily on her mind, and still others he was eager to push as far away as possible.

"I was thinking Hay," he said. "This would really be the perfect time for us to start our future."

With the bright sun shining behind her, he couldn't read her expression. He found himself trying to feel for it, interpreting her movements and body language. Her arms were folded and her left foot was crossed in front of the right, and was pivoting on a piece of driftwood that had washed up on the sand.

"Well, Hay? How do you feel about that?" Her eyes widened suddenly, as if she had lost all her breath.

"Well, I have to say that I'm a little surprised. Why all of a sudden this interest in settling down? Whenever I said anything about that, you shut right down. And, do you really think that with everything that has been going on between us, it's the right time?"

He sighed. There was a discernible angst in the way his eyebrows came together.

"I think it's the perfect time Hayley," he argued. "Especially now. Things have never been better, and I really need – I mean I really want to do this now."

They ate dinner at a little place just up the road. Small tables facing the ocean, arranged symmetrically under dim lights, and the sound of blues piano to soften the air. Hayley couldn't help but smile. They were miles away from their lives, and all of the things that encumbered their daily exchanges. No schedules. No commitments. No arguments. It was glorious. She was remembering the nights, long ago, and what had brought them together. His soft, inviting affectations. The way he made her feel, like all he could see was her. Cam was feeling good too. He now believed that if he could keep his mind from pausing on his indiscretion, it would tire and not return. If he could replace his ominous thoughts with those more pleasant, the former would simply disappear. He practiced this exercise the entire time they were away.

After dinner, they drove back to their room and sat outside, the salty air blowing gently across two wicker lounges on the terrace. They talked some more about each other, and about their vision for the future. They covered just about everything. Families. Their careers. Where they would live. It was easy again.

"This is nice Cam," she said, snuggling her head on his shoulder.

He sighed peacefully and nodded.

"And," she continued, "I have a little surprise for you."

She hopped out of her chair and scurried through the sliding glass door. He inhaled the salty air, filled his lungs and put his feet up on the railing. The stars, he thought, never seemed brighter.

"Here you go," she announced moments later. "Your favorite."

He grew deathly quiet, as though he were viewing some twisted parody of his darkest hour. He turned away from her. The moon, which had bathed them all night in soft, luminous hues, faded behind a passing patch of clouds. Even through the darkness she could see the slight tremor of his lips and the pallor of his profile.

"What's wrong? You always drink Absolut Raspberri."

He could hear the harsh undulation of the waves in the black of night and felt, at that very moment, a similar tempest brewing inside of him, one that would undoubtedly rise with ruthless rage and crash hard on shore, revealing, as a stormy ocean would, all of the mysteries kept hidden in the deepest corners of the sea.

"No, it's fine he said," shaking his head back and forth quickly as if to free his mind from the nagging misery. "I'm just not in the mood tonight, that's all."

Her face dropped a little and she sat up real straight.

"I don't understand Cam. What's going on?"

His gaze was fixed off somewhere beyond her.

"Nothing is going on Hayley. Why does me not drinking Vodka have to turn into such a big deal?"

"It doesn't Cam," she answered.

"Holy shit. I was just trying to do something nice."

He licked his lips and looked right at her now.

"Well, stop trying so hard Hay," he said. "Just stop. Please."

She couldn't help but think that they were going down that old road again already. Why was it so hard, all the time? She tried to move the conversation away from the subject. She prattled on about work, and about one of her friends who just had a car accident, and other mundane things that Cam just did not hear. Even her attempts at levity did little to chip away at his stolid expression.

"Tell me something I don't know about you Cameron Baldridge," she said, tugging playfully on the collar of his shirt.

"What?"

"Play with me Cam," she pleaded. "It will be fun. If we're going to be husband and wife, I want to know all about you."

"Come on Hay," he said shaking his head. "What are you talking about? I have no secrets. You know me better than anyone."

"Relax Cameron. What's wrong with you? I'm just trying to have a little fun here. Come on. Can't we still discover new things about each other?"

He cleared his throat, aware of his emerging discomfort, and with great effort, made an attempt to appease her.

"I'm sorry Hay," he said. "I know. You're right."

"That's better."

She pulled her legs up to her chest and leaned her head on her knees.

"Well?" she continued. "What do you want to share with me?"

He stood up and stretched his arms over the railing. He couldn't think. He wondered if mental fatigue was impairing his judgment.

"I don't know Hay," he said, shaking his head. "This is stupid."

"Please Cam. Just try. For me?"

"Okay Hay," he said. "Let's see."

He scratched his chin and rolled his eyes skyward.

"I got it. Here's something. You know what really bugs the shit out of me?" He formed a steeple with the fingers from both hands, as if he were getting ready to deliver a sermon or some sort of commencement speech.

"You *are* going to tell me, right?" she said, laughing at his deliberate approach. "Personalized license plates" he said. "Yup. That's it. Personalized license plates really bug the shit out of me."

He couldn't help but smile a little. She giggled.

"What? Come on Cam? Are you kidding me?"

"I'm dead serious. Come on You know I'm right. Who cares if you have '3 sons' or if you are a 'ski bum'? Are people so wrapped up in themselves that they think anyone really cares? It annoys the shit out of me."

She laughed at the faint note of seriousness that belied the absurdity of his comment.

"You have got to be kidding me," she said biting her lip. "That is friggin' nuts."

"It's not so crazy," he protested. He scratched his chin again and his eyes narrowed.

"Well, Miss Hayley," he asked. "What about you? What bothers you? You know, a pet peeve? Weird obsession? Something I should know about?"

She looked away. He took her hand, vexed momentarily by what he perceived to be her unwillingness to play fairly. She laughed, and did have a little trouble at first answering him.

"Vacuum lines," she finally said. "Definitely vacuum lines."

"What are you talking about?"

"Vacuum lines in the carpet," she explained. "I vacuum in a very precise way. In rows. After I am done, there are a series of nice lines etched in the carpet. I like it that way."

"Fascinating," he said.

"Hey, I didn't tease you," she complained.

He laughed loudly before taking both of her hands in his. "Okay, I'm sorry. I'll play nice. But I don't get it. What's the problem then?"

"The problem, Cameron James," she said shaking her fist, "is when someone walks across the lines and leaves *his* footprints in the carpet. It's very messy."

They laughed most of the night. It was cleansing. Then, under a brilliant sky filled with stars, they made love on the terrace, moving in unison to the sound of the ocean beating against the moonlit shore. It was the first time Cam was with her since that fateful night. She was different from what he remembered. Her smell, her taste. Why had she changed? He felt a little different himself, almost like he was using someone else's body. As he sped through the interlude in rudimentary fashion, it occurred to him, much to his horror, that maybe it wasn't her at all. Maybe it was him. He certainly felt strange, like part of him was missing, or guarded, inaccessible or locked away forever. Had Nikki taken the best part of him with her? He wondered secretly if Hayley could tell.

That night, as he lie quietly beside her, he felt something happening to him, like little doors opening and closing inside of his body. Hellos and goodbyes. Beginnings and endings. Everything felt like it was shifting, moving with the push and pull of the tide outside the window. It was unsettling, and he thought he might be sick. But he felt fortunate all the same, lucky to have escaped certain disaster and blessed to have this opportunity now to just move on. Lucky, that is, until on his way back from the bathroom, he read a text message he had received earlier that night. It had come from Nikki's phone.

Comfort Inn – Thursday 6:30...

He gripped his Blackberry tightly, beginning to lose presence of mind. He was stiff in every limb. He had never felt such suffocation, such desperation, until he read the second message, which all but brought him to his knees.

We should talk.

EIGHT

The skies were aberrant that next morning, producing heavy thunderstorms replete with sheets of lightening that flashed like a series of mini explosions all around them. Cam was disconsolate, and drove silently, furiously, as if he were racing to reverse the damage he had done in hopes of preserving the unused portion of his life. His throat was tight. It bothered him, hurt almost, but not nearly as much as the realization that he loved Hayley, and really had all along, and now his self-betrayal had turned what should have been a clear path to happiness into a narrow trail fraught with all sorts of hidden hazards. It was suffocating him.

"Cameron, did I do something wrong?" she asked. Her fingers drummed her knee in time with the wipers.

He shook his head.

"Because I feel like we went to bed last night happy, you know, and then this morning, out of nowhere, everything was different."

He was miles away, far-flung and spellbound.

"What? No, No Hay," he protested, rubbing her thigh. "You didn't do anything wrong. I'm just in a mood. Sad, I guess, to be leaving."

"Because if you have changed your mind, and don't want to-"

"Changed my mind? Are you kidding? Listen, let's not go down that road. Okay? I said I want to do this, and I mean it. In fact, I think we should make an appointment at the jewelers when we get home. Look at some things that you like."

She smiled, took his hand in hers, leaned her head back and closed her eyes. She wanted to say something else, and thought that she might, but she was not sure what it would be.

He managed, the next couple of days, to assuage Hayley's nagging uneasiness, but she was not totally convinced. Neither was his mentor John, or the rest of the people with whom Cam worked. He was a shell of his former self, consumed by the specter that someone else knew his secret, and could destroy him at any second. Who could it be? And how did this person have Nikki's phone? Everyone he spoke to became a suspect, every comment fodder for analysis. It was torture.

"What is it with you?" John asked as the two of them sipped coffee in the faculty room while bantering about the latest professional development courses the administration was force feeding. "You really are not yourself."

"What?" Cam replied. "I'm fine. What are you talking about?"

"Come on Cam, it's me you're talking to."

John went on, crushing his cup and dropping it in the garbage next to his chair.

"You know, it's okay to grieve for a student. It's normal. Nobody is going to think any less of you for it."

Cam liked John, but was always bothered a little by his air of superiority, the way he would raise his eyebrows and curl his lip whenever he thought he had unearthed a hidden truth.

"What, you think *that's* what bothering me?" Cam asked.

"Isn't it?" John persisted.

"Well, it's upsetting obviously John," Cam explained, "but it hasn't devastated me or anything."

"Nobody said anything about devastating Cam. But look, I know you guys were close. Everyone could see that. It's got to hurt a little. We all have students like that at one point or another."

Cam tightened up, trying to keep John at a safe distance from his emotional orbit.

"Look John, I don't know what you or anyone else thinks, but Nikki and I were not that close. Why would you say that? She was just a kid in my class. That's all. Just another kid. Like I said, it's sad, but life goes on, you know? I have other things to worry about, like paying for an engagement ring for Hayley, wedding plans, all that crap."

John's lids sunk a little and wondered silently about Cam's affect, and his emotional disarray, the general fuzziness that seemed to shout out that this young man whom he had mentored and grown to love and admire was no longer recognizable.

"I know all that. It's just hard, that's all. I mean it's in our faces every day, with the police questioning everyone and all. Nobody could blame you if-"

"That doesn't bother me John," Cam answered. "Why should it?"

John sighed.

"Okay Cam. I get it. You're okay. But remember, if you need anything, anything at all, or if you just want to chat, you know where to find me. I'm the old guy hooked up to the coffee maker."

With the self-combative proclivity of one who is at complete odds with himself, Cam struggled the next few days with even the most basic interactions. He screamed at the parking lot security guard for not moving the flow of traffic quickly enough outside the school, had an argument with Mrs. Murphy, the sweetest, most senior member of the cafeteria staff, and balked at his chairperson when he learned that he needed Cam to switch classrooms for the day to accommodate some special program going on. Even the students were feeling his distemper.

"Mr. B?" Melanie Randolph said, approaching him with peculiar concern. "Are you alright?"

"What do you want Melanie?"

She was holding her books tightly against her chest.

"Can I talk to you a minute?" she asked.

His face was perplexed.

"Look Melanie, I'm really busy here. I really do not have the time."

"I know, I know. It's just that I feel really bad about something and I really want to talk to you. It's important. I know what it feels like. To be upset I mean. And I think I may even be able to help you."

His laugh was cold and sardonic.

"Oh yeah, right," he said, dropping his pen on the desk with deliberate intent. "*You're* gonna help *me*? Look Melanie, you're a sweet kid, but I really do not have time to talk about Girl Scouts, or Photo Club, or whatever it is you do. So please, just go away and do your homework for class or whatever else will take you away from here. You cannot help here. Trust me."

"But Mr. B. I just want to-"

"Please Melanie. Just go."

The girl's heart beat down heavily. She lowered her head, so that he could not see the tears forming in the corners of her eyes; then she turned away, and walked out of the room without another word.

Despite Cam's growing uneasiness, and his inability to control the unflagging fear festering inside, he and Hayley marched on. Their life together was taking shape, beginning with a romantic dinner at Luigi's where Cam asked Hayley to be his wife. Sure, he was far from having completed his emotional and psychological convalescence. He was doubtful that it would ever happen. The walls of his memory still retained Nikki's shadow and his mind was filled with desperate visions and secret weavings, all tied now to that ominous message. He couldn't imagine who had sent it, and what this person could possibly want. But as one day spilled into the next, without any further correspondence, Cam began to convince himself that perhaps it was all just a cruel joke, one that it had run its course. So he pushed on, safely ensconced in the haven that denial often provides, and continued to make plans, trying to satisfy this escalating pressure to fill each day with significance, as if the present could somehow eradicate the past. They set a date, booked a wedding hall, chose Bermuda as their honeymoon destination and even talked about moving into a bigger place.

"What's gotten into you Cam?" she asked, on the night he insisted on driving over an hour just to hear a band he thought they should hire. "I've never seen you this way. I have to say, with the way you were acting a few weeks ago, I am thrilled how into all this you are."

"Come on Hay, are you kidding me?" he mused. "You know that nothing's too good for my girl."

Each day brought them a little closer to their new lives, and Cam a little further from the tiresome mania which had faded but still trailed him. He felt as though he could finally make real plans for the future, that the fear of the unknown, which he had built into a wall that had all but suffocated the outside light, was not a wall at all but a door to the world, open again should he have the good sense to walk through. Suddenly, in the glow of the afternoon sun, as he slipped into his car and pulled away from the school, he knew it was all good, or at least that it would be. He had somehow thwarted karma, cheated the universe, and escaped without punishment for his sins. It was such a liberating thought, as vast and limitless as the promise of felicity in the bright wide sky before him. But oftentimes the cosmos are fickle, a lesson he learned with breathless consternation after his Blackberry vibrated, and everything changed once again.

I haven't forgotten… public library… upstairs reference… tomorrow 5:00

The next night, weary with concern, Cam excused himself, with some difficulty, from his appointment with Hayley to select invitations for the big day and arrived at the library at precisely 5:00 p.m. His thoughts were racing and leaped with torment with every person he passed as he made his way upstairs with much deliberation. Was it him? The guy with the mustache and tortoise shell glasses? What about the guy in the tan sweatsuit? Maybe it was him. Yes, that seemed plausible. Of course, it did not have to be a man. He knew women could be just as devious. Maybe it was her -- the one sitting with her legs crossed, thumbing through a travel magazine. She looked a bit off. It could definitely be her. Or the other five women he noticed loitering by the book stacks. They seemed a little sketchy as well.

The more he surveyed the people there, the more he realized how futile his efforts were. How would he ever really know? Worse than that, what would he do or say when he finally did? Once upstairs, he stood for a second in the middle of the room, gritting his teeth while his eyes scoured the area. There was a middle-aged man with a bald forehead and heavy overcoat standing in front of one of the shelves. His dark, heavy eyes perused a row of books before eventually finding Cam's, and quickly Cam directed his stare elsewhere. His eyes shifted in a different direction, to a woman who was already looking at him, although seemed to be doing so with great difficulty. She was working at one of the computers, her mouth twitching slightly on one side, one of her hands now nervously attending to the wisps of hair falling across her face. Cam looked away, then looked back one more time before he made his way past the odd woman and around the corner to the reference section. His heart was loud in his ears, and his palms a sweaty mess. As he walked, and continued to look, the growing fear seized him, surrounded him, almost as if it were right there before him, tangible and somehow assailable. He felt as though he could grab hold of it, master it at least for the moment, when his focus was arrested by a familiar face.

"Uh, hello Samantha," he said, his head continuing to swivel. "What are you doing here?"

She looked out of place, sitting there dressed in ripped jeans, a black Lady Ga Ga T-Shirt and sunglasses on top of her head. She offered a half smile and shrugged her shoulders.

"It's a library Mr. B, and I'm a student. Remember?"

He laughed nervously, continuing to survey the area. "Thank you Samantha," he said curtly, "for that earth shattering revelation. But that's not exactly what I was asking."

Her face was still, frozen in an almost cadaverous calm.

"I like the library," she said, leaning back in her chair. "It's quiet, and organized. Everything is always just where it should be. You know what I mean?"

"Are you working on something for school?" he asked, his glance dancing between the open air and the somewhat vacant space before her.

"Nope," she said. "Not at the moment."

Cam paused, frustrated now by the idle chatter and the girl's inadvertent intrusion.

"Listen, I have a pretty important meeting here," he said with a detached look. "Right here, in fact. Maybe, if you don't mind Samantha, you can sit someplace else."

The girl hesitated awkwardly, like something important was hatching in her mind. He could not understand why the girl was being so obtuse. Wasn't he clear enough. It must have taken her a good five minutes before she finally stood up, gathered the couple of books and papers scattered around and threw her bag over her shoulder.

"You know Mr. B.," she said, just before she walked away. "I could sure use some help on that *Scarlet Letter* explication assignment."

Cam was not even looking at her.

"Some other time Samantha. Not now."

She stood for a little while longer, waiting in vain for him to acknowledge her, before leaving quietly, without uttering another sound. Once the girl was gone, and it was safe again, Cam sat down and waited. He watched one of the librarians shelf read the entire reference section with the anal precision of a neurosurgeon. In between impatient glances at his phone, he observed the dynamic of the study group across the way, marveling at the differences between high school girls and boys. Why were the girls always so much more advanced? And of course, with each minute that passed, he studied every other person he saw, wondering silently if the mystery texter was already there, and was just toying with him.

He got up, stalked into the stacks, circled the quiet study areas, then made his way back to where he had begun. Still nothing. He thought of Hayley, and how pissed off she was about him skipping out on her.

"So now I'm picking out the invitations myself? Are you starting this again?" she complained before he left the house. Cameron, you are really something else."

He beat himself up for a while over his decision, and grew more and more restless with each minute that passed. He repeated his circling of the study areas three more times, but in each instance, he returned, only to find the same thing. Two hours later, there was no emotion left on his face – just a tightening of his jaw and a narrowing of his eyes. He had wasted far too many hours worrying about this meeting, and now more time actually sitting there, for what now looked like some sophomoric, mindless prank.

"This is bullshit," he whispered out loud. "I'm out of here."

When he returned home, he dealt with Hayley's wrath as best he could. Then he tossed and turned all night, still angry that he had complied with a request from someone he did not even know. Once or twice he got out of bed, and contemplated calling the number, just to satisfy the nagging uncertainty, but decided that perhaps that's exactly what the person desired. So he did not. His insides were still steaming the next day at school when Samantha came in to see him in his classroom on his off period.

"Hey Mr. B," she said, bouncing through the door. "How was your meeting last night?"

He thought he might explode.

"It never happened Samantha," he replied. "The person never showed."

"Well, that sucks," she said. "I hate when that happens."

He was trying to complete grading his last set of vocabulary quizzes and was not in the mood for company. He felt like if he did not get away from her immediately, his skin would split open and all that burned wildly inside of him would be exposed to the light for the world to see. He had just about formed the words to excuse himself when he remembered that he had promised to help her with the assignment he had given last week.

"So where's the assignment?" he asked. "You know, the one you need help with?"

Her expression remained unchanged; it seemed as though she had no idea what he was talking about.

"I don't have it with me," she said. "That's not why I'm here."

"Well, look Samantha, I'm real busy, so if it's all the same to you-"

"It's my boyfriend," she blurted out. "We're not getting along so well. I'm kind of upset. I was sort of hoping for some advice."

Even if Cam had been inclined to do so, there was nothing he could have said to help the girl. The truth of the matter was that she was struggling with something even she could not understand. Samantha had been dating Bobby Albright for almost eight months, a veritable eternity in high school years. They met at a keg party the previous summer, at the house of a mutual friend. She had noticed him around school before, and he had seen her too, but they had never spoken.

"Hey, he said, you're Samantha, right? I think you were in my Study Hall class last semester. Mr. Jonas?"

"Yeah, I think so," she answered. "You look familiar."

He stood there, admiring her full lips.

"Yeah, I've also seen you cheering for the football team," he said. "You're good."

"Thanks," she said, lifting a red cup of sudsy liquid to her lips. "Too bad there wasn't much to cheer about this year."

They both laughed. They spent the next few minutes exchanging funny stories about other teachers they shared. She found it easy to talk to him. His interest in her made her feel special, like what she had to say mattered.

"What other sports do you play he asked? his hands busy setting up the next round of beer pong.

"Just cheering," she answered. "That's enough."

He was holding two cups and smiling.

"Ever play this before?"

She tilted her head back and put her hair up in a ponytail. Her smile was deliberate and devilish.

"Are you kidding me?" she laughed. "Have *I* ever played beer pong?"

They spent the next two hours drinking until neither one of them could really stand. When it was time for everyone to go, they walked out together, hand in hand. He was already a half hour past his curfew, but she was not finished with him.

"Let's go out back," she said, pulling him by the hand. "On the deck."

He had not even attempted a response before she had him on a lounge chair, flat on his back. She undid his pants, and smiled when the moon illuminated his eagerness. Then she kissed his mouth hard, climbed on top of him and began rocking back and forth, her violent gesticulations punctuated by a running commentary of all the things she wanted to do to him.

"What about protection?" he whispered in her ear? "I don't have anything."

"Forget it," she answered him, arching forward so that he could reach her breasts with his mouth. "I'm on the pill."

At first Bobby found it exciting that she was so aggressive, and that she always had to be on top. Samantha was unlike any other girl he knew. She was always talking about sex, and was usually the one who initiated their encounters. It amazed him. But he had some desires of his own, and thought that he might like to be in charge some times. At first he let the idea go, but eventually he found it too difficult to hold his tongue. She did not take kindly to his discontent.

"What's wrong with the way things are?" she said, her eyes wild with fire. "I thought you were happy."

"I am," he said. "I just thought that maybe you might want to try something new."

She wrinkled her nose and laughed.

95

"Now you know who's in charge here," she said, nibbling his neck to the point where it almost hurt. "When I want something different," she explained, "I'll ask for it."

They continued to see each other regularly. Bobby figured that he could live with the monotony. After all, how many seventeen-year-old guys are going to bitch over getting laid just about every day? Where, when, and position were just minor details. It was the other things, however, that began to bother him. Like when she insisted on tying his hands so that only *she* could touch *him*. Or like the time she doused his balls with beer, and began using the loose skin of his scrotum as a reservoir, drinking whatever liquid remained. As her twisted strain began to emerge, and take a tighter hold of their intercourse, he became more and more alarmed, even disgusted.

"I am feeling a little weird about things Sam," he told her after their last session. "I don't know. Maybe we should just chill for a while."

A warm flush surged in her cheeks.

"What are you talking about?" she fired back. "What is so weird?"

"I don't know," he tried to explain. "I just feel like I don't want to do all the crazy shit anymore. Like maybe we can just have sex. You know, like normal people?"

A trembling sense of urgency possessed her. She clenched her fist, and thought she might punch him in the face. He was trying to manipulate her, bully her into doing what he wanted to do. She tightened her fist even more, but then she saw the look on his face. The utter disdain for her. He was serious, and she really liked him. The quandary made her sad.

"Okay Bobby," she finally said, releasing her fingers one at a time. "Next time, we can do it your way. Promise."

Samantha was going to ask Cam all about the things Bobby had said and to explain how she felt like she was being treated unfairly, and that it was making her miserable, but she just could not find the right words.

"I'm afraid I'm not very good with advice on relationships Samantha," Cam said. "That's not what I heard," she scoffed under her breath.

He didn't catch what the girl said but was tired and just wanted to be left alone.

"Besides, I have a ton of work to do here. Maybe tomorrow, okay?"

His drive home was miserable. Road construction and a sudden rain shower had stalled traffic to a virtual standstill. He took out his phone and dialed Hayley, hoping that she could pick up dinner. Maybe pizza, or burgers from the diner. She did not answer. He cursed his day once again, staring at the sea of red lights glowing in the misty air before him. He placed his phone on the seat next to him and busied his fingers with the radio. He surfed from station to station, but nothing suited his mood. He tried to reach his briefcase, so that while he sat there he could perhaps read the three memos his chairperson had just put out; but the bag had fallen off the back seat after one of his sudden stops, and the handles were now just out of his grasp.

"This is just great," he screamed out loud. "Fucking perfect."

He finally decided that he would fill the idle time by cleaning out his glove compartment when his eye caught his phone. He reached for it, then pulled back. He was not entirely comfortable with what he was thinking. He must have done the same exact thing a half dozen times before a sea of frustration washed over him, and he could no longer stand it. He scrolled though his messages, found the one he was looking for, hit reply and typed.

What happened?

The second he hit send, he regretted it. What was he doing? Why was he playing this game? He felt wounded inside now, like something was leaking. He hated himself for being so weak, so easily controlled. He was right in the midst of beating himself up when the phone vibrated with another message.

Mistake. Be there tonight. 8.00. Same place.

His anger over the traffic and his loss of power now dominated his thoughts.

Why should I come? How do I know you will show?

This time, the reply was instant.

Be there, or be sorry.

Cam and Hayley had the Mexican leftovers from the night before after she got home around six. They talked briefly while they ate.

"So you know my new boss," she began. "Mr. Pinkert? He's turning out to be a real asshole."

She told him how he had asked her to work on a new project. It had taken her two days, but she came up with some great stuff. Then, at their weekly officers meeting, he took credit for all the work.

"He is a pompous ass Cam. I don't know how much more I can take."

He shook his head, and told her all about the traffic he sat in, about the parent who would not stop calling him, and how he had to go out later in a couple of hours, to get some books to use in class for his lesson tomorrow. She was tired anyway, and was going to bed early.

"Okay," she said. "If I'm not awake when you get home, kiss me goodnight."

There was a fine, cold drizzle falling, and the wind, which had previously blown in intermittent puffs, rose up and became a steady push. He watched, as he pulled into the parking lot across from the library, several people walking miserably through the misty night, on their way here and there. It was exactly eight o'clock. For some reason, he was a lot more at ease this time. Perhaps it was because somewhere in his mind, he thought that it would be another "no show", and he knew he would not be back again. He wasn't even halfway up the stairs when he saw her, again. *What is with this girl?* he thought to himself. She noticed him too, and began waving as if she had not seen him in weeks.

"Hey Mr. B.," she said, her face lost in some far away meditation. "Funny. Here we are again."

He was less than cordial this time.

"Samantha, don't you have cheerleading, or dance, or something like that? What are you doing here again?"

She was sitting with nothing in front of her, her head turned slightly to one side.

"I could ask you the same thing," she said.

He was in no mood for games. Not tonight.

"Look Sammy, I told you already I cannot help you. I'm here for a-"

"A meeting? Right?" "Yes, a meeting. I have a meeting, Right now."

A strange look attached itself to the girl's face.

"I know all about it," she said, displaying with smug certainty a cell phone he had not seen in weeks. "Be there, or be sorry, right?"

She leaned back in her chair, folded her arms and smiled.

"Why don't you have a seat?"

Cam's thoughts ate at him with savage curiosity. It was *her*? How? It made no sense. None at all. He sat down across from the girl, still wrestling with the tangled reality in front of him. Samantha? How? Why? It couldn't be. Yet amidst all of what he was feeling, relief was somehow a part of it all. She's just a kid, he thought. It could have been so much worse. He was certain that he could reason with her, or at the very least, manipulate her into doing what he wanted. If there was one thing he was good at, it was getting kids to do what he wanted. He knew that.

"So, what is it that you want to talk about Sammy?" he asked.

What Cam didn't know, couldn't possibly know, was that Samantha was polluted by a past that was cruel and unforgiving. She was barely eleven years old the first time it happened. Her mom was out for the evening, at a neighborhood pocketbook party. It was just her and her stepfather, Bill. She had just come out of the shower. Her hair was up in a towel, and she had another one wrapped tightly around her middle. She didn't even hear him come into the bathroom. She was looking at her toes, thinking about going to the mall the next day with her friends to buy those new boots she had seen in the Hollister catalog, when she was assaulted by the sudden smell of stale cigarettes and whiskey and the sound of his asthmatic breathing next to her ear.

"Hey kiddo," he said, grabbing a hand towel off the counter. "Let me get your back for you."

"Uh, okay," she said.

Her shoulders stiffened, and her head began to throb behind her eyes. She frowned as she caught a glimpse of his reflection in the steamy mirror, fuzzy and slightly out of focus. He placed one of his hands flat on her bare shoulder while the other dried her back in a slow, circular motion. She could see his face more clearly now. His eyes were closed, and his head was tilted slightly to the side. It was creepy. She also found it weird that it was taking so long, and that his breathing was getting louder and louder.

"Okay, thanks Bill," she finally said, turning around to face him. Her arms were folded now tightly against her chest. "I think I'm gonna get dressed now."

He would not let her leave.

"You know Sammy," he said, sliding in between her and the doorway. "You're very pretty. Yes you are. It's okay that I say that, right? Because we're like family, and family should be able to say nice things to each other, and do nice things for each other too. Right?"

Samantha said nothing. She just stood, arms still folded, eyes spinning with hysterical terror.

"Ah, come on Sammy," he said, backing her up against the countertop. "There's nothing to be afraid of."

He looked at her now ravenously, like a tiger just before a kill. He put his hot lips to her ear and whispered something about special secrets and good girls and then his fingers were in her hair, on her lips and before long inside of her.

"Shh," he whispered. "It's okay. It's okay. Nothing's gonna happen."

His perversion became more and more unshackled over the years. It seemed to feed on itself, becoming more and more rapacious each time he imposed himself on her. She was never safe. He wandered into her room at night, sat next to her when they all watched T.V., and skulked around the house, especially near the bathroom, the place that remained a favorite haunt of his. She tried to tell her mother, but she would not, as she said, "entertain such fantasy." Samantha hated her for it.

"Sammy, stop being such a spoiled little bitch," her mom chided. "This jealously thing has got to stop. I mean really. Bill is a grown man, and you're just a kid. Please, what would he want with you?"

The helplessness and lack of control just ate away at her, and the despondency she felt grew exponentially at the hands of the unholy, unvarying repetition. It was in her head, all of it, as she sat with her teacher.

"Well Mr. B, I think we should talk about Nikki," Samantha said, "and exactly what it was that you found so appealing about her."

He looked first at the shadows under her eyes and then around the library before answering.

"How do you know about any of this anyway?" he whispered.

"That's not important right now," she said drawing closer. "We have other things to discuss."

There *were* other things she wanted to talk about, including the fight she and Bobby had, and how he had just dumped her. She was angry. His words still stung.

"I told you Sammy, last week, that I did not want any more of the demented shit," he said just hours before. "Then you come here, to my house, climb on top of me and pee all over me? You must be kidding. Are you out of your fucking mind? Did you not hear what I said to you last time? What kind of a fucking freak are you anyway?"

She was still reeling over the severity of the assault as she sat there with Cam.

"Look, Sammy, I really don't know why you're doing this," Cam replied. "But please, I'm asking you to just forget about what you think you know. This does not involve you. Come on. People could get hurt here. It doesn't have to be like this."

There was something about his desperation, his vulnerability, that stoked her twisted fires. She could feel a distinct hopelessness in the quiet that followed each of his overtures.

"So, what you're saying is that you want me to help you out here. You know, bury the truth, so to speak? Is that what you would like?"

"Honestly, yes, yes. That is exactly what I want Samantha. We have all suffered enough."

"Okay," she said. I can do that."

She was just staring at him. His eyes were still traveling around the room, but he was breathing a little easier now.

"Good. Now, tell me how you know all this. And where you got Nikki's phone."

She opened her purse, removed a cherry lip gloss and applied a few strokes to her lips, then placed it back safely.

"No, I don't think so."

Cam appeared stumped for the moment.

"And what about what happened last night? Why did you tell me tonight, and not last night? Why did you have me come here yesterday for nothing?"

"I *wanted* to tell you last night," she explained. "But, I don't know. It just wasn't right."

"And tonight is?" he asked. "Tonight is so different?"

"Yes, she said. "Very."

She remained staring at him, her mouth partially open, her eyes lit by some unknown devilry.

"So, let's cut through all the bullshit here, okay?" she said. "You want something from me, right? A little information? And for me to just forget about what I know?"

He nodded, and began to rock slowly. He just wanted to go home.

"Okay," she continued. "I think I can do that."

She reached across the table and grabbed his hand, as if to steady her spiraling thoughts with the touch of it.

"But, first, you will have to do something for me."

The two of them sat for several more minutes, Cam listening intently as Samantha revealed to him the alarming depths of her consternation regarding his relationship with Nikki. She sat perfectly still, her shoulders back, hands folded in front on the table. He just listened. Her eyes were small and feverish, and burned oddly in the torpor of the moment. Then she stopped talking, and her gaze locked on him for several seconds. Nothing else was said. He wanted to die. He had almost decided to get up and leave when without any provocation whatsoever, he saw an alteration of mood spreading across her face. It was very slight at first, beginning with the raising of her eyebrows and the slight movement of the corners of her mouth, as if she were straining to hold a smile.

"So, did you get to fuck her?" she asked, her entire face exploding now with shining delight.

His shoulders slumped and his heart beat slower now with each breath, diminishing steadily like a fading echo.

"What?" he asked.

"Come on, you heard me," she replied. "Did you?"

"Come on Samantha. Do we really have to do this?"

"Was she good?" she continued. "Hmm? Did she take you in her mouth Mr. B? Huh? Get it all wet and hard before climbing on top of you and riding it until she couldn't stand it anymore?"

A feeling of utter disgust seized him. He gazed at her with bewilderment, unable to comprehend the depths of her sordid intentions.

"You know, cheerleaders are very flexible," she continued, smiling proudly. "I can bend in ways you can't even imagine."

A breath of hot air passed from her lips. She was rife with this unconquerable swell of manipulation.

"What is it that you want Samantha?" he asked her. "Huh? And for God sakes. Where did you get Nikki's phone and why the hell are you using it?"

"What I want, Mr. B., is to know why all of a sudden it is appropriate for teachers and students to date. Seems to me you said something very different to me a while back."

He said nothing.

"You guys were dating, right?"

"Look Sammy, let's just-"

"I also want you to wonder, every time you see me, what I am thinking. To know that we have a special sort of bond now – and that I sort of hold you in the palm of my hand."

She laughed out loud.

"Sound scary? Oh, it could be. It really could be," she went on. "But you don't have to worry. No. No worries. I'll be good to you. You can trust me."

"Look, Sammy, I am really not-"

"Just one hookup," she announced. "That's all. No big deal."

A nervous laugh escaped his lips. "You're kidding me, right? You cannot be serious."

Her thoughts swirled hazily in front of her, then came together in one clear impression.

"Do I look like I'm kidding? I'm sure if you think about it long enough, you will agree that what I'm asking here is fair, especially for a girl who has to carry such a heavy secret."

Cam sat quietly for a while, as if waiting for the spell to be broken. His mind labored greatly with the disorder of the scene. How could this be happening? He felt himself drifting even further from the natural world. But for all the horror and chaos, he could not help but entertain, on some remote level, the idea of putting the issue to rest. He hated what she was saying, but for the moment, he could not stop thinking about it.

"This is crazy," he finally said. "You know that. Besides, why should I believe you?" How do I know that you're not just playing games with me Sammy? That there is something else here."

She was relatively undeterred by his challenge.

"You don't," she said smugly.

She placed one of his fingers in her mouth. She moved it back and forth, in rhythmic fashion, running her tongue along both sides before finally releasing it.

"But, I really don't think you want to take that chance now, do you?"

So great was the helplessness kindled deep within him that he could not help but bury his face in his hands. She had him. He tried again and again to wiggle free from her twisted design, but to no avail. All he could do was sit across from her, picturing the hazardous boundary he was to cross again, unable to do anything about it. He sighed and nodded fecklessly. Then, under the soft glow of the library lights, with whispers tinged with degenerate fears and roiling resignation, Cam relented and the unholy agreement was forged.

NINE

Hayley was fast becoming the prototypical bride to be, consumed by all of the tasks germane to the big event. She sat most nights at the kitchen table, outfitted in her black aerobic pants and pink sweatshirt with MONTAUK in white letters across the chest, perusing catalogs, and the latest editions of *Modern Bride* and *In Style Weddings.* In the feeble light cast from the scented candles she had picked up at the last bridal expo she attended, she wrote feverishly, marking the pages in her purple notebook with ideas and tips that had previously escaped her ever watchful eye. There was so much to do. Flowers, food, wedding dress, photographer. The list went on and on. And somewhere in her mind, amidst the many strands of celebratory preparation, was the emerging concern for Cam, who had grown increasingly reticent and emotionally distant. He had become less and less interested in sharing her fastidious vision for their special day, more often than not deferring to her judgment regarding monumental decisions like Venetian Hour or cookie and fruit platters at each table, lobster or prime rib and live band vs. D.J.

Some mornings were worse than others.

"Do not forget that we have an appointment tonight at 5:30 with the florist," she said, measuring out a precise amount of chicken and lamb kibble before dropping it into the cat dish. "Hurry home. I do not want to be late."

Cam, fully aware of her budding volatility, flushed a bit before delivering his news.

"Uh, don't be mad Hay," he said, stirring his coffee with inordinate attention so that he should not have to look directly at her. "But I just found out that I have an emergency union meeting following the regular faculty meeting today. Something about contract negotiations. I think I am going to get stuck there."

"Are you shitting me Cameron? Not again!"

"I'm sorry Hay. I am. But it's not my fault. I have to be there."

"You *don't* have to be there Cam," she fired back, slamming her breakfast plate in the sink. "You don't. Where you have to be is with me. Remember me Cam?"

"Why do you have to blow this out of proportion this way?" he asked. "Holy shit Hay. I don't get it. We're just talking about fucking flowers here. It's not the end of the world."

"Yeah, you *don't* get it. You really don't. And you're acting like a real asshole besides. What don't you understand? I do not want to do all of this shit by myself. It sucks."

She began to cry -- soft, big tears – and tried to walk away, but he grabbed her by the shoulders and held her still with both hands.

"Look, I said I was sorry," he whispered, kissing her forehead. "I don't know what else to do here. I can't help it. I can't get out of it. But I promise, everything else that needs to be done, we will do together. Everything. After tonight, it will all be cool. Okay?"

She lingered a second over her thoughts, with so many words hovering around her lips. Then, with an expressionless face streaked with melting makeup, she simply nodded and went into the bedroom to get dressed.

That evening, Hayley went to meet with Claude the florist by herself, and Cam kept his appointment as well. He met Samantha at 6:00. They parked just outside the footpath of Meadow Lake and talked a while, the spider and her prey, measuring each other's mood under a black, starless sky that had hatched a menacing moon which shone now, stark and swollen. Cam looked at her, fighting at every turn the hollow emotion that was gathering inside of him. She was ugly. Sure, she had long, silky hair, full painted lips and bright eyes. Her body was also more like a woman's than a girl's. But she was ugly just the same, and it assaulted him with alarming vigor. He felt sick, deep inside his stomach. He could barely look at her.

"So, what now?" he asked, sliding the cloth covered panel shade across the moon-roof window in a desperate attempt to drown the heartless light.

"What do you mean?" she replied. It was considerably darker now, but he could still see the outline of her arched brows and wanton mouth.

"What do you want to do?" he said, trying to navigate the painful inevitableness.

She frowned.

"I have to say, this isn't very romantic," she complained. She ran her hand across his thigh.

"Do you really have to ask?"

"Listen Samantha, you're the one who wanted this. So if it's all the same-"

"Why don't you touch me," she said. "Touch me, the same way you touched her."

He clenched his lips, horrified by the animal pleasure glinting in her eyes. He heard what she said, and his brain had issued the command, but he could not move. He was frozen. It was as if his entire body had risen up in opposition to this most unholy union, staged an insurrection so powerful, so masterful, that he could not scarcely imagine ever moving again. Nothing worked. His eyelids were cemented open. His breath seemed to halt, his legs went numb, and the thoughts inside his head were titling with such fury that he thought his brain would surely pop and start leaking from his ears. His fingers, however, seemed the most defiant, most intractable, unable to strike the first chord.

He couldn't help but think of Maleigha, and how young and beautiful she was. She was an angel, soft and gentle, and when she looked at him, her eyes touched him somewhere so deep, so special, that his entire body came alive to meet her loving advance. It was like being caught outside, on the beach during a storm in July. All his senses were in play. It was a true union of souls. He was certain that that final night they were together would not only have been his first time, it would have been the first of many times, a lifetime of love with the angelic beauty. That should have been their night. She was supposed to be the first and should have been his last.

Sitting there, in the throes of paralysis, he considered Nikki as well, and how she too had managed to touch him in ways that he thought were other worldly. There was something wonderfully ineffable about her as well. It was her beauty, no doubt, and the way she smelled. But the longer he sat there with Samantha, whose breath was hot and strong, he realized that the physical beauty of both Maleigha and Nikki was intensified exponentially by an innocence, the journey into the unexplored, something that cast a sort of heavenly glow over both girls, setting them apart from the damaged mien of others like Samantha. He continued to sit there, unable to move.

Frustrated, and unwilling to contain herself any longer, Samantha finally initiated the exchange, grabbing his hand and bringing it to her breast; there was nothing warm or inviting about it. He tried to mask his repulsion, fearful that the girl might do something even crazier than what she had already planned. He turned to face her, pulling her toward him so that their cheeks were touching and that his face could not be seen. His hands slowly came to life, and began the work he knew they had to do, and with his eyes now fixed vacantly on the faint image of his own reflection cast in the glass in front of him, the desire to fulfill his part of the agreement and get out of there superseded the torrid aversion, and he gave in to, at last, the loathsome interlude.

The feel of his touch on her body created in her an instant stir, as if an electrical switch had been thrown, sending the off-beat girl into a fit of reckless ardor. She grabbed his face and kissed him hard, her tongue a darting flame that flickered all across his lips and teeth. He returned her kiss, his vexation ever present as her hands worked feverishly at the button of his jeans. He found himself ashamed that his body was responding to her at all. Deep inside his brain images of Hayley, and Nikki and sweet Maleigha refused to let him be. His chest was tight, like hands of a criminal on prison bars, and a wave of dizziness rose in him to the point of near unconsciousness. He was thinking that he would just stop it here, maybe try once again to reason with her and find another way to do this. Shit, there had to be another way. But then she licked her palm, smiled, and reached for him.

"How does that feel Mr. B.?" she whispered, chewing playfully at his ear lobe.

His erratic breath became a low groan. His body was full now of unnatural vigor and intent. Her lips found his again, and he kissed her, running his hands under her sweater and across her back, trying desperately to navigate the moment. She sighed with pleasure, kissed his neck, his chest, and looked deeply into the vacuity in his eyes before lowering her head and disappearing in his lap.

He sat with head back, his head filled with swirls of regret and self-loathing, realizing now what was so distasteful about the girl. In previous encounters with women, he always felt a sort of symbiosis, like at some moment during the dalliance, he and his partner became of one mind, one soul, melting into each other so that it was impossible to know where one began and the other ended. This was not the case with her. She had this quality, bereft of name, a very tangible yet curiously impalpable aura that had risen between them and sealed him off. If she sensed this, it did not seem to bother her, for even when he pushed her head away, and whispered his growing displeasure, she proceeded with unrelenting purpose, removing her sweater, hiking up her skirt and climbing on top of him with winded admiration.

With a mixture of dutiful indenture and sheer disdain, he sat perfectly straight, except for his head, which was tilted slightly up against the soft cushion of the headrest just behind him. Samantha was unhinged, rocking back and forth on him, narrating with winded effort every last sensation coursing through her body. The whole experience depressed him more than he could have ever imagined. The more she got herself off, the further he felt from the universe, like a single molecule of the earth's atmosphere being sucked irresistibly into the outer reaches of space. It was enough. He had had enough. But his body has betrayed him; he knew that as long as he was physically engaged, up to the task, there could be no end. He felt like Samantha could go on forever. He shivered at the thought, imagining another hour or two of this interminable imprisonment.

It was that thought that finally awakened him, spurred him to action. A sudden irony rose up and almost made him laugh out loud. All these years, he had devoted himself to *Maxim* articles and internet forums about lasting longer. There were so many theories and suggestions. He implemented those which he could master and discarded the rest. But the information which had served him well on so many occasions had now undermined him. He knew there was only one way out. So, like a groggy dreamer at the moment of waking, he began to stir. His movements were slow and deliberate at first, beginning with a gentle touch of her hair, followed by a more rigorous stroking of her shoulders and the small of her back. Then, he let out a sigh, placed both hands on her rounded bottom and with the unruliness of a feral horse suddenly unfettered, began thrusting wildly, deeper and deeper inside of her. Her hair was in his face now, but he could see, through some breaks in the redolent strands, the shadowed, copper edge of the moon reflected oddly in the cloudbanks just beyond the tree tops across the water. He kept his gaze there, watching curiously until the tinged cluster dissolved at the precise moment of his convulsive release, and in the flatness of the minutes that followed, he was at peace with himself, knowing, at long last, that he was free and that the desecration of the night was finally complete.

TEN

When he arrived back home, Cam stood in the shower for a good while, staring down at himself and crying, hoping that somehow all the anguished moments of the past two months would just melt away from him. His fingers were restless and worked feverishly, scrubbing his beleaguered body time and again until his skin was pink and shriveled. There was nothing left to do now but accept the circumstances that had befallen him – begin anew, starting with softer thoughts of he and Hayley and the life they would now pursue. She was right for him. She had to be. What had once frightened him, and made him question the tenor of his life, had now charmed him, given him something to fight for.

He dried off quickly and joined her in the kitchen. She was seated in her usual spot, a sea of magazines and charts stretching from her fingertips clear to the other side of the table. Her chin was resting on her hand as she shuffled some papers from one pile to the next. Her hair was up and she had retired her contacts for the night in favor of glasses. He came up alongside of her, kissed her cheek, then sat down in the chair directly across the way.

"How was your meeting?" she asked, eyes glued to her work.

"Okay," he said. "Nothing special."

He sat comfortably, brow raised, the thrust of his jaw far less severe than it had been earlier in the day.

"So, what did Claude say?" he asked.

"He said a lot of things Cameron," she replied, finally lifting her head to face him squarely. "Had you been there with me, you would know exactly why I'm flipping out over here."

"What do you mean?" he asked. "Is everything okay?"

"Oh, sure, everything's just great," she answered, holding up a stack of papers and waving them above her head. "Everything is just fucking great, as long as I don't plan on going to work the next few days."

"I don't understand?" he said. "What's the problem?"

She breathed in methodically and exhaled in the same manner. She was much quieter physically but her mind continued to shriek uncontrollably.

"The problem, Cam, is choices. Thousands of choices. I wanted long – petalled orchids for my bouquet, but if we do that, then we have to change the corsages for our mothers, so everything matches. Except we can't do that, because my mom is allergic to orchids. So then Claude suggested a combination of Peonies, Tea Roses, Tulips and Ranunculus, but I wasn't crazy about the Tea Roses. I could always take out the Tea Roses and replace them with Lily of the Valley, but then that would not go so well with the Ranunculus, which would then have to be replaced by Carnations or Gardenias, both of which I hate. So, I have been sitting here, for the last forty five fucking minutes, staring at these flower charts, and honestly, I want to kill myself."

His eyes were darting between the swell of papers and her crumbling expression. Her appeal suffered in the wake of the outburst. This was the Hayley who he had grown to loathe. She was always worrying about something – could never just live in the moment. The more time that passed, the more neurotic and controlling she became. He found it very off-putting. He remembered the first time he had witnessed this side of her. They had only been dating a few months. It was a brilliant April morning. The air was warm and sweet, and the sky an electric blue canvas with only a few wisps of gauzy white stretched across here and there. They were riding on Ocean Parkway, on their way to Port Jefferson for Hayley's cousin's wedding. Cam always loved to take this route when traveling out to the island. It gave him the opportunity to drive past some of his old haunts, like Tobay and Gilgo Beach. They had exchanged some idle conversation about the bride and her future husband, most of it of the critical nature, and even began speculating about what it would be like should the day come when they were the ones about to tie the knot. He had just told her what a beautiful bride she would be when her face morphed in the morning sunlight; she was unusually agitated.

"Which way are you going?" she asked.

"I always take Ocean Parkway," he said. "It's a nicer ride."

"But it's so much longer this way," she protested, checking her watch before drawing his attention to the invitation she was holding in her hand. "We cannot be late Cameron."

He was really taken off guard.

"We're not going to be late Hay," he said. "Relax. Just enjoy the ride."

"Didn't you hear me say that I *MapQuested* the directions?" she asked. "Southern State Parkway is much more direct. Everyone knows that. Why would you take us so far out of the way Cam? It doesn't make any sense."

He fought against the impulse to just start screaming at her. He couldn't believe she was making such an issue over directions. Her outburst rattled him a bit. He wondered if she was really upset about something else.

"What is wrong with you?" he asked.

"Next time, just let me handle the directions," she said.

Frustrated, and on the verge of tears, she slammed her hand against the car door and did not say another word to him the rest of the way there. Since then, he had learned to navigate her mood more prudently.

"Listen Hay," he said, reaching across the littered table top for her hand. "We can do whatever it is you want. And I will help – with everything."

The stillness of her face was disturbing. He thought that perhaps she had lapsed into some sort of self-imposed stupor.

"Hay, did you hear what I -"

"Yes, I heard you Cam," she answered, removing her glasses and rubbing her eyes with the palms of her hands. "But I'm beat. I can't do this anymore. What do you say we call it a night? We both have to be up early tomorrow."

He undressed quickly and got into bed. With his head propped up slightly by an extra pillow, he watched her in the dim light of the bathroom doorway, as she ran through an abbreviated version of her usual routine before slipping under the covers beside him. She was warm. He kissed her softly, once on the nose, and again on her lips. She was hopelessly lost in the tilting world of wedding appointments and deadlines, guest lists and dinner menus. Somehow, despite the pall of all her idiosyncrasies, her heartfelt exposure spoke to him tenderly.

"Goodnight Hay," he whispered. "Love you."

"Love you too," she responded with heavy eye lids. "See you in the morning."

She turned on her side, the way she always did, and he curled himself around her, molded his body so closely to hers that he could feel her heart and hear her thoughts as her breaths slowed steadily to soft, rhythmic modulations while she drifted off.

Lying there, beside her, he began contemplating things with a cold, ruthless clarity. He still wondered about the police, and if they would ever really close the case. He often found himself thinking about the motel room, and how he had missed the phone. He also tortured himself over the possibility of having left behind something else – a stray vestige of the interlude that could place him there. It was certainly possible. The uncertainty haunted him with merciless vigor. He was also plagued by the many eyes at school that seemingly judged him at every turn. It made him so uncomfortable. And of course, there was Samantha. He just could not rid himself of her face. He still smelled her, tasted her. And the lingering doubt that she was truly satisfied, and would really leave him alone, was the one thought, more than any other, that kept him suspended the entire night in the lonely chasm between consciousness and sleep.

ELEVEN

Despite all that had happened, things at school began to right themselves. Mr. B. was his old self again, brimming with that signature confidence, animation and charisma. He was completely energized, like a shipwrecked traveler who had been rescued in the eleventh hour, just as the rising tides threatened to swallow the tiny sandbar on which he stood. It was easy again. He could not have felt any better.

He was always most comfortable when he was in front of the room. It was his world, one that he could manipulate and control however he liked. It was ordered, familiar, and there for the taking. One of the greatest allures of the profession was that no matter how chaotic and lawless the swirling winds became outside his room, he could always close his door, and for the next forty two minutes, rule the universe.

"Man, you are mad crazy Mr. B.," Jonathan Keppler blurted out, as the ebullient teacher flew around the room in a fit of uproarious histrionics, acting out a scene from *Lord of the Flies.*

Cam could execute a lesson plan to perfection, but he was at his best when he abandoned the rules of conventional instruction and just went with the fire burning in his gut. Those were always the lessons that the kids remembered.

"Crazy?" he repeated, grabbing two rulers before jumping on his desk and striking a warrior's pose. "You guys ain't seen nothing yet!"

He growled and postured, and was just about to launch into yet another episode when the sound of laughter coming from the doorway diverted everyone's attention.

"He is definitely crazy class." John said after wandering by Cam's classroom and stopping momentarily in the partially open doorway. "But he's the only teacher here who will paint his face and jump on desks, just to get you guys to learn something."

Everyone laughed, including Cam, who tapped his makeshift spears on a desktop before addressing his friendly intruder.

"Come on Mr. Volpe," Cam teased, pretending to sharpen his weapons. "You can play too. You're actually just in time. How are you at walking on all fours and making pig noises?"

The class laughed again, this time louder than before. Cam could really work a room.

"Never mind that," Volpe answered. "I'm more of the chalk and talk type."

Cam rolled his eyes, and pantomimed a yawn. There were more laughs. The playful waters of teenage humor rushed at John for a moment, and he shook his head and smiled.

"Don't you worry about me now Cam," he fired back. "Just stop by my room after class. I need to speak to you about something."

Cam found John thirty minutes later, sitting in his chair, buried behind a daunting stack of term papers that teetered precariously on the edge of his desk. On the board behind him were the chalky remnants of the day's lesson, something about Sartre and Existentialism. Cam tried to make it out but his curious gaze was interrupted by the gravity in John's voice.

"Oh, I'm glad you're here," he said, removing his glasses and placing his red pen on the paper in front of him. "I really need to talk to you."

"What's going on?" Cam asked, collapsing into the seat across from John's desk. "Everything okay?"

John winced a little bit, his eyes somewhat pensive and objectionable.

"How's everything going in class these days?" he asked.

"Everything's great John. Shit, it's never been better. You saw for yourself today."

After a moment's reflection, John lifted himself up in his chair so that his back was now perfectly straight. He folded his hands neatly on the desk; his mind opened suddenly with a rush.

"Samantha Brocking came to see me the other morning Cam," he said. "We spoke for a while."

A thought floated to the surface of John's mind, like a piece of ravaged wood breaking free from a sunken vessel. He walked around his desk, his face an open book on which his feelings could be read, and silently took a seat next to Cam, whose voice remained collapsed beneath the fury of his angst. The emotional scabs which had only just begun to form had now suddenly ruptured, causing his wounds to bleed anew.

"Yeah?" Cam finally managed to answer. "Why should that concern me?"

"She *is* your student, right?"

"I have a lot of students John," he said anxiously. "So what?"

"Look, this is probably none of my business, and I'm sure you are more than capable of handling your own affairs, but-"

"*Affairs*?" he interrupted. "What affairs?"

"But, I was saying, you should know that she told me that she thinks you don't like her, and that she feels as though she cannot go to you for help, or anything else she needs."

Cam stood again with nothing to say, anesthetized by the unexpected entrance into his private chamber.

"So what's the deal with this girl?" John continued. "Is she a problem?"

"A problem?" Cam repeated furiously, like a fighter battling his way back off the ropes. "No. There's no problem. Why would there be a problem? She's just a little strange John. That's all. One of these needy kids who is never satisfied. I treat her the same way I treat all my students."

"I don't know about that," he said. "I think there's something else going on there."

The image of his future collided sharply with the events of the recent past.

"What is that supposed to mean?"

"She's crying out for something," John continued, "for some reason. I don't think you should ignore this. One tragedy this year is enough."

Cam was looking down at the discolored tile beneath his feet.

"Honestly John, I think you're making too much of this. The girl probably had a fight with her boyfriend, or got grounded by her parents for being out past curfew or something amazingly tragic like that. It'll pass, and she will be okay. Really."

John sighed, and sat meditatively, looking at the knotted expression before him, frustrated by his inability to make Cam see what he was saying. In all the years that they had known each other, it had never happened.

"Look Cam, she seems like a fragile kid," he said. "Christ, you should have seen that look in her eyes. I've seen kids like this before. Plenty of them. I know the signs. And even in the worst cases, I never saw the look that this girl has. Maybe you can watch out for her. Give her a little extra attention. I mean, what harm can it do, right? Besides, that's your forte. I hope you don't mind, but I told her that you were very approachable, and that she should go to you, privately, and talk about what's bothering her."

"You did what?" Cam wailed. "Why? Why would you say that?"

"Because she is your student and-"

"Do me a favor John will you? Huh? Just stay out of my business, okay? I got this covered. When I want or need your help, I'll ask for it."

Less than an hour later, Cam was sitting in his own classroom, his face swamped with anger and disgust, when the girl appeared before him. He didn't even hear her come in – just smelled her perfume, looked up, and there she was.

"Mr. Volpe said you wanted to see me?" she asked, clicking her tongue while wrapping an errant strand of her hair around her index finger.

His outrage now was not so much directed at her as it was at his own infirmity and impotence against her clever machinations.

"Not exactly Samantha," he replied. "But, uh, as long as you are here, let's go over a few things."

"I was hoping you'd say something like that," she answered, pulling a chair up in front of his desk. "I've really missed talking to you."

His jaw opened slightly, just enough to expel a quick breath of disbelief.

"Are you out of your fucking mind?" he whispered sharply. "Are you? Do you really think I want to just sit here with you and shoot the shit? You have to be kidding me. Don't you get it? There are not going to be any social visits Samantha. There's nothing going on here. We had an agreement. That's it. Now it's time for us to move on."

The silver chain attached to her belly button ring caught the top of her jeans and cut into her stomach. She fidgeted in her chair in protest and shifted her gaze for the moment from him to the row of classroom windows. Outside, a gentle afternoon light slipped through the courtyard of trees, and the limbs gave the edifice just behind them a gauzy, ethereal look.

"You haven't been very nice to me," she finally said, her eyes still fixed on some point off in the distance. Then she sighed loudly, licked her lips, and faced him once more. "I think I deserve better than that."

"Is that right?" he said. "And why would you think that?"

"I know we had an agreement," she explained. "But what we did together was special. I had no idea I'd feel this way. Come on. You feel it too. Now I know there's the whole teacher-student thing, and the age difference and all, but that doesn't matter. When something is right, this special, nothing else matters."

"We don't have anything special Samantha," he replied. "Blackmail is not special."

"What are you talking about," she went on carefully. "Don't you remember Mr. B.? The two of us, by the lake? It was amazing. I felt it. It was like our bodies and our minds had become one. I know you felt it too. Stop denying it. There are so many more things I want to do with you. I haven't been able think about anything else."

"Stop," he said. "Stop. Stop right there. There are no joined bodies here – no joined minds. You understand?"

He got up and closed the door.

"It was a one shot deal. Remember? At the library? You said it – one hookup. That was the deal. Now I'm sorry if you are having trouble with this, but we had an agreement, and I expect you to stick by that."

"What do you mean?" she asked, delighting in his emerging uneasiness.

"I mean, it has to stop. All of it. The thirty five emails you send me every day, the texting, the conversations about me to other teachers, the weird looks in class. It's enough now. It has to stop. I know you don't want to hear this, but it would be best for both of us if we just went back to the way everything was – you know, before this happened. And before someone gets hurt."

119

She was happy to be sitting with him, despite his distemper, and was charmed somehow by his loss of control.

"I guess we can do that, but really, you don't have to be such a dick about this. I have feelings too."

He laughed mockingly. She tried to order her thoughts. The prospect of never being with him again, and his utterly flippant attitude assailed her.

"You guess we can do that?" he repeated. "No, you are not going to guess anything. You *will* do it. And you will do it because I said so, and because that was the deal."

She did not answer at first. He stared at her quizzically, at her face, which masked emotions that he just could not access.

"I don't know if I *can* do that Mr. B.," she finally said. "It's a little more complicated than that. A feeling is a feeling."

She licked her lips and sighed before continuing.

"What was the line from that poem we read in class – let's see, something like 'I have found the paradox, that if you love until it hurts, there can be no more hurt, only more love.'"

Her movements were odd, easy and confident. She just kept looking at him, waiting for something to happen. He was suffocating, was being strangled by an overwhelming sense of failure.

"What about Bobby?" he asked desperately. "I'm sure you guys will get back together again. Why don't you focus on that?"

Her face contorted.

"Bobby is a fucking asshole," she said. "He's just a boy. So immature."

Cam sighed heavily. The whole world seemed to be twisting upon itself. He watched as the girl played with the silver ring on her thumb, releasing soft jets of air through her nose. She looked like she was holding back a smile.

"Look Samantha, an agreement is an agreement," he said. "It is. You can't go back on your word. Not now. It's not right."

"Why?" she asked, batting her lashes. "Tell me why?"

"Why?" he repeated? "Why? What kind of person would you be if you did that?"

With a disturbing warmth of pleasure, she rose from her seat and moved toward him, her face awash with anticipated concern. Her words proceeded to fall on him like the emerging shadow of an eclipse.

"I'm thinking," she said with a low groan of triumph, "no worse than the kind of person who would take advantage of a young girl, then leave her dead body rotting in a motel room."

TWELVE

Hayley unpacked a box of printed invitations, pulled one out, and read it aloud. It was perfect. Everything was falling into place. Despite the multitude of tasks and errands engendered by the wedding, and the day to day rigors at her job, she was feeling good about life right now.

When Cam found her, she had already lost herself in a bottle of Falling Star. She had come a long way from the life she had grown up with. All the fighting. The drunken outbursts and broken promises. All the crying. She still thought about it now and again, but the longer she lived, the more it seemed like it was some else's past she was recalling. She stared at herself in the mirror, peering in at what to her was now an awesome stranger. She embraced the beauty of her feeling and circumstance, then set down her glass, lifted her sweatshirt and turned sideways, staring at the noticeable results of her wedding diet. Yes, everything was perfect.

Things kept getting better as the date grew closer. The excitement was certainly building. What had seemed like something so remote had become imminently stirring; the reality of the event sprung seemingly from nowhere and grabbed hold of her by way of the myriad matrimonial harbingers such as dress fittings, song lists, wedding favors and the steady flow of RSVP's.

Cam was only too happy to embrace the excitement for it gave him something else to think about besides the barrage of twisted emails and text messages he was still receiving. He had watched with alarming disbelief, over the course of a few weeks, as the frequency of Samantha's daily correspondence grew from a dozen messages to thirty five or so to a staggering sixty three most recently. It seemed that the more he ignored her desperate attempts to contact him, the worse it got. She began text messaging him as well, and leaving him long, unhinged voicemails professing her love for him and her desire for the two of them to be together forever.

Hey lover. Can't avoid me forever. When I see you in class, you know what I'm thinking. It's not enough. I want to see you – alone. You know, the two of us - just like it used to be. Don't make me wait too long. I'm getting a little impatient. Sometimes, when I'm being fucked with, I get angry. Don't fuck with me. Now look what you made me do. This is no way for lovers to behave. I'm sorry. Do you forgive me? I hate to be like that, but it's for your own good. I have to go. Hugs and kisses. Love you babe. Call me.

He felt spiritless and dirty, like nothing would ever make him clean. His soul was smudged with anxiety, indelible disquiet that he swore would eventually burn through his thinning veneer. The only thing he had was hope – the absurdly improbable notion that eventually she would somehow lose interest and the insanity would stop.

"Hey, there's my sexy bride to be," Cam said, slipping his arms around Hayley's waist. "If you get any skinnier, that dress is going to slide right off you."

"Well, I still have one more fitting," she said, sliding both palms over her stomach. "So either way, I'll need to maintain whatever it is I have going on here until the big day."

"Looks to me like you got it down," he said, kissing the back of her head before skipping out to the kitchen, where he grabbed a drink from the fridge, popped the top, then sat at the table and started to go through the day's mail.

"Hey, what's happening at work?" he called to her, as he sorted through the bills. "Everything squared away for the honeymoon?"

"I told you yesterday," she said, coming around the corner with a stack of papers in her hands. "Kathleen is going to handle my appointments while I'm gone, and Jodi is going to take care of any paperwork that pops up for the new account. We're golden. The only thing I have to worry about is which bikini to pack and what SPF is best for the Bermuda sun."

He was more than happy to consider the thought of being miles away.

"That does sound great Hay. But aren't you getting a little ahead of yourself," he said, continuing to sort the mail into neat piles. "Did you forget about all of the seating arrangement drama, and the 'I'm not coming if so and so is' bullshit?"

Hayley steadied herself in front of him, breathing deeply while mimicking in pantomime the relaxation exercises she had acquired from her last yoga class.

"I decided that I'm not going to let it bother me," she said. "I am in complete control here. No more outbursts, crying, irrational fits. It's all good. This is our day, and I'm not going to let anyone spoil that."

Cam laughed suspiciously.

"So I'm guessing that you did not receive any more responses today," he said, rolling his eyes.

She ceased her attempt to center her emotional core with the universe and laughed along with him at the transparency of her previous statement.

"Nope. Not a single response. So, like I just said, today, it's all good. The only other thing that came in the mail is a manila envelope addressed to you."

"Yeah? Who's it from?"

"I don't know she said," removing the article from the counter and tossing it in front of him. "Here – see for yourself."

In the dimmed light of the kitchen, with legs crossed at the ankles beneath his chair, and with Hayley now busy in the other room, Cam surveyed the outside of the envelope. Typed label. No return address. Queens postmark. He hated these marketers. They were relentless. Professional parasites he called them. If they weren't calling the house, they were either cluttering up his email inbox with all sorts of shameless sales pitches or stuffing his mailbox at home with their pamphlets and fliers. Real estate agents. Insurance salesmen. Mortgage brokers. They were all the same. They all had something that you could just not do without.

He sat there, frustrated already by that which was out of his control, thinking with sharp distaste of how sick he was of dealing with these people. He had given out his information just the one time, only to get the 20 percent discount that went along with applying for a certain credit card. And now, despite a blood sworn promise by the sales associate that his personal data would not be shared with anyone else, his vitals had been splashed across the commercial superhighway, and were twisting out in cyberspace, just there for the taking.

He would have ripped the envelope in half and plunged it into the garbage immediately, the way he always did, but the unusual weightiness of the contents piqued his curiosity. He slid his finger under the glued fold and ran it across the top of the envelope. The smell found his nose instantly. It was familiar. So was the handwriting on the pages inside. It was all *too* familiar, yet he had never seen anything like it. Twenty six pages – each hand written in purple ink. It must have taken her hours. He looked over his shoulder before skimming in cursory fashion the psychotic contents. He surveyed the rantings and observed with horror and incredulity the series of hand drawn cherry colored hearts containing his initials – fanatical impressions that filled both margins – and he knew he was not finished with her. She was not going away. She already knew where he did his grocery shopping, and what barber did his hair and when he typically went. She even managed to appear at the pharmacy he frequented the last two times he went in to fill a prescription.

"You have to stop 'just showing up' wherever I am," he warned her one evening when she just happened to be standing outside the Chinese laundry. "It's getting a little more than weird Samantha."

She did not appreciate his candor.

"You didn't think it was so weird when you were inside of me," she said softly, raising her eyebrows with curious amusement.

"This doesn't change anything Samantha," he said. "We had an agreement. I'm just going to keep saying no."

John's assessment of the troubled girl was far more accurate than the old timer could have ever imagined. He was right. The girl was even a lot sicker than Cam himself had ever considered.

I cannot live without you lover and *I'll have to do whatever it takes* were just two of several repeated phrases in her letters that rendered his knees weak and erected the hairs on the back of his neck every time he read them.

Sitting there, he could not believe what was happening. He chewed at the inside of his mouth and slouched in his chair. The reality that the girl's obsession had now leaped the previous boundary and touched him where he lived, made all his blood rush to his face. There was no telling what she would do next.

"Cam, you want to give me a hand in here," Hayley called from the other room, shattering his silent wonderings. "The closet door came off the runner again."

He grimaced, and shoved the twisted correspondence back into the envelope, casting about in his mind some way to handle the urgency here without tipping his hand to Hayley.

"One sec Hay," he called back. "I'm just finishing reading this."

"I can wait if it's something important," she answered.

Something important? If only she knew. He lifted the soda can to his lips and took a long swallow. It seemed to him that there should be a right thing to do here. Some proper action that would free him from this immoral quagmire. Sitting there, perplexed and stone-like, his thoughts held hostage in a haze of uncertainty and disgust, he found himself unable to think of anything except more lying and deceit.

"No, it's nothing," he said, slipping the envelope underneath a pile of takeout menus in the junk drawer. "I'll be right there."

THIRTEEN

When she was not actively pursuing her fantasy, Samantha spent most of her time hold up in her bedroom, a modest yet well-furnished space that had become the headquarters for her twisted ruminations and calculated tactics. As she sit back on her bed, staring at the American Teen poster on the wall behind her dresser, the landscape of her mania emerged with alarming clarity.

All of the sacred objects with which she surrounded herself announced this wickedly delicious obsession. There was the shrine of photographs of Cam that adorned her dresser; a chain of images that she had acquired surreptitiously in class via her cell phone. When she first set up the display, she worried briefly that her mother would discover the unusual exhibit and question her. So she got into the practice of hiding the photos each day before she left the house, only to take them back out when she returned. This went on for a week or so, until she realized that her mother had not been in her room in days and did not appear to have any interest in doing so. This pleased her greatly, for the constant shuffling had begun to irritate her.

She also encircled her desk with copies of all the books that he had assigned during the school year. Each work, which she stood up on its edge, was a warm reminder of the man; collectively, they served as an emotional conduit to the classroom where she had spent so many hours of late pining for him. The same was true for the bottle of Armani Code she would spray each day in her room; the redolence of his fragrance was sweet enchantment, some sort of intermediary that afforded her mind's eye the necessary fuel for her nightly imaginings.

Lying there, with thoughts of him dancing wildly through her mind, she was struck by a strange sensation – one that she had never felt before where he was concerned. As she scanned the many images of his face, and filled her lungs with his presence, she was suddenly overcome by the clear, smokeless rejection that had defined so many of their recent exchanges. The more time passed, the worse it got. Time to think only intensified her consciousness of the unrequited affection that assailed her at every turn. What was she going to do?

It seemed as though this latest rejection had set off a brushfire of anger and general discontent with everything. She thought about how odious her house was, and the way everything smelled. Like a rancid vanilla. It was those cheap fucking candles her mother was always buying. She hated them, and hated her too. The woman was weak, and easily influenced by the trappings of her stepfather, Bill. Samantha tried to tell her, long ago, that Bill was no good, for either of them, but the woman would not listen. He had stopped touching her, and posed no real threat anymore, but the damage was done. Her mother's refusal to listen just made it that much worse – not because the woman was stupid and stubborn, in which case she would have deserved the life she had chosen for herself, but because Samantha knew, despite her mother's impassioned denial, that this person she called mom, the one charged with protecting her and keeping her out of harm's way, knew exactly what was going on.

Samantha still remembered that night, shortly after her thirteenth birthday. She just wanted to be by herself. She slipped out to the pool in the yard shortly after dinner. It was just getting dark, and she climbed up into a tiny raft, completely out of sight, save for her hands, which were busy trying to catch the fireflies that were hovering just above the little boat. The air was cool, and the water that managed to find its way into the inflatable raft was warm against her skin. She had just unclenched her fist and opened her palm, revealing a tiny spark of light, when she heard him.

"Mind if I join you?" he asked, slipping into the water. "I was watching you from the window."

She lifted her head to see exactly where he was. The sight of his nipples, fully erect through the tangle of chest hair matted now by the water, repulsed her. So did his blood shot eyes and stained teeth, both which flashed abhorrently in the emerging moonlight as he waded closer to her.

"Come one, I'll give you a ride," he said, placing his hands on the float.

He spun her around the pool a few times, until at last his hands moved from the outer portion of the boat to her. He touched her hair first, then her arms, her legs, and told her how pretty she was as he pushed her bathing suit bottom aside. She stayed perfectly still, staring up at the stars as if somehow they could rescue her, lost in silent desperation as his fingers moved across the soft folds of her skin. She could hear him breathing hard, and could feel the vibration of the water caused by his other hand, which was busy beneath the surface.

"I love the way you feel Sammy," he whispered. "You're my special girl."

Her eyes continued to scan the face of the sky, moving from one constellation to another. They appeared to her to be hovering just above her face, and once or twice she was tempted to reach out and grab hold, to somehow wrap her fingers around one of the white diamonds and catapult herself out of the water and into the safety of the deepening night sky. She had all but decided which one she would choose when she heard her mother's voice, calling from the back door.

"Sammy, are you out there?" she said, flipping the switch to the flood lights. I'm home early."

The illumination was unforgiving; she saw her daughter's horrified expression instantly. At first, she could not imagine what was wrong. She thought perhaps she was just spent from too much time in the water. Samantha got that way when she was tired. Then, he emerged from behind the raft, and she knew.

"Mom, I'm, uh, so glad you're home," the girl called from the pool. "Come in the water. Please. Please come in. I really want you to. Please. You have to."

She did not move, just kept staring at her daughter, whose face was colored by a stain of wild alarm. She wanted to move, to go to her child and release her from the unspeakable torment that assailed her. But she was afraid. Afraid that what she thought was happening was indeed the case – afraid of what he would say or do to her if she let on that she knew.

"You, uh, know I don't like the water Sammy?" she finally said. "Don't be foolish. I just did my hair. Besides, I have a million things to-"

"That's right Alicia," Bill fired back. "Go back inside. Just take care of your business in the house. We're fine out here."

She stared blankly out at the water, paralyzed by a sudden nausea that stole her voice and buckled her knees.

"You heard me dear," Bill repeated. "Stop leaning up against the door and go inside. And turn off those friggin' lights, will ya? The neighbors will be complaining about us."

She stood for a while longer, weighing one world against another, before turning around and walking inside.

Samantha thought of how hopeless things were. Her life at home was what it was. It would never change. And now Cam was being awful to her as well. He had rebuked her unmercifully with such detached cruelty. The sting of rejection was killing her.

"I don't understand Mr. B.," she implored as the now distant teacher packed his bag one day after school. "All I'm asking is that we see each other."

"Forget it Samantha," he answered, with a look characterized now more by anger than astonishment. "I told you, it's not happening."

"But why?" the girl persisted. She was reacting to the pulse of desperation throbbing within. "You still have not really explained why."

"Yeah, I think I have. I have explained it. About a hundred fifty times."

"Is it Nikki? Do you still have feelings for her?"

He huffed loudly. "Look Samantha, I'm a busy guy. I have some appointments this afternoon. I don't have time for this. I need to get out of here."

He grabbed his coat from the closet, flung it over his shoulder and pulled his keys from his pants pocket.

"It's Hayley, isn't it?" the girl said deliberately.

The words came like the cold shadow of an eclipse.

"What did you say?" he asked, turning from the door.

He stepped slowly in her direction, moved close enough to her so that he only needed to whisper now.

"Don't even go there Samantha. Just don't. I swear to God, I will-"

"It's not your fault sweetheart. I know. I know. She couldn't possibly understand. You're vulnerable, and she's turning you against me. I can't believe I didn't see it before."

His tongue, now hot and tingling, passed quickly over his chapped lips, and his eyes narrowed so that she looked significantly smaller standing in front of him.

"I'm telling you for the last time you fucking psycho," he said through clenched teeth. "Stay away from me and the people I love. You will be sorry if you don't Samantha. I mean it."

He left her standing in the classroom by herself, her eyes swollen with the rush of hot tears. A weakening in her knees threatened to bring her right to the floor; she steadied herself against a desk as she recounted the past few weeks. What had she done, but love him like no other could? Surely, no one loved anyone like she did him. Somehow, he just could not see it. This love for him was boundless, inexorable, matched only now by the raging anger banging away at her insides. There must be, she thought, something she could do to get him to finally notice her – pay attention to her and all that she had to offer. She turned over a thousand scenarios in her head, but all lead to the same fruitless conclusion. Being sweet and thoughtful was not working.

She remained in her bedroom for the remainder of the night, each hour that passed producing more frustration than the one before. There would be no emails tonight. No phone calls or text messages. She just wasn't up to it. There had been enough rejection for one day. She decided to call it a night, and was all set to turn down her bed when her eyes stopped their roving and were still for a moment. She sat up pensively, then slowly turned on her side, digging her elbow into the mattress before finally resting her head on her open hand. Her face, previously disfigured by all sorts of black emotion, erupted into a toothless smile as the scorned girl became curiously smitten with a slightly different idea. Her thoughtful stratagems had failed. It seemed to her, as she prepared to sleep for the night, that she needed to alter her course of action.

FOURTEEN

John and Cam sat in a booth at the Tower Diner, sipping coffee and talking about department matters, like Regents grading and duty periods. Despite their age difference, Cam and John shared many of the same interests, including baseball, classic rock and roll, and of course the love of language. They spent many hours talking about all of these things, and others as well, but even though they promised that they would not talk about school, the conversation always seemed to find its way there anyway.

One of the things that neither one of them could resist discussing was the exasperating consortium of women they worked with and their penchant for prattling on about things that they classified instantly as minutia. Cam had been there three years and it seemed to him that with each one that had passed, things had gotten progressively worse.

"I bet our meetings could be over in half the time, if they would just learn to shut their mouths once in a while," Cam grumbled.

"Shit, it's torture." John smiled. "They do love to hear themselves talk," he said.

They continued excoriating their less than likeable colleagues, and laughed wickedly about all the ways they would love to punish them, but did manage to take a break from their grousing when one of the waitresses stopped for their order. She barely acknowledged Cam, but gave John what Cam described as a hero's welcome.

"Hey there John," she said, her face exploding into one big smile. "What'll it be today? The usual?"

John frowned.

"That depends Lisa," he replied. "Will you tell everyone I'm boring if I say yes?"

She rolled her eyes and shook her head.

"Now what's so boring about a chocolate chip scone, huh?" she asked.

He thanked her for her kindness, as gratuitous as it may have been, and introduced her to Cam.

"Pleasure to meet you Cam," she said.

132

"Likewise," he replied.

She pulled a pencil out from behind her ear and raised her eyebrows.

"Young Cameron here is the pride of Hillcrest," John boasted. "One of the best teachers I have ever seen. You are in the presence of greatness here Lisa."

Of all the waitresses there, she was the most expressive.

"Well then, forget you old timer," she said, fawning all over Cam. "What can I get for you sweetheart?" she asked.

All the attention sort of cut against Cam's grain. He fidgeted in his seat while he decided.

"Well," he said, taking a final look at the back of a menu before answering. "As exhilarating as the scone sounds, I think I'm going to take my chances with a piece of apple pie."

She scribbled something on her pad and scooped up both menus.

"Can I get you fellas anything else?" she asked.

"No Lisa, that'll be fine," John said. "But maybe you can freshen up our coffees when you get back."

While they waited for their food, John moved the topic of conversation elsewhere.

"Did you hear about the scholarship Guidance is creating in Nikki's name?" he asked. "

Yeah," Cam said. "I did. Mary Eckers asked me if I wanted to be involved in some of the fundraising."

"That's great," John said. "I'm sure the family will really appreciate that."

Cam brought his coffee cup hesitatingly to his lips. He took a sip before deciding to speak.

"I'm not doing it," he said. "I can't. Too much going on right now, I mean with the engagement and all."

John busied himself with the napkin on his lap. The tension hung like smoke in the sudden quiet.

"You know Cam, there's nothing wrong with showing that you're upset," he said. "I keep telling you, it's alright to mourn Nikki's loss. She was special to you."

"I don't know why you keep saying that," Cam protested. "She was my student. Yeah I liked her. And I'd like to help out also. But I just can't John. That's all."

"Well, that's too bad," he said. "We sure could use your help. Seems that a group of our more parochial colleagues don't think it's right. I mean, with the latest police reports and all. I guess the fact that she was found in that motel room, and that there is now evidence of sexual activity, sort of makes her less of a tragedy for some reason."

Cam's face flushed.

"Sexual activity?" he asked.

"Yeah. Are you surprised? Come on Cam. What did you think she was doing there?"

"Oh, no, I kind of figured that. I just had not heard that it was reported. That's all."

"Yeah, but that seems to be all they have to go on," John continued. "It's a real mystery, although I suppose they could still be doing some DNA testing and stuff like that."

Cam's mind, unable to cope with the implications of the conversation, worked feverishly now, trying to rationalize his growing fear.

"Well, that's only if they got bodily fluids," he said. "Might be hard otherwise. These kids today are pretty smart. Seems that a condom would all but eliminate most of that."

John mentioned that he had not heard of any talk like that. Cam was just about to say something else when Lisa arrived with their food.

"Okay gentleman," she said. "Here we go. Chocolate chip scone for Mr. Excitement, and a piece of warm apple pie for the young superstar."

She placed the contents of their order on the table, filled their cups, and was off to take another order.

"I think you may have made yourself a friend Cam," John said, winking. Cam forced a smile, but his mind was clearly elsewhere.

"Look Cam, do you mind if I play the role of the garrulous old fart for a while, and try to impart some wisdom of days past to my young protégé?" John asked.

"I promise I won't talk with my mouth open."

Cam had barely nodded before John was off and running, taking Cam back to *his* first year at Hillcrest, some twenty nine years ago. He explained how he had just graduated college a few months before at the age of twenty one, and sort of fell into the position. He was all set to go to graduate school when a family friend told him that Hillcrest needed someone to teach senior English.

"So there I was Cam, just three years older than most of my students, trying to teach Shakespeare, poetry and Existentialism, to three classes of students who had no interest in anything except how old I was, where I lived, where I went on weekends. That sort of thing. They were always testing the boundaries. I tell you, it wasn't easy."

Cam's thoughts of both Nikki and Samantha only complicated his growing uneasiness.

"I really didn't have that problem John," he said. Not when I started. Not now."

"And the girls," John continued. "They were the worst. All the questions, the flirtatious comments. They were very forward. And I have to say. Some of them were very attractive."

John frowned at his empty cup, then motioned to Lisa.

"Cam, did I ever tell you about Marilyn Landers?" he asked.

John recounted for Cam how on the very first day he stepped foot in Hillcrest High School, a very ardent, five foot seven brunette knockout in his afternoon British Lit class made it very clear that she was interested in being more than just his student.

"She left notes for me everywhere," he recalled. "In my copy of the text we were reading, my jacket pockets, my car. Just about everywhere you can imagine. This girl, Marilyn, really had a thing for me."

Cam used his fork to push around the final piece of pie crust remaining on his plate.

"I didn't know they had stalkers back then," he said, forcing yet another smile.

"No, that's my point Cam," John said. "She was not at all weird, or creepy. She was beautiful, sweet, and really pure of heart. And I never told anyone this, but at one point, I really think, in some way, I was in love with her."

John's confession hit Cam oddly. He had never looked at John in any way but as the consummate professional. He was the quintessential English teacher, almost an absurd stereotype, right down to the glasses, graying temples and the jacket with the corny patches on the elbows.

"So what happened?" Cam asked. "I know you didn't marry her."

"Nothing happened," he replied. "I mean, there were several times when I was close to calling her, or meeting her. Hey, the allure of a beautiful girl is very powerful. Makes you feel invincible. So alive. But alas, I never did. And I am damn grateful that I had the good sense not to."

He paused a moment, taking the check from Lisa as she whizzed by the table with a tray of drinks. He reached into his pocket and threw a twenty on the table.

"My point is, these things happen Cam. It's not so uncommon. But it's what you do with them that counts. You understand what I'm saying here?"

Cam spent the rest of the day thinking about John. He wanted to ask him more questions, like how was it that he was able to say no. Not that it mattered, but he was still curious. He also wanted to tell him what was going on, and to ask him his advice, but he felt small now, even more so than before. It made him sad.

Later that afternoon, as he drove home, he thought some more about one thing that John had said. *It's what you do that counts.* Clearly, he had mishandled everything here. It was too late with Nikki, no doubt, but he could not help but wonder if he had had this conversation with John before the whole thing with his young lover had happened, maybe he would have been able to walk away. Or at least wait. But that ship had sailed. What he had to do now was focus on doing a much better job of damage control with Samantha.

FIFTEEN

Cam received a black lace thong in his school mailbox the same day Hayley discovered that all the windows of her Jeep had been smashed. She had headed out to the car a little before she was supposed to leave in order to get a box of folders she had left on the backseat that morning and was devastated by what she saw. She stared at the explosion of glass that littered the pavement and grass by her car. Under the strain of the shock her heart beat so brokenly that she looked as though she too would just shatter. She began to cry almost instantly. The cold hands of the fading sunlight assaulted her as well, leaving the frazzled woman shivering in the stiff breeze as she dialed her phone and sobbed hysterically to Cam.

"You have to get here," she said, struggling through spastic breaths. "It's my car. It's a mess. There's glass everywhere."

Cam arrived shortly after the police. He ran to her, kissed the back of her head and rubbed her back while one of the officers continued his questioning.

"And when did you first notice the damage" he asked.

"Right before I called you," she replied. "Everything was fine this morning."

The officer peered into the car and made a notation on his pad.

"Nothing missing from the vehicle?" he asked.

"No. Everything's here. My I-Pod, GPS, all of my CD's. Even the money in my console is still there."

"Rules out burglary then," the officer said, again scribbling something as he spoke.

Hayley turned to Cam, who had his arm firmly placed around her at this point. She was markedly more upset now.

"So what are you saying then?" she asked timorously. The officer tucked his pencil behind his ear and yawned.

"Looks like a classic act of random mischief," he said. "Senseless vandalism. Seen it a hundred times before."

His flippant announcement produced the same effect as a hand grenade, sending splinters of distress that pierced her with swift fury. She began to sob again.

"Just to be sure," the officer continued, "anybody have a thing for you miss?" You know, a grudge, some sort of problem?"

A sickening dread rose in her. Her heart was beating wildly.

"Oh my God," she began. "I think that maybe there is."

Cam stood with mesmerized gravity. His eyes glazed so that for a moment, he could not see straight.

"What are you talking about Hay?" he asked.

"Don't be ridiculous. Nobody wants to hurt you."

Her hands formed a steeple around her nose and mouth as she began to conceive the notion of a stalker.

"No, it makes sense now," she explained. "At least I think it does. I've been getting crank calls and hang ups at work the last few days. I say hello, and nobody's there. It must have happened at least twenty times yesterday. And on five or six different occasions, I have run into the same girl at my gym. She's young. Very pretty and blonde. First I saw her looking at me through the front window. Didn't think anything of it. But then it happened again. After that, I saw her on the street as I was leaving and two days ago she was on the treadmill next to mine."

"Come on Hay," Cam said. "Don't you think you're getting a little carried away here? What business would this person have with -"

Hayley continued to scroll through her recent memory.

"I think I may have even seen her at the supermarket."

"Do you know this girl's name miss?" the officer asked. "The blonde?"

She had stopped crying for the moment and was concentrating real hard.

"No. No, I don't. How would I know her name? I've never seen her before until recently."

"Well," the officer went on. "The only thing I can say is that if you think this girl is following you, ask around about who she is. Maybe start at your gym. If you get a name, or some information we can use, then we can bring her in and question her. It's the only real shot we have."

A tow truck delivered Hayley's Jeep to a nearby auto glass repair shop while she rode with Cam. The trip home was frenetic, with Hayley talking and gesticulating wildly about the officer's theory.

"I can't believe I didn't see it sooner," she kept saying, pounding her fists on her knees as he drove. "I knew something was not right."

A communicative discomfort flowed from his stoicism. He tried to minimize the real concern in his voice by looking straight ahead at the road before them.

"Listen Hay, I understand that you are upset, and a little rattled, but I don't think there's any need to get hysterical here. How do we know that what the officer said is necessarily true?"

"I'm really freaked out by all of this Cameron," she said, her eyes wide with hysteria. "I do not feel safe anymore."

"Come on Hay, you know I won't let anything happen to you," he answered. "I promise. I will make it right. I will. I will do anything to help you. We will get to the bottom of this."

"That's not possible Cam and you know it. I have some lunatic stalking me. What the hell are you possibly going to do, huh? You cannot be with me 24/7. I need to do something. I need something now."

"Well Hay, I'm not really sure what else-"

"A gun Cam. I want a gun. Nothing fancy. Just something small that I can carry in my bag with me. Just in case."

Cam sagged, as if all the air had suddenly left his body.

"Are you out of your fucking mind," he thundered. "A gun? You? Come on Hay. Be serious. That's fucking insane"

"I *am* serious. You said you would do anything to help me, right? Well, I am telling you I want to carry a gun. And I want you to get it for me Cam. Do what you have to do. Just get me what I need."

He was speechless for a moment.

"I don't know anything about guns," he complained. "Neither do you. How do you expect –"

"If you love me Cam, and really want to help me here, you will do this for me. And anything else that I ask. You will figure it out."

He was certain she would punish him for his initial response. She was out of control, battling the spasms of fear that were railing against her.

"First thing tomorrow, I am going to find out who this little bitch is. I have a few people who I think can help me. Shouldn't be too hard. Then we'll let the police take it from there."

Police. The mere mention of the word excited alarm. He tugged involuntarily at his shirt collar, checking his face in the rear view mirror to be certain his true feelings had not stained his countenance. He did not know what he was going to do; it seemed that every day this quagmire swallowed a little more of his soul. Yes, he was sinking fast, and was without an idea as to how to alter the terrible course. But one thing was for certain – one thing was for sure -- he could not have the police anywhere near this thing.

"Come on Hay, do you really think it's going to get that far?" he asked. "I mean, it's likely that this girl, whoever she is, and the person who smashed your car are not even the same person. And even if they are, which is really remote, don't you think that it's probably over now?"

She said nothing else the entire way home. His somewhat trepid response to her concern sliced what was left of her resolve. She sat with her back turned to him, staring out her window at the succession of telephone poles and the canopy of wires that connected one to the other; she was thinking somehow about her father, and about the misery that tinged so many of their moments together. She wondered, as one pole gave way to the next, about Cam as well, and her decision to marry him. She loved him, but she had misgivings. Was he able to be the sort of guy she needed? The familiarity of her past perhaps had slipped unnoticed into her consciousness, emerged without announcement, causing her to embrace the very thing against which she had rebelled for so long.

When they arrived home, they went their separate ways without exchanging a word. While she was busy in their bedroom folding laundry, Cam sat numbly at his laptop, staring at the icon which was swollen now with the proliferation of emails he had received that day. He sat there without any movement at all as an entire hour waned. The faint light of hope that had rallied so many times before in the last few months flickered inside his head. One hundred seventeen new messages. A quick click and a cursory glance revealed the escalating horror; they were all from the same source. His face grew harder as he slammed shut the computer.

140

When he found Hayley, she was sitting on their bed, a small stack of hand towels balancing on her lap. She was crying.

"Hay," he said softly with great trepidation.

"I'm sorry."

She did not answer.

"Listen, I understand why you are so upset. You have every right to be. When I said –

""You have no idea what this is like Cam," she said. "No idea. I feel so vulnerable. Can you imagine what it's like to have someone watching your every move? Knowing things about you that they shouldn't? Showing up the same places you are? And then you try to tell me that-"

He hung his head.

"What I'm trying to tell you *now* is that I will take care of this for you. I don't want you to worry. I will make things right. I will do all the leg work. I will find out who she is, and I will make all of this go away."

She looked in his eyes, judging him with curious ambivalence. Her heart was in a riot.

"Oh sure you will," she said bitterly. "Just like you took care of picking up the favor sample for *our* wedding. Right? Just like you help out with this mountain of laundry and the vacuuming and the dishes. Yeah, you'll take care of it. You care more about those kids at school and that cat than you do me."

"What is that supposed to mean?"

"I want that gun, you hear? Do that for me. Right away."

"What does that have to-"

"I ask you for things, for your help, and for your involvement in what is supposed to be our special day, and all you can say is that you're busy and pre-occupied. Busy and pre-occupied, that is, for me. I ask you for just a little time, and you can't. But you managed somehow to clear your schedule enough to get to the store to buy Othello a new collar. Very sweet. The hearts are a nice touch. Truly. But do you think you could have used that time for me? For us?"

He stood open-mouthed, as though he had just sustained a blow to his abdomen.

"Collar?" he repeated.

All the vapors of discord condensed into one instantaneous squall of panic as he searched for something to say – something to supplant the unceasing travail. He thought about sitting her down and telling her everything. Purging himself, once and for all. He was tired of carrying it all, everywhere he went. Or at least he could tell her about Samantha, and how she was destroying him with her evil manipulations. He would not have to go into all the details. Just enough to render him a victim too. That would eliminate some of the immediate angst he was feeling. Perhaps together, they could fight against the common enemy and figure a way out of this mess. Yes, he was sure he would tell her. Right then and there. Yet as his lips tried to form the words, he found himself envisioning her response and instead said nothing.

He imagined her crying, and punching and asking all sorts of other questions. Questions he just could not answer. The thought made him shudder. So instead of confessing, he said nothing. He just continued to stare dumbly into space. He would have to live another day with the haunting residue of his lies because he didn't have the strength or energy to deal with the fallout once he told her that the girl with the blonde hair was the one responsible for the collar.

SIXTEEN

Hayley was unnerved. In the distance, somewhere far away from the ocean of worry, she could see her life, the way she always thought it would be. It was perfect. She had laid it all out, the way she would her dolls when she was a girl, and it all made sense. Everything was just so. But somehow, despite her plan, she kept getting caught up in the current, and it kept sweeping her further and further from the vision she held so dear.

She laughed bitterly to herself when, while rummaging through a drawer on a quest for a sweatshirt she had not seen in a while, she came across the scrapbook she used to keep when she and Cam were first dating. It was all there. A cocktail napkin from Lucky's from the night they first met, the tiny black and white picture of the two of them kissing in a photo booth at Dorney Park, and the Hallmark card he had left for her on her windshield a month later, to mark their first milestone. Next to that was a pressed rose in wax paper and a postcard of Key West, something he slipped into a book she was reading, just because she said she always wanted to see a sunset there. He was so thoughtful back then, and she loved him like she had never loved anyone before.

"Why do you keep doing all these amazing things for me Cam?" she asked him.

He seemed so taken back by the question.

"Come on Hay," he replied, grabbing her with both his arms and smothering her with kisses.

"I love you. Nothing in this world is easier than that."

She continued flipping the pages. She smiled when she discovered the ticket stub from Shea Stadium, from the night they made love in the parking lot after the Mets beat the Reds in an exciting extra inning affair. On the next page was a photograph of a white sheet with some black and red paint on it. He had made it for her sometime after he had discussed the possibility of the two of them breaking up for a while.

"I just need a little space Hay," he told her. "It will be okay."

She was devastated, thought that she would never breathe again. It had only been about twenty four hours when, while driving home from the library the way she always did, she saw it. A big white sheet, tied to the fence just above the underpass on the Long Island Expressway. There was a message for her, surrounded by two red hearts:

I'M SORRY HAY
I LOVE YOU
PLEASE CALL ME

She remembered how he melted her heart that day. It was much easier then. They used to laugh all the time. She missed that, maybe more than anything. She pulled out the somewhat beaten up pair of 3D glasses, the ones she wore when they saw *The Adventures of Shark Boy and Lava Girl*. It had taken her two weeks to convince him to take her.

"Come on Cam," she begged, pulling on his shirt sleeve like a little girl.

"Take me. Please? It's so cute."

He refused, saying it was far too juvenile and just plain stupid. It was only a few days later, while they were at Lucky's listening to some awful Karaoke, that he relented, suggesting that the movie would cost her.

"I always wanted a pretty girl to sing to me," he said smiling. "I think it's really sexy."

"What'd you have in mind?" she asked, more than willing to play his game.

"How about Karaoke night, right here at Lucky's? Next Tuesday? I'd have you do it at my place, but it won't be half as exciting if there isn't a crowd to watch."

"Deal," she said, smiling. "You got yourself a deal."

That Tuesday at Lucky's, Hayley Lofton performed the most impassioned, provocative version of Debbie Boone's "You Light Up My Life" in front of a packed house at Lucky's. He was floored. He often said that it was that night that he knew he loved her for sure. Less than twelve hours later, with a tub of popcorn between them and colored cardboard glasses resting awkwardly on their faces, they sat in the last row of Whitestone Cinemas and watched Hayley's movie.

When she had relived enough of their past together to become sufficiently depressed, she turned her attention to a different endeavor. She found it easier to deal with Cam and the peculiar circumstances when she was immersed in their wedding plans. There was something about the routine of it all that appealed to her. Everything else was just an exercise in frustration. Her inquiry at the gym yielded no information about the mystery girl, and Cam was still being strange. He had, once again, faded from the world they shared together. She could not attach a name to his odd behaviors. And although she was still besieged by the crank phone calls, and a few other odd occurrences, somehow she persevered, undaunted in the face of the unsettling scenario.

Cam's approach to things was far more passionate. He was writhing in the grip of conflicting emotions. Underneath the sheer terror and helplessness he felt a beat -- a steady pulse of anger. He was tired of Samantha's antics – sick of being her play thing. He had decided that he would stop allowing her to control things. His manner conveyed a very clear exasperation.

"Meet me after school, in my room, 3:00 sharp," he ordered her. "Do not be late."

His head hurt, and he found it next to impossible to focus on his classes. He decided to give his students seat work, which removed the onus of interaction with them, but his detachment was more punishment than therapy, for it left him staring at the clock the entire day. The hours slipped by slowly, making it seem like days had passed when three o'clock finally came. He had just finished closing the blinds, and securing the area for their meeting, when she walked in. She dropped her bag, flipped the hair off her neck, and took the seat directly in front of his desk.

"Well," she said. "I'm here. And I'm two minutes early. Do I get extra credit for that?"

Her movements brought to his nose the distinctness of her perfume.

"I am losing my patience with you Samantha," he said. "I thought we spoke about this."

"I really don't know what you are-"

"Cut the bullshit!" he thundered, slamming his fist against the file cabinet next to his desk. "You know exactly what you're doing."

She gave a quick glance at the dent he had just made.

"You should really watch your temper Mr. B.," she said, shaking her head. "People are going to start talking."

"Why are you calling my fiancé?" he asked, suppressing the urge to place his hands around her throat. "And why are you following her? You broke her fucking windows. Who does that? Did you really think all that would get me to love you Samantha?"

"At first maybe," she said, her hands rubbing the back of her head. "But now it's not really about that.

"Really? Then what's the issue Sam? Let's just settle it now."

She smiled oddly. Then she bent her head and leaned in across the desk, as though preparing for a kiss.

"You fucked me, Mr. B.," she whispered. "Remember? Nice and hard. And I know you liked it. And you know what's funny? To be perfectly honest, now that I think about it, it wasn't even that good. For me anyway. But that's not the point. You took advantage of me, a vulnerable, teenage girl. Sort of like you did with Nikki. And now you want to just pretend like none of it ever happened. I don't know. Call me crazy, but that sort of bothers me a little."

He made a faintly audible sound in his throat.

"Look Samantha," he began, scraping at a spot on the desk with his thumbnail. "You are a beautiful girl. You are intelligent, fun to be with, and have so much to offer. You don't need me. There is a very lucky guy out there, someone your own age, who you can be with, without sneaking around, someone who can treat you the way you deserve to be treated. I care about you, which is why I need you to listen to me."

She was twirling her hair, and her eyes were fixed somewhere on the ceiling, as though she were storming the heavens for the right words to say to him.

"*You* have not been listening to *me*," she finally said. "I don't want some pimple faced poser who thinks he knows how to make me happy. I want you. I want us."

Cam felt his resolve draining, as if someone had just pulled a plug. He could barely see straight.

"You listen to me Samantha," he said. "If you touch Hayley, or anything of hers, or if you come near my house, or my cat, or anything else like that, you will be sorry."

She sat with her hands folded neatly, her eyes now lowered to the floor in silent reflection. She was laughing.

"So you didn't like the collar I bought for little Othello?" she said. "Hearts and rhinestones? I thought it was really cute."

Cam was paralyzed by exasperation. Except for swallowing and the nervous rubbing of his palms on his pants, he didn't make another sound until she got up to leave.

"Where do you think you're going?" he asked.

"I have things to do" she replied.

"I'm ready to go to the police Samantha," he said. "I've already put together a record of activity. You could get in a lot of trouble."

He wasn't sure why he said it. It just came out. The last thing he wanted to do was involve the law. But he was thinking of his life now in terms of a poker game. He was holding an empty hand, while she had a fist full of aces. The only shot he had left was to bluff – make her think that he had something on her, and that he was just crazy enough to blow himself up for the sole purpose of taking her down with him.

"What you are doing constitutes stalking," he said. "Not to mention harassment and criminal mischief. An acquaintance of mine down at the 105th precinct said a person could actually go away for things like that."

"Police?" she repeated. She shook her head histrionically and laughed again, this time out loud. "Did you just say that you are ready to go to the police? Is that what you said?"

She took a few steps back toward his desk. Her wild stare stretched its darkness over him. "I tell you what, Mr. B.," she said. "Why don't we take a drive over there right now? Together. Just the two of us. You know how I love your car. You can tell them all about me, and how I am – what is it you said I am doing – *harassing* you? Yeah, you can tell them all about how I am harassing and stalking you. I will sit right next to you while you are doing it. And then when you are finished, and the officer has written down every last detail, I will tell him a story I know. All about a man. A teacher, who seduced a beautiful young girl. Had a relationship with her – a relationship that included a trip to the Comfort Inn, where the two of them rolled around together, nice and sweaty, until the girl stopped breathing. Then this man just left the girl there to rot. Left her as she was, covered from the waist down, her legs twisted in the sheets, eyes and mouth slightly open, as if she were still trying to tell her story. But not before he cleaned up all the visible traces of his being there. Sound familiar?"

Cam shivered. His eyes sank into a face that was now ashen and drawn.

"Aw, what's the matter lover? You look upset? Did I bring back a bad memory for you – of the girl you loved and lost? Or, is something *else* bothering you?"

"How do you know all that? I mean about the room? And about what she looked like?"

She said nothing for a while, delighting devilishly in his escalating alarm. She thought about making a scene, screaming or weeping uncontrollably, just to test the true temperature of his present condition. She imagined herself sobbing, struggling to get the words outs that she desperately wanted him to hear, and him rushing to comfort her, either out of genuine love now or just the uncompromising fear of being discovered. For a moment, it seemed like a deliciously wicked approach. But somehow, her immediate sensibilities took over, and her final overture of discourse was anything but hysterical.

"You'll find out," she finally said. "I told you I'd be good to you. Soon, you will know everything there is to know."

SEVENTEEN

Time pursued its inexorable path. Nothing changed. Eager for some relief, Cam tried desperately to put some distance between himself and Samantha's dogged pursuit, but with the past all around him, trailing him, haunting his every action and every thought, each minute grew more heavy on the air.

"Hey, what's the deal with you Cam?" John asked one morning while the two of them sifted through the contents of their mailboxes. "And don't bullshit me and say it's nothing."

Cam stood stone like, arms crossed, shoulders hunched, his eyes restless and full of hidden torture.

"Why does something have to be wrong?" he replied, his limbs tired and heavy.

"I could ask you the same thing."

"Yeah, but I'm not having heated exchanges with students in my classroom after school, and on free periods, and in the hallway."

"I don't know what you're talking about," Cam insisted.

John moved back a step, as if he were trying to focus the picture before him. He thought about remaining silent, about simply walking away, but the uncalculated opportunity was too much to resist.

"You're screwing her, aren't you?"

"What?"

"Samantha. Come on Cam, I'm not stupid. And neither are the other people in this building. You are not being as discrete as you think. That's why I took you out the other day. You need to talk to me. Look, I'm not here to judge you – shit, I think you know that by now. I'm just trying to help you, before it's too late."

Ordinarily, nothing anyone said could have induced Cam to open up, even the slightest bit. But his heart had grown timid these past few months. His despair had leaped past all boundaries.

"I really don't know what to say John," he answered, dabbing his forehead with his shirt sleeve. "But it's not what you think. I really cannot get into it right now."

"All I'm saying is that it might help if you-"

"I know what you're saying John. Believe me, I do. And I appreciate your concern, and the offer. But you just have to let me handle this my way. I have to do this the way I am most comfortable."

"I'm not trying to make you uncomfortable Cam," John insisted. "I'm just saying that I will talk to her if you'd like. "Maybe she will listen to me. Sometimes it helps."

Cam clenched his teeth.

"Stay away from her John," he demanded. "I told you once before. Stay out of my business. Besides, you do not know what you're dealing with."

Comfortable? That was a place that just seemed to slip further and further away each day. He could not escape the quagmire, this unholy mess he had created. It felt as if both girls were inside him now, each struggling with the presence of the other. He was thinking more and more about Nikki, and what he had done. And dealing with Samantha was exhausting. It was getting more and more difficult to hide the exertion from Hayley.

"Cam, this envelope came for you today," she said one evening, handing him a fairly large manila envelope with the words DO NOT BEND written in red on the outside. His heart beat with physical defect when she handed it to him.

"Thanks Hay," he said, his tongue thick and chalky. He put the envelope under his arm and turned from her.

"What's the matter?" she asked.

"What do you mean?"

"Well aren't you going to open it?" she asked.

"Ah, it can wait. I, uh, am swamped with essays and quizzes. I think I'll just go in the other room and work for a while."

In the dim light of his office, with gray clouds gathering outside his window, Cam opened the envelope. His face convulsed wildly as he stared at the horrid images. He had forgotten just how sickening it was. There she was, beautiful Nikki, in that bed, eyes still open, lips pursed, like she was about to say something to him. He let his face fall into his hands and wept openly. When he was finished sobbing, he sat perfectly still, unable to move. His limbs were paralyzed but his mind raged on. It walked him through the valley of despair, a ravine of heartache that seemed to be widening all the time. His mounting panic, or whatever mysterious thing it was that had now seized him, rendered him on the verge of lunacy.

Hours later, he found himself a curious mixture of fear and loathing. Samantha was hunting him. That was her new game. And yes, she had him. It killed him to have to admit it to himself. She had outplayed him, at every turn. This young girl had revealed herself as quite a puppet master. He had everything to lose, and she knew it, as did he. He sat in the dark, lamenting his fate. Half his thoughts signaled the readiness to wave the white flag, capitulate to the girl's devious machinations, and do whatever it was she wished. It was the easiest solution, he thought. Still, the other half of his imagination, the part that continued to grow, vowed at that moment to fight -- to beat her at her game. Why not? He was smarter than she was, right? How could a kid really be any match for him? The more he thought about it, the more preposterous it seemed. He would attack now as well, threaten her in ways that even he had not considered until that moment.

The next morning he waited for her outside her homeroom. Standing there, watching the frenetic rush of students making their way to their programmed destinations, the landscape of his own youth began to present itself. He thought about Mr. Frattalone's Italian class, and of third period gym dodge ball, and study hall with his friends Dave and Brian. He could see vividly laughing at his lunch table with the guys from the baseball team about the cafeteria pizza, and recalled with alarming trepidation the daily Algebra quizzes that Mrs. Cavaletti always gave, and the way her breath always smelled of tuna during their extra help sessions. He remembered all the parties at his friend Sherry's house, and the ski trips he took with his friends. The good definitely supplanted the bad. If only these kids knew how glorious their lives were – now, right now. Oh, to have the worries of youth. He could also see Maleigha, sweet, beautiful Maleigha, and knew, in the very core of his soul, that if fate had allowed her to live by him, allowed her to go to school with him, his life would have never run the course it had presently taken. He had often thought about that and it angered him if he dwelled there too long. His frustration had just begun to reach its apex when the bell to begin homeroom sounded, without Samantha's presence.

Vexed, he went to class himself, satisfied that he would have to deal with her later on that day. He taught his first two classes, unable to shake the mounting reality that stopping the girl immediately superseded all else. Was it merely chance, coincidence, that she was not in school? Or was her absence, somehow, part of her morphing maneuverings? He abhorred her now more than ever.

By mid-day, there was still no sign of the girl. The seat she usually occupied in his class was empty as well. It was no different by late afternoon. Samantha Brocking was not in school. Knowing very well that he would have to wait until tomorrow to effect some sort of change in his circumstance, he threw his briefcase in the back of his car and sped off, his mind polluted with worry. Since that day at the library, Samantha had not missed one day of school. She had also never gone more than an hour or two without some form of correspondence. His heart sat heavy with an inactive dread; what was she up to? Being absorbed the way he was in all of this had enervated him.

When he arrived home, he dropped his bag on the floor and flopped on the couch. He reached for the television remote, and began clicking feverishly, his face partially lit by the frenzy of digital images running before him. He could smell lilac, or strawberry, and it bothered him until he remembered that Hayley had just refilled the plug-in air fresheners throughout the apartment. When his thumb tired, he decided that re-runs of *The King of Queens* would have to do. He loved Kevin James, and was in desperate need of a laugh. He set the remote on his chest, locked his fingers behind his head, and stretched out. It was one of his favorite episodes, the one where James' character gets caught lying to his wife so he can go play basketball with his friends. He had missed the first few minutes of the show, but it was of no real consequence, because within ten minutes of watching, his eye lids could no longer support the weight of his distemper and he was fast asleep. He slept hard, only stirred when he heard Hayley come in several hours later.

"Hey," he said, rubbing his eyes. "What time is it?"

"A little past ten." "Why so late?" he asked, sitting up in an attempt to get his bearings.

It took her a while to answer. She was wet, and cold, and seemingly stiff in every limb. Her hair was a tangled mess, and it looked as though a tiny runnel of blood had dried and settled in the left corner of her mouth. She breathed with great difficulty, almost in gasps, and for a moment it appeared as though her legs were going to quit, and she would topple over.

"Something happened tonight Cameron," she finally said, "Something real bad."

He could feel the inexplicable tremors in the earth that had shaken her.

"What is wrong with you Hay?" he asked wildly. "What happened?"

She stood blankly, tugging lightly at the collar of her coat with her thumb and forefinger, then directed her steps toward him. Her eyes were glassy, and her lip twitched ever so slightly, as though someone were tugging at it with an invisible thread.

"She's dead Cam," she whispered. "What? What did you say? Who's dead Hayley? Who?"

It took her a while to compose herself.

"It was an accident. Honest. It all just happened so fast."

"Hayley, talk to me. Please. Who is dead? What happened tonight?"

She was growing paler, and more unsteady with every word. At one point, she stopped speaking completely, unable to collect her thoughts. Then she filled her lungs, licked her lips, and unfolded the horror.

She had just come out of the gym, and was walking to her car, when someone came up from behind her, stuck a knife to her back, and ordered her to walk. There were people all around, rushing home or to appointments, and it was fairly dark, so nobody could see what was happening.

"She forced me into my car," Hayley continued, "and told me that she would kill me if I did not cooperate."

Cam's face drained of all its color. She was equally unnerved.

"Who Hayley?" he asked desperately. "What are you saying?"

She described, with great hysteria, the next sequence of events as something out of a low budget horror film. The girl was wearing a thick black jacket, zipped up half-way past her chin, so that her mouth was barely visible. She spoke through the makeshift mask, uttered things that chilled Hayley to her bone.

"She said all sorts of awful things Cam," she explained. "Things, things that made me sick. She said you were with her, and that the two of you were in love, and that both of you wanted to be together. And, and that it was me who – that I was in the way."

A curious silence fell across them, so that the only audible sound now was Hayley's breathless sobs.

"I still do not understand," Cam said desperately. "What the – oh no, you didn't use the-"

"The girl," she continued softly. "She's, she's dead. I killed her."

"Who is the girl? Who are you talking about?"

He stood uneasily, his foot tapping wildly, wondering if he were really watching the twisted blur that was now unfolding before him. She was off as well, and could barely speak, but after several failed attempts to catch her breath, she finally completed the horror.

"The blonde girl Cam. You remember. The one – the one who was following me. It's her. She's – she's dead Cam. She's dead. I killed her."

EIGHTEEN

When something someone has wished for suddenly comes true, his reaction may not be what is expected. Instead of euphoria, or even relief, the wisher is left with a feeling of emptiness, like there is a tiny leak inside of him, and what should have filled his recesses of sweet relief and jubilation has simply run right through, and puddled on the floor all around him.

After Hayley's announcement, she was too tired, too distraught to say anything else. He laid her on the couch, right where he had been before she came in, and before he had the chance to ask her even one of the thousand questions burning in his mind, she was asleep. He sat beside her the entire night, mired in self-induced torture, and kept the vigil, waiting for the moment when her eyes would open, and he could finally learn what had happened.

"Hayley?" he asked softly, the minute she stirred some hours later. "You have to tell me what's going on here. What happened. Who else knows about this?"

She was still groggy, and her lips were dry. Cam got her a bottle of water, and she gulped most of its contents instantly.

"I still can't believe it," she said, wiping her mouth on her sleeve. "It's a nightmare."

She was flushed and unsteady. He was wild with impatience.

"Hayley," he said, grabbing her by the shoulders. "Look, I cannot do this. I have to know. Right now. What exactly happened last night? I need to know everything."

She fussed a little with her hair and her blouse, and made an odd motion with her right arm, as though testing its welfare. Then she finally spoke. She explained, as she had done so the previous night, how the girl was skulking outside her gym again, and how she had considered calling the cops, but remembered Cam's request to leave the police out of it. So instead, she finished her workout on the elliptical machine, showered as usual, all the while pretending she had not seen the demented girl watching her.

"I told you Cameron," she said, deviating briefly from her narration, "that I was sick of this, and that I wanted it to end."

"I know, I know."

"No, you don't know," she persisted. "Saying you know doesn't make it so Cam."

There existed in his head an escalating horror that he had housed in the forefront of his mind. It was far more concentrated now, pummeling him unmercifully with unbridled vitality.

"So what happened?" he asked again. His eyes were twice their normal size.

She went on to describe for him the way she slipped out the back, instead of using the doors in front, mindful that the girl knew her usual routine. She crossed the street, without being noticed, then while the girl waited, arms folded and eyes affixed to the front doors, Hayley stole up behind her.

"Wait a minute," Cam said, his face a twisted mess. "I thought you said *she* came up from behind *you*?"

There came forth now from Hayley an involuntary shrugging of her shoulders.

"She did," she said sharply. "I mean, afterwards. Look, I'm tired, and upset. Is the order of things really that important?"

"No, I suppose not," he answered. "But I would like to know exactly what happened."

"She wanted to talk to me," Hayley said. "That's how it all started."

Cam's legs, which were already twitching, became even more spasmodic.

"She said, uh, that *she* wanted to talk to *you*?" he asked with measured breaths.

"Yeah, can you believe that?" Hayley replied. "I'm thinking that this lunatic who smashed my car and has been following me around is going to do some horrible thing to me, beat me up or rob me or something, and then she says that all she wants to do is talk."

His heart felt like suddenly it was too big for his chest.

"Well, what did she say?" Hayley was perched carefully on the end of the sofa.

"It's like I said last night," Hayley explained. "She tried to tell me that you and her were in love with each other, and that I was standing in the way. Some crap like that."

An unremitting shivering infected his heart and he struggled to suppress it. He wondered if she could tell.

"Hayley, you have to believe me. I am telling you that-"

"Relax Cam. Just relax. It's not an issue. I knew she was lying."

He tried to fill his lungs, to somehow meet the assault represented by what he was listening to, but still struggled. He could feel something, deep inside, rushing to the surface, like his entire body was trying to turn itself inside out.

"What else did she say Hay?" he asked. "Did she tell you that she has been cutting my class, and that all of a sudden she has this weird grudge against me? It has been so -"

"She is lying, right Cam?" she asked, as though the previous moment of silence that passed between them had ushered in some doubt. "About all the love shit. Because if you are not"

"Yes, yes. Come on Hay. Please. Of course she is. How can you even ask? She's just some misfit who is all confused. You know I wouldn't do something like that."

She lowered her eyes and shook her head.

"I don't know anything anymore."

She went on about the uneasiness that had tainted her last few weeks, and how she felt like she was going to simply explode, but his mind was racing, and he heard nothing she said.

"I just don't understand Hay," he went on, his hand resting on his head. "So she lied. Okay. I get that. But what went wrong? You killed her?"

Of the mixture of fear and pain painted on her face, only the pain remained.

"What the fuck is wrong with you Cameron?" she screamed. "Are you not hearing me? She had a knife. Look at me! Look! Do you think I wanted any of this? Huh? I told you. It was a fucking accident."

He sat idly for a moment, plotting his next move. There were things he had to know. But how? He needed Hayley to tell him everything -- but how would he accomplish that now, without tipping his hand? He started by apologizing for his insensitivity. They sat for a while after that, and said nothing. They both just sat vacantly, Hayley's eyes fixed firmly on the floor, Cam's gaze suspended in the collection of framed photographs displayed on the entertainment center. Happy faces. Happy times. Each shot seemed to mock his restlessness.

"Hayley, you have to tell me everything else that happened. I mean *everything*. For you, and for us. We have got to protect ourselves."

"It was all so fast," she said. "We went to my car, to talk. I said that. Everything seemed okay. But then she started in about the two of you, and your plan, and how I was in the way. It was all so weird. Then she took out a tiny knife again, from under her jacket, and grabbed me, and I think she was going to-"

His eyes were wide, his jaw agape. He sat, transfixed, as Hayley provided the rest of the gory details. She described the struggle, how the girl was stronger than she looked, and how close the twisted stalker had come close to overpowering her and plunging the knife in her chest.

"I really thought I was dead," Hayley confessed.

"So what happened? *You* stabbed *her*? You stabbed her?"

As he carried on, he felt the sting of hypocrisy deep in his throat, for as shameful as it was, he had been harboring similar thoughts himself.

"Relax Cam. I didn't stab her. And I didn't shoot her either. All I did was push her off me. I wanted no part of her. She must have lost her balance or something – hit her head on the window. I just remember the thud, and then grabbing the knife from her, and sitting there, waiting for her to wake up. I just wanted to find out more about her – where she lives, what she *really* wanted. I don't know."

His own feeling of dread was now echoed in her telling of the story.

"This is unreal," he lamented. "Did anyone see you guys?"

"I don't know. I doubt it. It was dark."

He struggled with Hayley's flippancy.

"So that's it? You're not sure? What about the body? What did you do with the body?"

He watched her wade through the recollection. He believed that she was still more or less in her right mind, but found the growing detachment with which she conveyed the experience troubling.

"I didn't know *what* to do at first," Hayley recalled. "I just drove around for a while, thinking, looking for a place to put it. I could not decide. I finally stopped over by the racetrack. There's a patch of trees and bushes on the Cross Island, around exit 26. You know what I'm talking about? I just wanted her out of the car, so I dumped her under a tree."

Cam gesticulated wildly, his arms flailing like helicopter blades.

"That's it? You just left her there? Right there, out in the open?"

Her nerves tightened and the ache in her head beat on.

"Well I didn't bring my shovel Cameron, if that's what you're asking. What are you thinking? Do you really think I knew *what* to do? The only thing that made any sense was to cover her up with a bunch of leaves and sticks. It looked good. You would never know she was there."

The more she talked, the more uncomfortable he became. He stared at her, as though he had never seen her before, and tried to reconcile silently the tempest of concerns still swirling in his imagination. *What's going to happen when they find her*? he thought. *What if they check her phone records? Or her e-mail? And the pictures. Where the fuck were those pictures?* He was tied to this thing in a hundred different ways. The speculation was killing him.

He moved closer to Hayley, and touched her softly on the cheek, trying to impart to her the urgency of the situation – to make her understand what was at stake here, all without implicating himself in a way that would blow everything up in his face. But he was out of ideas. Any more probing and she would definitely become suspicious. The best he could hope for now was a little questioning from the police, and perhaps a testimonial from him that the girl was obsessed with him, and that he wanted no part of her. Hayley would help with that, certainly now. And maybe John would corroborate his statement. That wouldn't be so bad. There was nothing really tying him to Samantha. He'd be cleared. It would be uncomfortable for a while, but he would still have Hayley, and the two of them could move on with their lives.

He was almost okay with that scenario, had convinced himself that it wasn't so bad, until he remembered again those pictures of Nikki, and all the notes Samantha kept, and whatever else she had. It was a horrifying recollection. He was screwed unless he could get near the body, and perhaps answer some of those questions. But there was no easy way he could suggest that. His entire body sagged until, as if his secret longing had been heard by some divine intermediary, she spoke the words that had stalled on his lips.

"I'm really worried Cameron," she said, placing her hands over her mouth momentarily. "I think we have to move the body. Tomorrow night. It's not safe. We need to go out and move it -- as soon as possible -- you know, someplace out of the way, where it will never be found."

She saw he was beginning to crumble.

"Come on Cam," she said, shaking his shoulders as if to rouse him from a sudden dream. It will be fine. Really. We will take care of everything. Nobody will ever have to know."

NINETEEN

The hours before sundown passed glacially, like the hands of the clock were scraping along the face of time. When they weren't trying to lose themselves in television or reading, Cam and Hayley watched the clock, paced the floors, and made steady visits to the window, cursing the interminable minutes while imploring the sky to drop her nightly veil. After they had exhausted all of those ploys, they spent the remainder of the time talking, mostly about their relationship. Hayley's thoughts drove most of the conversation.

"Do you remember when we were first dating?" she asked him. He was listening to the wind whipping through the hemlocks just outside the window.

"Of course I do Hay," he said. "What kind of question is that?"

"It was nice, right?" she asked.

"Yes," he said.

"It was great. We were both so happy back then."

She remained pensive, and seemingly at odds with herself.

"Remember that time when we went skiing, in the Poconos?" she asked. "At Hillside Lodge?"

"Yeah," he said laughing. "That was quite a trip."

"Yes, our one and only ski adventure," she added.

They both mused in a very palpable, melancholy manner about how she twisted her ankle on the first run they took, and how he lost a ski and got frostbite carrying her down to the lodge.

"You should have seen the look on that guy's face when you tried to explain to him what happened to your ski?" she said. "He thought you were insane."

"Who, old slope nose?" he said, mocking the peculiar attendant who greeted them once they came in.

"Yeah, he was really one to talk."

She laughed, then crossed the floor over to one of the end tables and picked up the picture of them taken at Niagara Falls. She held it in her hand, and thoughts of better days continued to wash across her.

"What happened to us Cam?" she asked. "What happened?"

Her nostalgic jaunt was tinged with a startling morbidity.

"When did things gets so bad? Really. Was it something I did?"

A whirling expanse of detail transported him back in time.

"I don't know Hay," he said. "It's hard to say. Things happen. People change. Things change."

He stopped himself for a second, mindful of where he wanted this to go.

"But listen, I don't think it means you can never get back what you had. It just makes it a little harder, that's all."

She stood with her back to him, so that he could not see her eyes, but he knew, from the sound of her voice, small and fading, that she had begun to cry.

"I don't know about that," she said.

He sat with great unrest, fidgeting as though the walls had begun to close around him.

"What do you mean Hay?" he asked. "Are you giving up? Just like that?"

She felt chilled and uncomfortably warm at the same time. Only a faint glimmer of light proceeded from her eyes.

"What do you want me to say Cam?" she asked, wiping the moisture from her brow with her shirt sleeve. "I don't know. Ever since I got back from my trip, you've been strange. Different somehow. Things are so weird. Strained. I don't know exactly what it is, but it's there."

"What are you talking about?' he protested. "I'm not different. I'm telling you I love you, and that I want this to work for us."

"Come on Cameron," she said sighing. "We've been through this a few times. It's not what you say. It's the other stuff. Like the way you touch me -- so guarded, like I'm going to shatter if you squeeze me too tight. And it's the way you look at me sometimes -- and don't look at me. Like the other night, when we were watching TV, and you were somewhere else. You don't even realize it. I swear you have made me so uncomfortable with myself. I just don't know what to do anymore."

She had come home that night with the idea that they would spend some time together, the way they used to. She made a bowl of microwave popcorn, crawled under a blanket on the couch, picked up the remote and ordered a movie on demand. Woody Allen's *Match Point* caught her attention. She invited him to join her, and he did, but something was clearly distracting him.

"It was like you weren't even there," she continued.

He shook his head. There it was again -- this struggle with the absurd irony. He was thinking the same thing about her. *She* seemed like the one who was distant. He recalled how she used to be the one to carry their conversations, regardless of the topic. They could giggle for minutes at a time about things like her OCD or his phobia of milk, and could wrestle for hours with far more compelling issues, like family, religion and the meaning of life. But that had all changed now. She was different. He thought that perhaps the anti-depressants she had started taking were to blame – that they had clouded her brain so that more often than not she was incapable of only the most rudimentary expressions. Sure, they had taken the edge off, but she was not the same. He wasn't certain that the Prozac was to blame, but he was at a loss to determine what else it could possibly be.

"I really don't think that's fair Hay," he said. "You aren't exactly yourself either."

Not much else was said. They simply waited dutifully for the right time, and when the horizon finally swallowed the sun, and all that could be seen was the steady glow of street lights and porch lamps, they ventured outside, carrying a large blanket, flashlight, hand shovel, and the guarded vision of correcting Hayley's mistake. Cam drove, while Hayley directed his course of action. She took him back to the gym, so that he could see for himself, step by step, exactly what had transpired the previous evening.

"Okay," she said, pointing to the spot in the tiny lot where her car had been parked. "That's where we talked, before it all happened."

After a brief deliberation over the possibility of someone having seen their struggle, Cam drove, with Hayley's assistance, the exact route she had traveled. They turned onto Springfield Boulevard, and then again at Hillside Avenue.

"I cannot believe you did this," he said, his fingers tapping restlessly atop the steering wheel. "You should have called me. I wish you had just let me handle it, like I said I would."

"Don't start again Cam, alright? You say a lot of things that don't mean shit. How long was I supposed to wait?"

"So, now it's my fault, is that right?"

She was staring out her window at the trees in the distance, bathed in the moon's glow.

"Well, did you take care of it, or not?" she fired back. "She's a girl from your school, right? Isn't that what you said you thought? I kind of think that means you're sort of responsible."

Sensing that she was unraveling, and becoming belligerent and alarmingly unpredictable, Cam swallowed his anger and frustration. They rode for a little while in silence, lost in a wordless fuming. The mood in the car was now galling him more than the reason they were there.

"Look, I cannot deal with this bullshit right now Hay," he said. "It doesn't matter. We have to take care of this issue before we find ourselves in a lot of trouble."

"Fine," she said, turning again toward her window. "Make a right in two blocks, and get on the Cross Island Parkway."

She continued to talk Cam through the events of the previous night, pointing out along the way all the places she had considered stopping before she finally did.

"Nothing looked right," she explained, after his loud sigh announced his resentment over the growing distance.

"I'm sorry. This is not easy you know."

"I didn't say a word Hay," he replied. "Just keep looking."

They had only traveled one more exit when the high beams of their car caught the exit sign she was searching for.

"That's it," she said, pointing ahead. "26D. Just to the right of the sign."

Something odd stirred inside Cam. The thought of disposing the body, and hopefully all his worry, stimulated his imagination and made the present suffering that much less acute.

"Pull over," Hayley said. "Just like I did."

"No, no way," he barked loudly. "Are you out of your mind? That is way too risky. We will have to get off up ahead, and double back from one of the side streets. We'll pull up as close as we can."

The car came to rest in front of an abandoned furniture warehouse. The place was a wreck. The roof was in a state of protest, revealing the many fractures that years of storms and harsh weather had dealt the old edifice. Virtually all of the shingles had fallen off the exterior, and it sounded as if the wind had found every last loose board that remained. It was creepy. Almost like the building had its own story to tell. He did not know why, but it really unnerved him, especially when the damp moonlight caught the jagged ends of broken glass still clinging to the casements, and for a moment, appeared to hang on the tiny shards like tears.

"Would you look at this place?"

Cam got out first. He was still eye balling the warehouse, but began scanning the area for activity. Not much was happening, save for a stray cat rummaging through a tipped trash can and a vagrant snoring on the corner. He called to Hayley to join him, and motioned to her to bring the flash light and blanket. Cam followed as Hayley tried to retrace her steps from the different direction. With the steady roar of traffic from the Cross Island drowning out their movements, they navigated the underbrush almost surgically, their every step lighted by the compliant moon.

"Are we close?" he asked her. "Does any of this look familiar?"

"I'm pretty sure it's just up ahead," she said. "In the clump of bushes by that tree, a little diagonal from the exit sign."

They pushed on a little further, careful to shield themselves from the wave of headlights spilling across the parkway. The thickets were denser now, and once or twice Hayley almost stumbled, and had to reach back for Cam's hand. He was tired, and now cut up, and the thought of why they were there rose up suddenly once more and oppressed him.

"I thought you said it was over here?" he asked. How much further?"

"This is it," she said, pointing at an area just in front of a large Sycamore. "Right there."

He grabbed the flashlight from her hand and jumped out in front of her, eager to cross the threshold of relief. He fired the artificial light all around the tree. She remained a step behind, so that she could not see the sort of inflammation that passed in his face as he dislodged a barrier of branches that housed nothing but more fear.

"There's nothing here Hay," he said, swinging his foot violently through a clump of leaves. "Son of a bitch! Where is she? What the fuck is going on?"

He was kicking at the ground and waving his arms. Hayley was still some distance away, just watching him.

"I don't know," she said. "I don't understand Cameron. This is where I left her."

He could feel his teeth straining against the inside of his upper lip.

"Well, where the fuck is she then? Huh? Where the fuck is she Hay? What did you do?"

He picked up the weathered remnants of an errant brick and fired it at the tree, all the while continuing to curse her. Her slight and previously submissive figure moved next to his, and suddenly became a more integral part of the scene.

"Hayley, where the fuck is she?" he repeated louder.

"I told you, I don't know."

"Well, that's just great Hay," he roared. Beautiful! "You don't know."

He turned his back to her, and glared out at the thin rays of light from the parkway that continued to spill through the sparse cover, all the while trying, with unflagging desperation, to untangle the snarl of awful thoughts and swelling rage.

"Well, let me ask you this," he said, turning to face her once again. "Are you sure she was even dead when you put her here?"

Hayley dwelled at some length on the tremors of the night. She had had all that she could stand. Cam's attack just made it that much more intolerable.

"You go fuck yourself Cameron," she screamed. "I'm done. You can deal with this shit yourself, you fucking asshole. I'm out of here."

"Are you kidding me Hay?" he said. "You're not going anywhere. Are you out of your fucking mind? This was your idea, remember? And you're the one who killed her – the one who is in trouble here. And you think you're just going to leave?"

"That's what I said."

For a brief time, no additional words were exchanged. They just stood across from one another, each bereft of expression. His eyes were pale and off somewhere in the distance. She was looking the other way.

"So that's it, huh?" he finally said. "You commit a fucking murder, dump the body, it disappears, and you don't give a shit now that it's gone. Is that right?"

"I've had enough of all this shit Cameron. You hear? Enough? I'm telling you I put her here. Right here. And she was dead. I don't know what happened. I don't know. Maybe somebody found her. Who knows. But I'll tell you something. What I don't need is you screaming and cursing at me. I'm upset enough. You being an asshole does nothing to help."

The silence that followed was thick and painfully awkward. Hayley just stood there, arms folded tightly against her chest. Her cheeks were stained with tears.

"Why are you crying?" he asked.

"You're a real prick Cam. You know that?"

"Look, I'm sorry Hay, okay? I didn't mean to yell. I am just out of my mind. This is serious shit here. Please. You have to think. Please. One more time. Are you sure this is where you left her?"

"Yes, yes," she said, wiping her face with both hands. "I told you, a thousand times, yes."

"Okay, then can we just look around some more? Please? Will you help me?"

He saw how angry she was. He considered that he had never seen her so upset. But at least she was not going anywhere; she was still standing there. She was not usually the type to forgive so easily. Rather, she was the sort who needed time to linger over the dynamics of an argument, to mull both sides of the issue and then weigh each of their roles in what had transpired. Sometimes this took days, and he could not even approach her, even if it was to apologize again, until she had reconciled in her head exactly what had happened and had decided what she wanted to do about it. Yes, this was not like her. But then again, nothing seemed as it should be.

"Okay," she said. "I'll help. Just for a little while."

She took the flashlight from his hand, and under a waxing crescent moon tinged with streaks of burnt orange, the two of them reconciled and spent the next three hours searching frantically for the missing girl.

TWENTY

Cam drove to school the next morning with the fears he had screaming in his mind like a gathering of prophets announcing his tragic fate. They had not found the body, and all of the questions he still had remained unanswered. His anxiety had grown both in scope and severity, something he did not think possible. *How much more can I take?* he wondered. Rhetorical as it was, he found himself searching for the answer when he saw two police cars parked in front of the entrance of the school.

The flashing lights ignited his imagination until it exploded with unrestrained speculation. *Why were they here? Had they found the body? How much did they know? And if he was asked about any of it, what would he say?* He had only just begun to wrestle with the possibilities when he found himself thinking again of Maleigha, and that night at the beach. *Why didn't he just stay with her in the water?* If he had only stayed with her, she never would have drowned. They would have made love, on the sand, the way they had planned. And maybe she would not have moved to Ecuador, and they would have been sweethearts, gotten married, and lived a life that was simple and pure.

The dam of regret continued to spew as he walked through the parking lot. Once inside the school, he moved swiftly. The halls were bristling with the usual morning activity. John was the first person he saw; he was standing just outside the main office. It appeared he had been waiting for him.

"What's going on John?" Cam asked. "Another drug bust?"

For a second, John found no words and could barely look at Cam.

"It's not good. The cops are in Sanders' office. He told me to get you as soon as you got here."

Cam blushed. He could hear the ticking of his heart, louder now than he had ever remembered.

"Me? Why does he want to see me?"

John shook his head.

"Not sure Cam. But I think it's about Samantha."

Peter Sanders was the long-standing principal at Hillcrest. He was a good man; professional, intelligent, and approachable.

All too often Cam had heard about school administrators who were sneaky and disingenuous, duplicitous micro-managers who were barely qualified. But then there was Sanders. He was just a good guy, always there to help. The two of them had a very good relationship, one that began when Sanders sat in on one of Cam's lessons, when Cam was just a student teacher. If anyone else had been in his room that day, things would have turned out much differently.

He was teaching *The Catcher in the Rye.* He had planned for hours the night before, and had come up with a killer lesson, one that included all sorts of creative variations. But despite his efforts, things somehow went awry. The CD of Bob Dylan's *Positively 4th Street* would not play. The photocopies of the lyrics were smeared and illegible, the photograph of the duck pond in Central Park had gotten wet in the morning rain, and he had somehow misplaced the old baseball glove on which he had written some short poems. Nothing he had planned was in order. He trudged on, and the kids were good, but all around him he couldn't help but feel that the floor was coming out from beneath him.

Afterward, he sat in Sanders' office, wanting to die. He was already thinking of all the other schools that might have a need for a slightly beaten up fledgling educator.

"I like your passion kid," he told him. "Really. I liked what I saw. Don't sweat the small stuff. I saw all that I needed to see today. There just may be a place for you here."

Cam never forgot that day. Or all the others that followed. He appreciated Sanders' humanity so much that the last thing he ever wanted to do was to let the man down.

"Good morning Cam," Sanders said, when the rattled teacher peeked his head inside his office. "Come in please. Have a seat."

The two officers seated on either side of him did not speak. They just remained silent, measuring Cam's entrance. Were it not for Sanders' warm greeting, Cam would have come unglued for sure. He was still weighing all the possibilities, and trying to figure out what it was all about, but for some reason, he began thinking about Father Mason, the pastor at his church when he was just a boy. Maybe it was the smell of Old Spice on one of the officers, or the framed watercolor of a country steeple hanging on Sanders' wall just above his bookcase. He didn't know. Whatever it was, it had him ruminating about hellfire and damnation and all the punishments that pious Catholics promise to those who transgress. He was cold and miserable again, as if he were sitting in the front pew of Our Lady of Lourdes Church on Sunday morning, listening to the apocalyptic rantings of the religious leader all the kids called Father Flames.

"Cam, I'd like you to meet Officer Kearney and Officer Spenser," Sanders said, pointing at each one respectively. "They'd like to ask you a few questions."

"Sure," Cam replied, rubbing his arms to get warm. "No problem."

His heart was pounding away inside his chest like a jackhammer and his head felt like a balloon, expanding so rapidly that his whole face stretched, and all he could see was a distorted amalgam of books and pictures and faces.

"Mr. Baldridge, Samantha Brocking is a student of yours?" the first officer asked.

"That's correct officer. Samantha is in my 6th period class."

"Have you noticed anything unusual about her behavior of late? Did she say anything to you, about any trouble she was in, or anything like that?"

"No, No. None that I can recall. Honestly, I have not seen her. She has not been in class lately."

Cam was trying to keep his eyes off Sanders, but could see, without even looking at him, the severity of his face.

"We're a little concerned about Samantha Mr. Baldridge," the other officer added. "You see, we found her mother last night. She was murdered inside their house."

Cam abandoned for the moment the contemplation of his immediate fate in favor of the shocking news. It made no sense.

"Samantha's mother was murdered?" he repeated catatonically. "That's awful."

"Yes, and we are having trouble locating the girl. Naturally, we are concerned."

Cam's head felt a little like it was returning to its normal size. "You don't think that the same person who killed her mother-"

171

"We don't know what to think Mr. Baldridge," the first officer said. "But it is certainly a possibility."

The focus of their attention had buoyed his confidence. He struggled to say something more, something else to place even more distance between himself and the girl.

"This is certainly terrible news, truly, but I don't understand why-"

"We're calling in *all* of Samantha's teachers Cam," Sanders explained. "I wanted to begin with you, because I know how close to the kids you are. I was hoping that she would have told you something."

His insides lurched with alarm.

"No Peter, it's like I said. I can't recall anything particular. I know that she does not get along so well with her stepfather, but that's about it."

The second officer removed a pen from his front pocket and scribbled something in a tiny notebook.

"Yes, we are trying to get a hold of him as well," Sanders said. "But Ms. Calderone, the social worker, just informed me that the stepfather has not lived with them for a few months." He paused for a moment for reflection. "Sort of makes finding him a little more difficult."

The meeting dragged on for some time after that, with the police trying to ascertain, with the help of Cam, any possible insights that could lead them in the right direction. They asked him all sorts of questions, about her grades, attendance, unusual habits and anything out of the ordinary that had happened to her recently. He was of little help, until an awfully clever, wonderfully sinister thought crept into his brain.

"Well, she did break up with her boyfriend a few weeks ago?" he said. "And I think she said it was sort of messy."

The minute the words left his lips he felt dirty. Bobby Albright was a good kid. He played in the band, was captain of the lacrosse team and had all but been accepted already at Johns Hopkins for the following year. He came from a good home, where all three Albright boys were celebrated for their academic and athletic accomplishments, as well as their service to the community. A better family there was not. But Cam was desperate.

"Interesting," the first officer noted. "Thank you for your time Mr. Baldridge. You have been a big help."

That afternoon, Cam waited impatiently for Hayley to get home from work, busying himself with the television news reports about the murder of Mrs. Brocking. The woman was stabbed nineteen times in the chest, then thrown down a flight of stairs. The police, it was reported, were no closer to finding the killer, although it was mentioned that they were looking to question the stepfather in conjunction with both the murder and the disappearance of Samantha. Cam felt a little guilty about how easily he had received the news, but it was sure hard to argue with the feeling of relief he was beginning to have over the amazing timing of it all. *This guy just may have saved my ass*, he thought.

Hayley was later than usual that night, but when she finally arrived home, she was amazed at what Cam had to tell her. They sat across from each other, with the boxes of Chinese food Hayley had brought home, and tried to make sense of it all.

"Can you believe all of this Hay?" he asked her. "It's like a movie or something."

She made an involuntary sound with her lips as she arranged the table.

"Yeah, it is pretty messed up," she answered, opening one of the white containers. "What now?"

"I don't know. I mean, they think it was the stepfather. If they're right, and they find him, then he will probably take the fall for Samantha as well – whether they find the body or not."

Saying it out loud sounded even better, although the whereabouts of the pictures, and perhaps any of Samantha's manic notes that had yet to be delivered still bothered him.

"I think we might be in the clear."

She took a long sip of wine and swallowed.

"And what if it wasn't?" she asked.

"What if it wasn't what?"

"The stepfather. What if it wasn't him who killed the mother? Then where does that leave us?"

He moved the food around on his plate methodically.

"I really can't say, although it seems that now there is enough out there to leave us in the clear. I think we should focus on the positive here, and just try and get back to normal."

Time for Cam proved to be somewhat of a tonic; so did the report that came almost three weeks later -- the one revealing that Bill Kalovich was picked up in Atlantic City and charged with the murder of Samantha's mother. It seemed like and open and shut case. Clearly, the contentious relationship the two had experienced provided the motive, and the murder weapon, a tiny knife that was part of a set that Bill had in his car at the time of the arrest, was still lodged in Mrs. Brocking's chest when the police arrived.

"I think they're going to nail Kalovich for Samantha's murder too," Cam said, after hearing the news. "Isn't that great Hay? "This is just incredible. We're home free."

Hayley was not as elated as Cam. She saw a great difference in him now -- in his words and manner, an alarming divergence from the man she always knew. It made her even sadder.

"Does it bother you at all that this man is going to take the blame for something that we, uh, I did?" she asked. "How can you be so happy?"

"I don't know," he said, considering her comment as though he had never before thought of it. "Does it really bother you?"

"Yeah, it does Cam," she said. "I mean, he's obviously a real scumbag, and she did stalk me, and try to kill me. But it just doesn't feel right. I don't know."

It was plain that his mind had been swept suddenly by thoughts that were now only his. He had come close so many times these past few weeks to just telling her everything, but somehow, he just thought, just knew, that the only way to move on was to bury all of it.

"I would think that the missing body would bother you more," he said. "Aren't you curious?"

"Why should that bother me more Cam?"

He really wasn't sure.

"I don't know," he replied. "I guess because it bothers *me*."

Hayley placed her elbow on the table and leaned her head against her palm. She closed her eyes for a moment, trying to rid herself of all that was awful.

"And besides," he went on. "What about us? We can finally move forward, right? Like we said?"

"Yes" she answered, opening her eyes once more. "I want to move on. Get my life back. We have a wedding coming up, remember?"

He wanted the same thing – was determined to embrace that very same thing. It was the reason why he had made plans for them to return to Montauk, a quick get-a-way that would put them both back on track.

"Yes," he replied. "Our wedding. Of course I remember Hay."

TWENTY-ONE

The two of them did move on. Hayley continued working and went for her dress fittings, and made all the final arrangements for the big day. She even began looking in the Sunday paper for a house that would suit the two of them once they were finally husband and wife.

But the doubts remained.

Cam's life assumed a more usual course as well. He busied himself with his classes, worked out at the gym, and he too began dabbling in the real estate market. His uncle's generous gift years ago had done well in the Oppenheimer fund where it was placed and he was eager now to parlay that into something that would make them both smile. He was convinced that he could pull it off, just forget all that had tainted them. For the most part, this optimism buoyed him, and allowed him to trudge forward, although the strained awkwardness festering between them, and impalpable uneasiness that remained nameless but very real, brought him back to reality far too often.

It was most evident when they were alone. The ease with which they spoke to each other was gone, replaced now by this insidious disquiet that had seeped into their private world. Their discourse seemed forced. There was very little laughter, or emotion, and on many evenings, they sat across from each other at the dinner table, picking at their food in silence, exchanging no words at all. He wondered if there was something prophetic in the silence, but did not ask, for fear of actually obtaining the answer. This retreat to nowhere was most evident in their bedroom, where for over a month, nothing more than an occasional good night kiss had been shared.

"What's going on with us?" he asked her one night. She had just crawled into bed after showering. She smelled good. He wanted to touch her, but could sense the angst floating between them.

"I don't know Cam," she answered. "It's still hard for me. We have not really resolved anything. A lot has happened."

His thoughts zigzagged all over the place. He felt suddenly like everything was moving away from him, like he was orbiting above the earth, watching as everything he knew drifted further and further from sight. It made him restless. The bed squeaked as his weight shifted, and he found himself sitting up, staring at the thin shadows cast on the wall in front of him.

"So, where does that leave us then?" he asked.

She did not answer right away. She was worlds away, somewhere remote and inaccessible. And when she finally did speak, he had trouble hearing what she was saying, for she was rolled tightly in a ball, her back to him.

"What do you want me to say to that Cam?" she asked.

"I don't know," he replied.

"Something? Anything? Just so I know that we are both thinking along the same lines here. I have to say, all in all, it does not seem like you care too much."

His brain was working much slower now. He studied with feint curiosity the movement on the wall of the intermittent light from the passing cars outside, as each narrow beam entered through the window, scrolled across from one side of the room to the other before disappearing forever.

"I can't do this tonight Cameron," she said, pulling the covers closer to her and wrapping them around her body so that she was now safely ensconced. "I am exhausted."

He felt like the victim of cruel irony once again, as he struggled with the realization that it was only now, after having fouled up things up so badly, that he wanted her more than ever. He began noticing things, like how her hours at the gym had rounded her ass so that it looked like a beautiful flower. She looked so good in whatever she wore – jeans, short skirts, dress slacks. He could not remember a time when she looked so good. Her breasts seemed fuller as well, and he had spent many moments of late admiring them as if they belonged to another man.

"Okay Hay," he said, reclining once again so that he could feel the coolness of the pillow on the back of his neck. "Whatever."

Things at school seemed off as well. Cam was still good old Mr. B. in the classroom. Yes, he could always turn the trick, regardless of what was going on in his life. No one would ever know that outside those four walls, his world was so disordered. John had not really spoken to him since the day the police were there. It was odd. It was as if he had decided, without any good reason, that Cam was linked to Samantha's disappearance and the murder of her mother.

"Are you sure that you don't have anything to tell me Cam?" John asked him that day. "I just want to help you."

"I told you John, the girl was just a little odd, that's all. Beyond that, I don't know anything about it."

"Look Cam, I know something was going on with you two," he persisted. "You inasmuch told me so. And now her mother is murdered, and she is gone – disappeared into thin air? This does not look good."

"So what now John? he asked. "Huh? You going to turn me in? Tell the police that you think I'm some deranged killer? Is that it?"

"Come on Cam, can't you see what is happening here? I'm just trying to help."

Cam shook his head.

"I told you already, more than once, I know nothing about it. And I do not need your help."

Cam returned John's dour expression, and recalled how his manner had grown more remote with each day that passed. The two had not exchanged anything more than just a casual hello since then. It troubled him. Then there were the others, the bottom-feeders. Those teachers who habitually compensated for their own boredom and dissatisfaction by skimming the floor of the fish bowl that is a high school building, searching rapaciously for something, anything, to fill the vacuity. The more salacious the gossip the better. It had always sickened him.

First it was Maxine Michaels, the young music teacher who received a DWI one Memorial Day weekend. It's all anyone could talk about, until Steve Slater and Kathy Benson were caught in the copy room after school one afternoon in varying stages of undress. Then they took center stage, only to be outdone by James Hannan, whose wife left him last winter break for another woman. That remained fodder for many a faculty room discussion for what seemed like an eternity. Now, Cam was certain it was him. Nobody had said anything, at least anything he had heard, but he could sense that it was brewing. All he could do now was thicken his skin, ride it out, and wait for the next scandal to render him obsolete.

Even some of the students had him thinking twice, including those who usually worshiped the very ground on which he walked. He could not decide if he was being paranoid, or if there really was something going on -- like somehow, they knew.

"Hey there Melanie," he had said to the querulous girl that morning. "I love your new glasses."

She could not have been more aloof.

"Thanks," she said, her voice rattling like the Indian bangle bracelets she wore on her wrists. Then she lowered her eyes and walked hastily past him.

Wow, he thought to himself. *What did I do to her*?

So bad was his general mood that he decided he would stop feeling sorry for himself and vowed, once again, to take charge of his destiny -- to take back his life. He was tired of lamenting his situation, just drifting though each day, waiting to feel bad about something. He had a beautiful fiancé, students who typically adored him, and a future that included a house and a family of his own one day. It was time to start embracing that.

He considered that all of the most wonderful things he envisioned began with Hayley. She was the one thing that would make everything else possible. He realized that somewhere, deep inside his being, he had known that all along -- and that he had been foolish to stray from her, despite the difficulties they had been having. He felt so fortunate to now, after all his indiscretion, be given another chance.

"What's all this Cam?" she said smiling, after coming through the door one evening to find the living room they shared lit by the flickering glow of a dozen candles. "Did I miss something?"

He didn't want her to worry anymore. He wanted to take away her consciousness, and all the cares housed within. He wanted, more than anything, for her to just let go, commit herself to him, and to them. To run with him through the rest of their days, without worry. He was sure he could do it.

"Since when do I need a special reason to be with my favorite girl?" he said, helping her with her things before guiding her to the sofa. "Welcome home."

They made love almost instantly, at his request. It was the first time for quite some time. He undressed her quickly, as if he were racing against some unseen deadline. He lost himself in her the way he had when they were first together; it was good, a complete escape, and it made him feel like himself again, yet as the fury of their lovemaking waned, and he was left with just his thoughts, and Hayley's blank expression, he was struck by the cold, unrelenting reality that something about her was still not right. When it was over, he felt thankful nonetheless that they had finally gotten over the hump, even though the interlude was a little quicker than he would have liked, and far less passionate than he preferred. Still, he was thankful. But as they lie next to each other, their bodies still tangled, he was powerless to dismiss the two things that now threatened to dull the shine of the moment: the galling realization that not once during their intercourse did she kiss him, or even really look at him, and that now, in the quiet that punctuated the aftermath of their union, thoughts of Nikki, and of course Maleigha, were swirling all around him.

"Hey, you're awfully quiet," she said. "What are you thinking about?"

"What" he asked.

"I asked you what you were thinking about."

"You, Hayley," he said. "Just you. I was just thinking about you."

He was motionless, listening to his own words, burning with the shock and shame of self-exposure. She was still as well; he listened for a few minutes to the steady ticking of the clock on the table, and was just about to ask her about the thoughts occupying her mind when she stretched her arms, yawned, and swung her legs around until her feet were on the carpet.

"Thanks, Cam, for thinking about me," she said, covering herself with a blanket before lifting herself up off the sofa. "I'm just going to run to the bathroom. Then we can start dinner."

He felt tired. It had been a long day. His thoughts shifted for the moment from Hayley to his briefcase, and the pile of essays that he promised his classes he'd grade and give back. How was he going to stay awake long enough to do that? He had fallen behind of late, understandably so, but was determined to correct that as well; all he needed was a plan. He was trying to divide in his head the number of papers by the hours he had left in the night when he realized he did not even know what time it was. He reached over and pulled his Blackberry off the end table. One push of a button revealed the answer -- 8:49. It was later than he thought. He also noticed that he had one unread message. The number was familiar, but the caller was unknown.

Nobody has to know, about either girl, but I do…

He opened his lips, as if he were going to say something, but nothing came. From where he sat, he could see the dark sky outside. His vast emptiness had begun to fill up with more suffering and uncertainty; he rubbed his eyes then shook his head. What else could possibly go wrong?

TWENTY-TWO

Cam managed to find some solace in the repetition of the devotional phrase *everything will be all right*, but it didn't take long for the predicament to swell into something even more hideous and unruly. He could not even begin to imagine who could be tormenting him now. He had never managed to get any information out of Samantha about how she knew about Nikki, or where the pictures had come from. The unknown was like a steady pulse, a faint hammering beating incessantly at his temples. He tortured himself over his inability to put the pieces together, something that rattled his very core until he could scarcely think.

He spent the better part of that afternoon reeling, sitting quietly in the dim light of the kitchen, searching desperately for a way to escape the inexorable advancement of the encroaching walls. Sitting there, mired in fear and self-pity, the horrors that surely awaited him flowed like the vodka he and Nikki had shared that night. Why couldn't he have seen this coming? Hours later, he was no closer to discovering anything that resembled a way out. He was flushed and raged. The rush of energy that had always fueled his passions had become the same force which now threatened to eat him alive. He thought he might begin tearing himself apart when his eyes found the magnetic business card from ERA Realty that Hayley had brought home and affixed to the refrigerator the day after Cam told her about his trust fund and suddenly the darkest, most barren region of his imagination was lit by a glimmer of hope. *Could this possibly work*? he wondered. What if it were as easy as money? A lot of money. For a moment, the idea became too much for him. Overwhelmed him. It was just as crazy as the rest of it. But the longer he sat, considering his fading vision for the future, the more he realized this was the only way.

We can end this. 100K if you keep quiet.

The hamburger and fries he had eaten for lunch sat heavily in his stomach, expanding with each minute that passed. He crossed the kitchen floor, his steps barely audible on the checkered linoleum, trying to occupy his mania while he waited. He sifted through the pile of mail on the counter, rearranged the contents in the dishwasher, and began organizing the eclectic mess in their junk drawer. He moved from one inane task to another, careful to check his phone every few minutes. It had been a while, longer than he had hoped, and once again all sorts of doubt began creeping into his consciousness. What was he thinking? He wrinkled his nose, let go an explosive sigh, then sat back down at the table.

Feeling weary now, he crossed his arms and placed them on the table, making a comfortable place for him to rest his head. Then he closed his eyes, and drifted off for a spell, only to be jolted from his momentary slumber by the vibration of his phone.

Not enough. Make it 500K and you got a deal.

Cam tried to mask his emotions, careful to nurture the façade so that no one should gain entrance into his private hell. He worked, helped Hayley with the remaining details tied to the wedding, but fought, with every ounce of his being, the fact that he was, months later, still a faithful soldier to his sin. It bothered him of late, more and more, that he should have to go on like this – bothered him so much so that the initial impulse to panic and wallow in self-loathing and pity over the ransom request soon dissipated, and was replaced by a virulent anger that buoyed his defiance. *Fuck this*, he told himself. It was enough. He was through playing the fool.

The next morning he got up earlier than usual. Then, after his daily run, he stopped at the local bagel shop to get coffee for Hayley. She loved the coffee from there, and he thought she would be appreciative of his consideration. While he was there, he picked up a few dozen bagels for his morning classes.

"What all this Mr. B?" one of his first period students asked as she was greeted by the wonderful smell. "Party?"

"No, no party," he said, smiling. "Does there have to be reason to do something nice for my favorite first period class?"

Later on, Cam was in his classroom absorbed in creating a power point presentation to go along with his introductory lesson on Edgar Allan Poe, when Evan Mauer came in. The young man had actually been standing at the desk for a few minutes before Cam realized he was there.

"Oh, hey Evan," he said, his eyes still fixed on his computer screen. "What's up?"

"Not much Mr. B.," the boy replied.

"Did you need something?" Cam asked.

"No, I just wanted to share a little news with you."

Cam stopped what he was doing and watched as the boy reached into his backpack and removed a letter. He smiled uncontrollably as he handed it to Cam. Then he just stood there, chewing his thumb, as his teacher began to read.

"Hey, *Who's Who*, huh?" he said. "Congratulations Evan. Well done."

The boy smiled again, then motioned with his eyes for Cam to keep reading.

"Look at the bottom part," Evan instructed. "To the right, where it says something about an influential teacher?"

Cam's eye scanned the letter quickly, and discovered with little difficulty the real source of Evan's excitement.

"Now this is one of the nicest things anyone has ever done for me Evan," Cam said, reaching out to shake the boy's hand. He was a little choked up. "I don't know what to say."

He was distracted by Evan's thoughtfulness, and for a moment felt more like his old self again. He was enjoying this respite from the daunting specter that seemed to cloud his every move when, on the sixth day after the ransom request, he received in his school mailbox a legal size brown envelope with the word CONFIDENTIAL marked in red. He made idle conversation with the two other teachers who were in the mailroom at the time, entertaining comments about the last faculty meeting they had had and some rather petulant remarks about the rumor they had heard concerning a sign in sheet that all of them would have to use both before and after school. Then once they had left, he removed the envelope from the box, buried it between some of the other notices and announcements that he had yet to read, and with the entire pile in hand, stole away to the men's room.

Once inside, he walked to the last stall and locked the door behind him. Then he sat down with the envelope, undid the metal clasp, and removed the contents. Pictures. The same ones he had already seen. Nikki, at the motel room. His heart sank. When was it going to end? He looked at each one, the same way he had before, this time steeling himself against the latest assault. What did these pictures mean anyway? He was not tied to any of them – at least not to the outside world. Why should he care?

He flipped through the photographs. He had seen these before. Then he reached the final shot in the pile -- one he had yet to see -- Samantha and him in his car, taken that awful night at the lake. He sat there sweaty and silent, staring at the photograph. She had played him good. With the feint redolence of soap cakes inside his nose, he began to piece together what her plan had been. She had set the whole thing up. Lured him to Meadow Lake, then orchestrated the taking of the picture, all for the purpose of stringing him along afterwards. Who knows how long it would have gone on had Hayley not derailed the plan. He knew now that the one who snapped the picture had picked up right where the Samantha had left off. He was in for more cloak and dagger bullshit, only this time, the stakes were much higher.

He studied the picture, hoping to catch a glimpse of the photographer in the reflection of the car glass. He remembered seeing that in a movie once. It worked for Matt Damon. Why not him? He scrutinized the photograph, and thought for a minute he was onto something, but all he could see was her, and the damning evidence. Everything began to lose focus. He also noticed, after holding the picture up to the light in one last desperate attempt to uncover some clue, that there was writing on the back. There was a message.

This isn't a game. Don't fuck with me. You have 48 hours to get me my money. 500K. Put it in a bag and leave it behind the pile of old tires at the Exxon station on Hillside Avenue. 10:00 p.m., Thursday. If it's all there, you'll get all photos and the memory card in your mailbox at school. Nobody will ever know. No games. No cops. No witnesses.

Now time just seemed to stop. His horror and sadness had been replaced by an utter incredulity, an absolute inability to grasp the leap that all of this had just taken. It was surreal. This was so screwed up. Two dead girls. Photos. Now extortion as well? It was all impossible. Yet there was something oddly reassuring about this blackmail.

Money was tangible, something to be counted and valued. It was something that was finite as well. An honest to goodness one-shot deal. That was never the case with Samantha. He always knew, in the darkest recesses of his mind, that the girl would have always wanted more -- that she could never be satisfied. But this other person, whoever it was, was after something more practical, logical. Surely the motivation here was selfish, but not psychotic or malevolent. It was a shit load of money, no doubt, and he would have some explaining to do to Hayley when the day came when she asked about it. He still was not sure, and would have to consider it some more, but was a large part of him was beginning to think that it was worth a shot. What else did he have?

TWENTY-THREE

Hayley was driving on the expressway in the middle of the afternoon, blasting Alanis Morrisette's *You Oughta Know* while mouthing the words; she had taken a half day at work so that she could sneak over to Bridal Treasures to try on her gown and veil one more time. The wedding was only three months away, and she was getting more and more uptight about all the little details. She also took the opportunity to make a few other stops, including the A & S Pork Store, where she purchased all the key ingredients to prepare a special dinner for her and Cam. She got all his favorites; stuffed peppers, fresh mozzarella and tomato, homemade manicotti with a Bolognese sauce, and for dessert, a chocolate cream pie from Sergio's Bakery.

It was all waiting for him when he walked through the door. He was so engrossed in the particulars of the clandestine monetary transaction he was about to execute that he did not even notice at first. He had spent most of the previous hour on the phone with an agent from Merrill Lynch, making the arrangements. Social security number, date of birth, mother's maiden name. The list went on and on. It was only the melodious tone of the agent's voice that made the transaction bearable.

"Are you certain that you want to wire the entire amount Mr. Baldridge?" she kept asking him. "This is a lot of money."

"Yes, yes," he responded each time. "All of it, to my savings account at Astoria Federal Savings Bank. The account number is 3307006748."

"And you are sure that you want me to go ahead and make arrangements for them to have that money available to you Thursday, in cash?"

"Yes, thank you. I would really appreciate that. It is one less thing that I have to worry about."

He could hear her on the other end of the phone, punching the keys on her computer. He scrolled through the varied images from his past as he waited, bristling each time the montage presented something that he recognized as foolish or destructive. There was much to regret.

"Okay now. You are all set Mr. Baldridge," the agent finally said. "You just may want to call ahead to Astoria before you go, just to verify that you are coming and that they are ready for you."

"Okay, thank you."

"Is there anything else I can do for you today sir?" she asked. "No, no thank you," he replied. That will be all."

Her name was Earlina, or Estefana. She was sweet, and very helpful. Her voice was so soothing to him, made him feel okay, especially considering the circumstances. She sounded like Maleigha. He smiled. He wanted to believe that was a good omen.

"Ta da!" Hayley yelled, standing by the table with her arms spread wide to greet him. "What do you think?"

The vision of the photograph of him and Samantha and the printed words on the back was stuck like a splinter in his head; as a result, everything else that he had seen since remained out of focus.

"What's all this for?" he asked.

"I thought about what you said the other night. About me and us? I think we both should try harder. That's all. Besides, I'm just feeling very happy tonight," she said, popping the cork of a new bottle of merlot. "And, I have something so incredibly exciting to tell you. I can't wait but I will. You're going to flip out when you hear."

He threw his bag on the sofa and sat down across from her. Everything smelled wonderful. He considered that he would be organizing a dinner like this of his own in a day's time, once he put the worst part of this nightmare behind him.

"Try one of the peppers," she said. "They are amazing."

In the faint light being thrown from two pillar candles, she cut a small piece of his favorite appetizer, just the way he liked, handed him the plate, and watched him bring it to his lips.

"Well?" she asked. "Awesome, right?"

"Yeah Hay. Tastes great."

She took the plate back, cut a few more pieces, and returned it to the space in front of him.

"So, why don't you tell me about your day Cam. What's happening at school?"

"Not much," he said, taking a sip of wine from his glass. "Same old."

"Well, that's good, right?" she continued. "I mean, things with the search for Samantha have died down? Things are finally quiet again?"

"I guess so," he answered.

"Well, has there been any more talk about-"

"Look Hay, if it's all the same to you, I'd rather not talk about school. Okay?"

He could see the severity of his demeanor reflected in her eyes.

"Hey, I have an idea," he said, observing the sudden alteration in her mood.

"What?" she asked."

Why don't you tell me about *your* day? Judging by that smile you had when I came home, it's bound to be better than mine."

She began talking about how her boss, Mr. Pinkert, the one whom she had described to him as a pompous asshole, had been real nice to her. Complimented her on a report she had just submitted, mentioned something about a promotion of sorts, and actually let her go one hour earlier than she had already asked for that afternoon.

"That gave me extra time to try on some things at the boutique -- and to stop at A & S, the bakery, and the liquor store."

The latter part of her commentary was not so much a declaration of enthusiasm as it was an attempt to take him to task about his apparent lack of appreciation. He got it.

"I'm sorry Hay," he said. "Really. Everything is great. It is. I just had a real shitty day. That's all."

"That's okay," she said. "That will make what I am about to tell you that much better."

His eyes squinted a bit and he wrinkled his nose.

"Come on Cam! That great news I said I had?" she repeated. "The thing that you were going to flip out over? I told you about it ten minutes ago? Remember?"

"Yeah, yeah Hay. I remember. Tell me. What is so spectacular?"

She scooped up her glass of wine and placed her back up against her chair. She was smiling, as if she was just about to announce the surprise of the century.

"Well, I also made one more stop today that I did not tell you about." She was bursting, almost gloating.

"Yeah?' he asked, motioning with his hand. "And?"

"Oh, nothing that unusual. I just happened to stop by that ERA office and dropped off a check – just a little something called a binder on a cute little cape I saw last week in Valley Stream."

His face grew pale, paler than the moonlight that was creating a series of twisted shadows on the maple tree just outside the window. Anyone watching the scene would have sworn she had shot him right through the heart.

"Oh, you should see it Cam," she went on, oblivious to his agony. "Grey fieldstone in the front, pretty white shutters, and a yard that is to die for. And you should see the inside. The kitchen has-"

He could hear none of it over the thumping in his chest.

"You should not have done that Hay," he said, only after the pounding of his heart returned to something that resembled a more normal beat.

"Why Cam? You said that I could go for it if I found something I liked."

"Yes, but I didn't tell you to go buy it, now did I?" he fired back. "We can't afford a house right now. What were you thinking?"

She looked up at the ceiling with mounting irritation.

"First of all, I didn't even tell you how much it's going for," she snapped. "What is wrong with you? You said that you wanted to move forward, right? You said that you wanted to know that I was on board. Remember? So what is your problem now?"

She threw her fork down on the table and spoke now through a tight jaw.

"And just for the record, *both* of us have been talking about this house thing. Did you forget?"

"That's not the point!" he screamed, pounding his fist on the table. "You should have told me. What gives you the right to spend my money without even talking to me?"

Hayley glared at him through emerging tears.

190

"You just continue to be an asshole Cameron, you know that? A fucking asshole."

"Are you kidding me?" he fired back.

"Me? Me? You're the one who's wrong here."

"Really? *Your* money?" she repeated. "Is that what you said?"

"Don't pull that shit with me now Hayley. You know what I mean."

"Yeah, I know exactly what you mean."

His forehead was wet and his legs weak. The steady leaking of life rushed now with more intensity, yet he surprised himself somehow with the strength and severity of his voice.

"Hayley, that trust fund has been in my friggin-"

"That's okay Cam," she said, her fingers curled in a fist which hung by her side. "It's fine. Really. Don't you worry yourself about it now. You keep *your* money. Spend it on whatever it is that's going to make you happy."

Her exit was wild and untamed, punctuated by the slamming of the door behind her. He sat for a while by himself, breathing in a series of audible spasms, as he recalled bitterly all of the fighting that had gone on in recent months, something that steadily became more and more intolerable in the wake of the reproachful silence that lingered in the apartment the rest of the night.

TWENTY-FOUR

Cam struggled to fight off the rising wave of calamity that seemed ready to crash over him. He did not need Hayley's blessing regarding the allocation of his trust fund money; those wheels were already in motion. He knew that she'd get over the fight they just had, and he would somehow find an excuse to explain the disappearance of the money, if he decided that he was actually going to go through with it -- some clever way of explaining to her how he had lost the money, but only when the time was right. It would be okay, although he continued to torture himself over his antics and the possible damage they had caused; she was so excited about that house, and his reaction to her news had shattered her.

After school that Thursday, he went right home. He poured himself a drink, took a passing glance at the day's mail, and sank into the sofa. There, in the living room, he sat, hunched over like a wounded animal, surveying the space with reddened eyes, all the while continuing to battle the kaleidoscope of past images filtering through his mind. There were phases in his life that he found himself reliving, or at least examining.

He thought about the time in fourth grade when was sent to the principal's office after gluing Alfred Spade's math book to his desk when the kid, who just happened to be the bane of little Cam's existence, was absent one day. The next morning, all the kids laughed when Alfred tried to remove the book, and wound up tearing the insides right out. Cam recalled feeling this sense of power – a real rush. He had executed revenge and had done so with impunity. But on the day of the infamous caper, unbeknownst to Cam, Rachel Weinman had come back for a bag she had left behind, and without being noticed, saw everything. She ratted him out later that day.

"Well, what have you got to say for yourself young man?" his father asked.

"I don't know," he answered, chewing nervously at the inside of his cheek.

"You mother and I are not happy with you Cameron," he went on. "We're very disappointed."

He could remember sitting there, at the kitchen table, staring dumbly at his father, uncertain as to what it was his old man wanted him to say. I mean sure, he imagined that under the circumstances, any parent would want his child to say "sorry" for what he had done. It made sense, and certainly would have been easy enough. The problem was, he *wasn't* sorry. With the exception of the trip to the principal's office, courtesy of Miss Rachel Weinman, he loved everything about what he had done. Stepping outside the parameters of acceptable behavior made him feel so alive. It was like being awakened from a sleep he did not even know he was in. How could he be sorry? Aside from getting caught, which wasn't even that bad, he was thinking that it was no big deal at all. Then he looked harder at his father, who was actively deciding his fate, and he grew a little uncomfortable. He began weighing the thrill against the possible cost. Sitting there, waiting for his sentence to be dispensed, he decided that perhaps he had misread things. Maybe all the excitement was not worth it after all.

"Just don't do it again," his father finally told him."

"Is that all," young Cam asked. "That's it?"

"Yes. I'm sure you realize it was wrong. Now run along young man, and watch yourself."

And that was it. No punishment. He always wondered why his father looked the other way, and somehow knew, now more than ever, that facing the music was a lesson he really should have learned.

Other reminiscences were not as detailed but just as troubling, like his second place finish in the sixth grade spelling bee, making the last out in the Little League championship game, and of course, swimming with Maleigha. There were so many others as well, including the first text-message exchange with Nikki. If any one of them had not happened, he ruminated, things for him would surely have been different. So he hated all of them, wanted nothing more than to hurl stones at each one as it surfaced, for he saw now the role each one had played in shaping his reality – a reality that had betrayed, at every turn, the vision he had always held for himself; a vision that he would be great in this world. He had been fooling himself. It had all been a lie. Just a miserable, fucking lie.

Now, all he could do was try and salvage what was left of the disaster he had created. So he just sat there, on the sofa, torturing himself with these ghosts from the past, until his timorous heart could no longer support the weight of the act. Then he went to the closet, emptied all of his softball gear from his New York Jets duffle bag and drove to the bank.

He was back before Hayley arrived home. He stayed by the window, one eye watching for her, the other affixed to the trunk of his car. His insides were in knots; three hours was a long time to have to wait. He had a couple of beers to take the edge off, and watched some television. He flipped through the different stations. He caught a little of a college basketball game, lingered on the remote long enough to watch the final scene in *Rocky*, and got the weather for the next day on a local news channel. The distractions helped a little, but his steady trips to the window every few minutes made it impossible for him to lose himself in anything. He was also anxious about how he was going to get out of the house once Hayley got home. He had been making a lot of excuses lately, and felt at a loss to create something original. He was wrestling with a few different scenarios when his cell phone rang. It was her.

"Listen Cam, I got held up here," she explained. "I don't know exactly when I'll be home, but it looks as though it won't be until after eleven."

He exhaled loudly. The unexpected development made him feel a little better; one less thing to worry about. From his window, the night seemed at peace with itself. He could hear through the glass the hum of a steady wind, and the moon was full and bright, bathing the trees along the street in long ribbons of brilliant white. It was the sort of night that he loved, the kind where he would walk with Hayley, or jog by himself, invigorated by the crisp air and the warm calm falling all around him. There were very few things that made him feel better. He sighed, then put on his heavy coat, the one with the high collar, pulled a baseball cap down over his brow, and headed out.

He pulled up across from the Exxon Station at ten minutes to ten. Much to his delight, nobody was around, but he felt foolish anyway, walking up to a gas station so late, with no visible purpose. He thought about pulling his car in for gas, or up to the air hose, but decided that either one would be far too forced. The last

194

thing he needed was one of the attendants noticing him, or becoming suspicious about him being there. He sat for a little while longer, scanning the premises for anything he could use as cover for a trip across the street. The clock on the car dash read 9:57, and he was beginning to panic. Only the discovery of a soda machine on the side of the building, exactly where he was headed, saved him from a full blown meltdown.

With the duffle bag in one hand, and a dollar bill in the other, he crossed the street – a haggard, solitary figure drifting through the darkness with eyes still restless and a mouth, chalky and dry. His nerves stirred wildly now, rising up from the buried depths that had been silent the past few days out of necessity. He had done a good job carrying on, as if nothing were happening. So good, in fact, that on several occasions, when he let his mind go blank, and immersed himself in the immediate events surrounding him, he himself forgot the turmoil he was battling. But that was over. There was no hiding the aching now.

With great deliberation, he stood before the massive Pepsi machine, flattening the edges of his dollar bill before inserting it into the slot. His finger moved down across the row of lighted buttons, pausing momentarily before settling on the one that read Aquafina. He twisted off the cap and gulped wildly, looking over his shoulder before wiping his mouth and slipping around to the back.

Behind the little station it was dark, and the air was rife with the stench of old rubber and cat urine. He stood for a few seconds, his legs weak now from the immediacy of moment. *Okay*, he whispered to himself. *This is it*. Standing there, as the candy wrappers and newspapers swirled in the dark alley -- way behind the building, Cam heard the harmony of the past, as if the wind had whispered it in his ear. He missed his old life.

The chocolate bar wrappers made him think of trips to Hershey Park; the sea of discarded soda bottles also took him back in time, conjuring images of neighborhood stickball with Jimmy Sullivan and the rest of the gang. They would play for hours, one game after the next, until they could barely throw another ball. Then, they would hop on their bikes and make the short trip to the corner deli, where they would sit around, indulging in the sweet reward of either Orange Crush or Dr. Pepper, all the while discussing the fantastic feats of athletic prowess they all had witnessed just moments before. It was the most pleasant of his recollections, until his restless foot dislodged an old bottle rocket from a random pile of refuse. He smiled. He was transported back in time instantly. It was the 4th of July; he and Maleigha were sitting on the curb in front of his house, holding hands as they marveled at how the quiet street in Massapequa where he spent the first fourteen years of his life had been transformed into an outdoor theater; throngs of neighbors and their relatives lined the sidewalks with lawn chairs and picnic benches in joyful anticipation of the Independence Day fireworks display, courtesy of Freddy Lamonica, the neighborhood butcher and part time pyrotechnic enthusiast.

As darkness stretched across the neighborhood, everyone settled in their seats, craning their necks to the heavens as flecks of red, white and blue phosphorescence streaked across the night sky to a chorus of *Celebration* and other festive melodies. Each explosion that flooded the row of tiny houses with luminous hues of festive colors elicited a raucous concert of clapping and whistling. They were mesmerized.

"It's so beautiful Cam," she said, squeezing his hand even tighter.

It *was* beautiful. So was she.

"Haven't you ever seen fireworks Maleigha," he asked her.

"Not like these," she explained.

"Once, I saw them on T.V., but it wasn't the same."

Afterward, the two of them slipped away into his backyard. The grass was smooth and the evening dew was cool on their bare feet. They sat together on a lounge chair – he leaned back, so that he could still see the colorful sky, and she did the same, positioning herself between his legs, with the back of her head resting gently on his chest. They said nothing to each other for quite some time. The moment was just too perfect for words. It was only when the fireworks had finally ceased, and thoughts of the fleeting pace of summer slipped into their consciousness, that he finally felt the need to speak.

"The summer is going very fast already," he said.

She knew what he meant.

"Yes, it is," she answered, leaning forward and turning around so that she could now see the moon's glow reflected in his eyes.

"But we have time Cam. We do."

He wanted to tell her that he knew that, but somehow, he also knew that it would just never be enough.

"I think I love you Maleigha," he said, touching her softly on her cheek. His heart was racing. "I really do."

She had tears in her eyes.

"I love you too Cam. And I think I always will."

It was the first time each of them had made the thrilling confession. But that was a long time ago. His life had changed drastically since then.

He thought some more about Maleigha, and a few other pleasant reminiscences, but when he decided that he had tarried long enough, he moved further into the darkness, his feet scraping along the soiled pavement. The pile of tires was right there, just as he had been told. He felt now like a man on a sinking boat, one that had been cast away in shark infested waters. As the waves spilled over the sides, and the cold water collected in the bottom by his feet, he shivered, not so much because of the temperature, but because of the sad reality that he was left with nothing but two choices: remain and do nothing, and go down with the boat for sure, or jump off, swim like mad, and give himself a chance to make it safely to shore, even though it was likely that he would still drown, or be ripped to shreds by the legion of man-eaters. What a quandary. He just stood there for quite some time, trying to decide what to do.

Then, with a chorus of crickets and a ticking clock mocking his idleness, he came to a decision; it was the only one that made any sense. He would swim for it, with all his strength, and hope that the duffle bag he had just placed behind the pile of tires would serve as a life preserver instead of what it felt like now, yet another anchor affixed to his ankles.

TWENTY-FIVE

Six weeks before the wedding, Hayley appeared to be buckling under the oppressive nervousness thrust upon her by the calendar's inexorable march. She was often moody, and distant, and Cam found himself lamenting the fact that they were right back where they had begun when all of this started. So ill was her frame of mind that she even began neglecting certain things germane to the final arrangements for the big day. The bill for the flowers was still unpaid, the menu for the rehearsal dinner was still undecided, and she had yet to submit her final list of songs to the DJ. It just seemed to get worse with every passing day.

"We got a phone call today from the church Hay," he told her. "They said we still owe them for the organist."

"I know, I know," she said huffing.

"Well don't you think you should be tying up of all these loose ends," he said. "I mean, we are just a month and a half away."

She came right back at him, her eyes afire.

"Excuse me, but is this *my* wedding, or *ours*?" she asked, waving her finger in his face.

"Maybe you could do some of the tying up around here Cam. Seems the last time I tried to do something for us, I was scolded for spending *your* money irresponsibly. Remember?"

"That's a cheap shot Hay," he responded.

"Well, what do you want me to say Cameron, when you attack me like this?"

"It's not an attack Hay," he explained. "I'm just trying to find out what is going on here."

Life in their bedroom was no life at all. She was cold, almost alien like, in her responses to him. He would lie in bed next to her, waiting for her to show some sign that she wanted to be there – that she had not simply resigned herself to a life with a man for whom she had no love, no passion. The longer he waited, the more he thought about Maleigha and Nikki, and how his time with each, albeit brief, was filled with this soothing warmth and breathless excitement. He missed that.

He always wound up rationalizing his unhappiness, reminding himself that he was in an adult relationship now, and that things were not always about thumping hearts and butterflies. There would be times when he would have to work at keeping the fire burning between them. It was ruminations such as this that allowed him to keep trying.

There were other things he couldn't wrap his mind around as well. Five days passed without any sign of the pictures or the photo card he had been promised. Each day at school, every chance he got, he ran down to the mailroom like a child on Christmas morning, certain that there would be an envelope waiting for him. But each time, he left empty handed, more dejected than the time before.

On the sixth day, he could no longer tolerate the unflagging injustice. He made one final trip to his mailbox that afternoon before leaving school, then stomped out to his car, and sat in the parking lot, phone in hand, pressing feverishly on the mini keyboard.

You got your money, but I don't have my pictures. Honor our agreement. Drop them off at school or else.

He sat for a few moments longer, holding his breath, eyes fixed on the tiny display. Each minute that passed fanned the flames of irrepressible suspicion. *I'm not getting those pictures*, he thought to himself. It occurred to him that this person, even though he or she had nothing to gain by holding on to the photos, still had no real reason for releasing them. The money was paid. Why then should he expect anything? He turned the ignition, buckled his seat belt and bid a tearful farewell to any peace he could ever have hoped for just as his phone vibrated

Okay, the message read. *Tomorrow.*

Cam and Hayley had retired for the night in the usual fashion, with Hayley retreating to her side of the bed the minute the light had gone out. He was struggling with the thought of yet another night of disappointment and frustration. Only on this particular night, he was fueled by a different feeling – a desire that was calling to him, imploring him to take back that which was rightfully his. His hand moved beneath the covers and found hers. She let him linger there, but did not offer any sentiment of her own. With the curious drive of a creature both wounded and vengeful, he turned on his side, so that he was now hovering slightly above her, and moved his hand up her arm, then across her stomach, where his palm remained, rotating in tiny circles.

"I miss you Hay," he whispered to her.

She didn't say anything.

Undaunted, he continued to massage her stomach, until he felt a surging deep within him that lead his exploration elsewhere. He moved quietly, eagerly, up to her breasts, where his finger began making tiny circles around her nipples, sliding effortlessly across the silky canvas of her nightgown. She was perfectly still, and did not say a word, but her breathing was faster now, and Cam accepted that as permission to advance. His hands became more inspired, roaming all over her body. Her skin was soft, and her hours in the gym had definitely toned and sculpted every inch of her. He marveled at how beautiful her body was, something he told her softly as his lips took the place of his hands.

She closed her eyes and rested her hands on his back while he devoured her, his lips and tongue gliding across her breasts and stomach in a fury of delight. He kept talking to her the whole time, whispering short expressions of his admiration for her, but she still said nothing. It was only when he climbed on top of her that she made any sound at all, and when he brought his mouth to hers, desperate to taste her, she turned her head the other way and lifted her body up to his, so as not to have to look at him. He found her behavior troublesome, but did not let the pall of the moment deter him from finishing.

Afterward, he considered the full ramifications of what had just transpired. She was increasingly distant. He spent several minutes trying to put a name to the strange alteration. Maybe she's just tired he considered, or nervous about the wedding, or about something at work. That was probably it – just stupid worries about stupid things. No big deal. It was certainly preferable to the damning alternative. Yes, the alternative was something he had considered privately for some time, even kept secret from himself. But she was still there. That's all that mattered. There was no need to think about the alternative – that she was already gone. He would have to see how things played out. Her job. The wedding. And naturally, the lingering effects from the whole ordeal with

Samantha. Murder and a missing body were not things to be dismissed so lightly. He understood that.

But lying there, alone with his insecurity, his mind could not help but wander back to the idea that their time together seemed to be over. He continued creating in his mind this list of other possible reasons for her detachment, trying desperately to assuage the riotous fear that she had given up on him. But in the end, when he finally shut the light, he found himself even more despondent than usual, for he could not help but feel, as distasteful as it was, that he had been with her for the very last time.

TWENTY-SIX

Hillcrest High School held a vigil for Samantha Brocking, one designed to garner support for the continued search for the missing girl, as well as raise money for a reward leading to her whereabouts. As the hope of finding her waned, the need for the gathering became apparent. In addition, many members of the Hillcrest family began donating money in order to help defray some of the expenses Samantha's aunt Katherine had incurred; in the absence of any other blood relative, the forty eight year old single mother had stepped forward as the next of kin in order to help post fliers and mobilize a search party for her wayward niece.

It was nothing like the other vigil Cam had attended, years ago, for his first love. Sure, there were tiny candles, and Samantha's cheerleading team had baked cookies and cupcakes, and the orchestra played chamber music. People sat around, talking about both of the tragedies that had befallen their little school community recently, and everyone shared what money they had in their pockets and the brimming hope that the girl would undoubtedly return unharmed. But for Cam, who knew all too well the futility of the event, the gathering had a different feel.

The night they all assembled on the beach for Maleigha was far more poignant. He could remember the sun going down over the ocean, and wondering if Maleigha could see the brilliant splashes of orange and red that looked as though they had been applied by a thousand celestial brushes, transforming the familiar horizon into a stunning work of art. When the sun had finally sunk into the darkening vastness, and night began to fall all around them, a few people went around the area that had been cordoned off, lighting torches that had been driven into the sand in symmetrical fashion so as to provide definition to the small gathering.

The water was calm that night, and the redolence of salt and citronella was strong. Even though he knew almost everyone there, he talked to no one. He sat well behind most of the action on a weathered log, his feet buried in the cool sand, his heart desperate for a miracle. He could still recall staring out into nothingness, his senses altered, lulled by the undulation of the surf and the thought that at any minute, Maleigha would come walking out of the waves, covered in sand and smiling, ready to relay the details of her great adventure. Once or twice he thought he saw her, when the wind caught the artificial flame from one of the torches and threw its light seaward, where it rode atop a tiny wave, illuminating what appeared to be his sweet beloved, a stirring image that made his heart leap, leap with the promise that she had returned to him, a promise that was all but revealed when the wave crashed into the beach, taking with it the light and the beautiful image cast in its glow.

He sat there the entire night, pining for her, certain that she was coming. It didn't matter that most of the others had already left, and that the Coast Guard had called off the search. They did not know Maleigha the way he did. She was coming for him. And he would be there when she arrived.

She never did. The emptiness filled him to the point of near suffocation. He was certain that he would remain at that beach forever, join his beloved and drift with her forever in the capricious tide, when toward the end of the service, a slight woman with wavy hair and dark eyes sat next to him. It was obvious to him that she had been crying, and that her world had been altered too by the same loss he was experiencing.

"Are you Cameron?" she asked softly, adjusting the direction of her gaze to match his. The two of them struggled momentarily, bathed in both the amber glow of the torchlight and the seriousness of the moment.

"Yes," he said, his eyes still searching the restless water.

"I wanted that I talk to you," she said. He said nothing to her. If she wanted to talk, that was okay. He would listen, but go on, just the same, wedded to the tide.

"I am Marisol, Maleigha's mother," she said.

She spoke with a heavy accent, but her voice was soft and gentle.

"I want very much to meet you."

It was darker now than it had been all night, and he could only see the faint outline of her mouth and nose flickering in the dying light of the torches as he turned to face her. His stomach was burning, and he could feel his eyes filling up. He was trying his hardest not to cry.

"My Maleigha, she tell me about you," the woman began. "Said you was kind to her. And that you love her and watch after her while she were here."

He could not speak. The words were too big for his lips. All he could manage was a nod of his head.

"We all upset Cameron," she continued. "It's okay. We loved Maleigha. Very much. She was special girl. You knew that. That's why you love her. Thank you."

She reached over to him and placed her hand on his arm. He could feel the warmth of her skin through his shirt. Her touch was electrical, and seemed to release the flow of emotion that he had, until that moment, managed to arrest. The tears came fast.

"And I want you to know Cameron," she said, as he began to crumble before her, "that she love you, too. She did Cameron. She tell me, many times, in her letters."

That old memory came creeping back now that he was forced to mingle with the crowd that was assembled for Samantha. He did not want to. He felt nothing for the girl, except relief that she was gone, and found feigning hope that she would return a most onerous task.

"Quite a nice turnout, eh Cam?" Principal Sanders said as the two men stood by the raffle table being run by the PTA. "It's really touching when a school pulls together like this."

"Yeah," Cam said, trying desperately to care. "It's really something."

The two men continued chatting about a variety of things, from the upcoming budget vote to the success of the basketball team, but much to Cam's dismay, the conversation kept returning to Samantha.

"You know, the police are no closer to finding her," Sanders told Cam. "I would never say this to any of these people, especially not tonight, but I have to admit, it's starting to look a little bleak. There are absolutely no leads, and her stepfather still insists that he had nothing to do with the mom's murder, or Samantha's disappearance. I don't know. I just can't tell what to make of it."

Cam nodded, then slid his hand out of his pocket just far enough so that he could steal a peek at the time.

"Well, it is unfortunate," Cam said, shaking his head while he spoke. "But I guess all we can do now is hope for the best."

Just beyond the table where the PTA was selling ribbons, John stood silently, helping to dispense the commemorative red and white reminders while watching Cam from a safe distance. He was lurking like a tiger, waiting for an opportunity to get Cam by himself. He watched, in what appeared to be a bottomless darkness lit only by feeble flames that struggled in the night air, as Cam slipped away quietly after Sanders exited.

John moved instantly.

"Hey Cam," he said, surprising him from behind. "How's it going?"

"Okay John," he answered. "How are you?"

"I'm good, I'm good Cam. Just a little surprised to see you here, that's all."

Cam was desperate to leave.

"What is that supposed to mean?" he fired back.

"Hey, you need to relax Cam," he said. "You're the one who told me that things were complicated, and that you could not talk about it. It's not like I'm making this shit up."

The smell of burning wax created a bothersome smell in the cool night air, one that Cam was suddenly unable to tolerate. He rubbed his nose and frowned.

"You know what John, you need to stop bothering me, okay?" he said, tilting his head to one side as if the alteration would somehow drive the point home at last.

"Okay? I have had enough of your shit, good intentioned or not. So please, for the last time, just leave me alone."

Amid the chorus of lamentations for the lost girl, and Cam's belligerent salvo, John's face contorted for a moment, as if he had just been kicked in the shins. He thought about responding, and actually began forming the words on his lips, but never did. He stood silently, watching the myriad figures milling around on the lawn, struggling with the mystery that was locked inside his friend. This need to know was mastering somehow – stronger than anything else he had ever felt. It had become his dominant drive, far more virulent than hunger or sleep. In Cam's eyes he saw something deep and dark. It was calling to him, but he could not answer. He did not know how. All he could do was shake his head, swallow his frustration and walk away, leaving Cam standing by himself in the waning light of the burning candles.

TWENTY-SEVEN

The longer the commotion about Samantha went on the more anxious Cam became. His face, which was dotted here and there with dried specs of blood from his morning shave, told the story of his uneasiness. He was jittery and irritable and felt most often like he would explode if one more thing, regardless of how minute, went wrong.

All that changed, though, the morning he received the envelope he had been waiting for. In just about every possible way imaginable, the atmosphere surrounding him seemed to soften. Things were still far from good, but he was certain, as he held the delivery in his hand, that this was certainly a step in the right direction. He left everything else in his mailbox behind, and rushed to his car to examine the contents of the precious parcel.

The envelope, he noticed, was lighter than he expected; he frowned at the unforeseen disappointment and had begun to really panic as he walked when he realized that perhaps it was just he who was a little lighter, now that the weight of worry had begun to lift. He had hardly closed the car door when he began working the seal, ripping it open with just one hasty tear. It should have been different from that moment on. This was to be his liberation – his ticket to freedom.

He was stunned by the unforeseen calamity. With dark eyes that signified something dim inside his soul, he saw with a more acute anguish than ever before the wicked world to which he was now condemned -- a world with no paths, no light, just shadows and caves. He leaned his head back and exhaled loudly. There were no pictures. The envelope contained only a note, typed on pink Xerox paper.

Sorry. Changed my mind. At first, the idea that nobody had to know seemed reasonable. But the more I thought about it, the more I realized that actually, everybody should know. What you did is pretty fucked up. So, I'm giving you a list of people who I think really ought to know. They are in the order in which I will begin telling them. Hayley, Mr. Sanders, Mr. and Mrs. Dillinger, NYPD, Daily News. I hope you don't mind, but I'm keeping the money. Good luck.

He had felt an array of emotions since the day all of this began: fear, uncertainty, self-loathing and pity, anger, arrogance, hope, and most recently, a twinge of relief. Sitting there, with the paper still in hand, all that remained was despair. Complete and utter hopelessness. There was nothing left. He was out of ideas, bereft of energy, and altogether unable to fight it any longer. He knew he now would do what he should have done long ago.

Hayley came home that evening to find Cam on the sofa, cradling an empty bottle of wine in his lap. His hair was messed, and his eyes were vacant, staring off in the direction of an idle television. His mouth was twisted, and partially open, as if he had just said something, or was about to speak. She noticed instantly his desperate state.

"What is wrong with you Cam?" she asked, moving closer with small, tentative steps.

He turned and acknowledged her slowly, as if waking from a dream.

"We have to talk Hay," he said, with the trepidation of a trapeze artist. "We have to talk. Right now."

She dropped her briefcase on the floor, took off her coat and threw it over the arm of a chair.

He turned to face her as she took a seat beside him; the enormity of his impending announcement hung heavy on the air between them.

"What is going on Cameron?" she asked. "Why do you look so awful?"

"I want to talk about Samantha," he said, rubbing his eyes. "We need to talk about what happened."

"Look Cam, I am still upset too," she said. "I mean, I'm the one who killed her. I'm the one who has to live with that the rest of my life. And every day I wake up, I think to myself that this will be the day that the police find her body, and come knocking on our door."

The muck of despair was spreading through his veins like an advancing illness.

"It's not just that Hay," he said, staring at her with hopeless surrender. "It's me. It's me Hay. I can't. I just can't do it anymore."

"What are you talking about?" she asked.

A prevailing gloom settled upon him.

"I made a bad mistake Hay," he said.

In his head raged a cinematic catastrophe, a montage of grievous scenes ranging from sobbing and hysterics and a complete emotional breakdown to a violent, unhinged protest, one that would render him defeated and powerless. His mind spun in sweeping circles the way it always did when he was buzzed.

"Before I say anything else, I want you to know Hay that I love you. I really love you. I realize that now more than ever."

She arched her back and began to yawn, but checked the impulse when she noticed his twitchy shifting from foot to foot.

"I lied Hay," he said. "I lied to you."

She was as engrossed in his words as she was affected by them, as if somehow, she knew what he was about to tell her.

"What are you talking about Cameron? Lied about what?"

"Samantha," he replied. "She was right. We were together Hay. We were together."

"What are you saying Cam?"

"I – I had sex with her. Just once. I should have told you. I know. But I was scared. I couldn't explain it then. But I need to now. I do. I'm sorry Hay. So sorry."

He sat in the chair next to the loveseat, hands clasped behind his head, waiting for the explosion. She appeared stunned, for nothing immediate passed her lips. He continued to watch as blinding tears filled her eyes, then spilled down her face. He thought she would just fall apart right there in front of him. He reached for her hand, but she swatted it away. Then her crying ceased, and she faced him square, with a more hardened look. The condition of her mind was not easily discernible, and her posture became a curious mix of sorrow and purpose.

"I want you to tell me why," she said with unusual disaffect. "Tell me why."

"What?" he asked.

"Why?" she repeated. "I want to know why you did it."

"I had to Hay," he said.

"You had to?" she asked. "You had to?"

"Yes," he said, lowering his head. He could barely speak the words. "That's the other part I need to tell you."

Cam spent the next hour purging, explaining things even he had not thought of until that very moment. He killed himself over not seeing Samantha's manipulation for what is was, right from the start. He swore to Hayley that he had tried, on several occasions, to put a stop to all the blackmail.

"I should have gone right to the police," he said. "I know that now."

The longer he spoke, the more convoluted his confession became. He sobbed as he recounted his days with Maleigha, and how he had never gotten over her drowning that night. He wanted Hayley to believe that although it was so many years ago, he loved the girl with all his heart. He needed her to believe that a part of him was also lost that night, and that he still did not totally understand it all.

"You told me that that girl moved away?" she asked. "How come you never said anything?"

He shook his head, and admitted that he was always too afraid to tell her the truth.

"I don't know," he explained. "I guess I just thought I was over it, or that if you knew, it would make things weird with us."

It was that same fear, he explained, that made him run from her when they were struggling, a fear that lead him into the arms of young Nikki Dillinger. He begged her to understand, to believe him when he said that he never intended it to get that far. But he lost her the minute he mentioned Nikki's name.

"Oh, this is just great Cameron. This just keeps getting better. So you fucked *two* girls? Two? Is that what you're saying?"

"You don't understand Hay," he said desperately.

"I don't understand," she fired back. I don't-"

"Yes, I was with Nikki. I was. It just sort of happened. I know it was wrong. But I stopped it. Or at least I tried to. You have to believe me. I was all set to tell her it was over when she had that attack. I'm sorry Hay. I had feelings for her. It was all mixed up, with Maleigha, and you, and even Nikki herself. She was hurting. I don't know. I guess I really wanted to help her. It all got mixed up somehow."

Hayley cringed.

"I never meant to-"

"You are a fucking piece of work, you know that?" she said. "Feelings? Is that what you said? You had feelings for her? You are pathetic. You know that? Is that why you left her rotting in a motel room, by herself? Because you had feelings? And then lied about all of it? You came home to me, night after night, and lied about it? Please. There's nothing mixed up here. You wanted to fuck her Cameron, plain and simple. And it blew up on you, and now you hand me all this psycho-babble about being confused, and afraid, and all the other shit you've just spent the last hour dishing out. You are just like all the rest. What am I, some sort of fucking idiot?"

She picked up a picture frame and fired it against the wall. "You are disgusting."

He ran through his mind again the twisted sequence of events, wishing at every turn that he could take any one of them back. All he wanted was for her to try and forgive him. He wanted her to see him – who he really was, and where he wanted to be.

"I know Hay, I know. I understand why you're hurt, and angry. I do. I'm sorry. I am. Please you have to-"

"I have to do what Cam? Listen to you? Understand? Forgive you? Pretend it never happened? Is that what you expect me to do?"

"I don't know what I expect Hayley," he said. "I just want you back. I need you."

Her expression was entirely blank.

"And I needed a man Cam, one who would be honest with me. You have lied to me, for months, involved me in something dirty and illegal, and made an absolute asshole out of me. And for what? A couple of cheap thrills? And after all I have told you about my father, and what I had to watch my mother go through. This is unbelievable."

"It's not that way Hay," he pleaded. "Please listen to me, there's something else I have to tell you."

"You mean that's not everything," she said. "Oh, this is great Cam. What else are you going to tell me? What other little secret have you been keeping from me? Are you already married? Or did you get another one of your students pregnant? Don't hold back now, lay it all on me."

His calves ached. There was a few minutes delay as he stood up and stretched his legs. He was thinking that all his blood had rushed to his brain to support the most egregious endeavor he was now undertaking.

"Somebody else knows," he began in a hoarse whisper. "There are pictures. It's bad."

He spent the next few minutes detailing all of the cryptic text messages, and how he was desperate not to lose her. He barely had enough energy to tell her about the ransom notes, and the trust fund. He was fading, his heart barely beating.

"So not only did you fuck two of your students, and leave one dead and me with no choice but to kill the other, you lost all of our money as well? Is that it? And the whole thing is still not over? Is that what you're telling me Cam?"

What could he say? It was asking a lot of Hayley to just accept all that he had told her. He stood quietly now, just looking at her, trying to keep his desperation in check. He was certain he had lost her, but satisfied that he had beaten the mystery torturer to the punch. He thought about the list, and how Sanders would be next; his days at Hillcrest were surely over as well.

All he could do now was salvage what was left of his dignity, say goodbye on his own terms. It was killing him. He watched Hayley storm off to another part of the apartment, and knew that the deep, dark emptiness into which he was thrust was here to stay, and he could not do a damn thing about it.

TWENTY-EIGHT

Cam sat in his classroom after school, after everyone had gone home, looking out into the courtyard and marveling at the tree just outside his window. He could still remember the day it was planted because it was the same day he was hired. It was all part of a beautification program at the Queens high school. He often joked that he was brought in for the very same reason.

He loved that tree, not just because of its fragrant white and yellow flowers in the spring or its awesome scarlet and burnt orange leaves in the fall. Sure, he liked that too. But he loved that tree for no other reason than its reflective qualities. He often thought that he and that tree would travel together on the same journey. He would watch it grow, and the tree would do the same with him. An awesome way to mark each passing year of his career. Sitting there, staring aimlessly at the once tiny Amur Maple, he could not believe how much bigger it had already become.

When he had sat long enough, he began going through his desk drawers and file cabinets, placing all of his belongings in empty Xerox boxes he borrowed from the copy room. He had amassed quite a proliferation of handouts and lesson plans in just a few short years. He felt odd as he transferred each unit folder from its original resting place into a box. He worked quickly, wanting to finish as much as he could, but every now and again, he stopped, opened up a folder and peeked inside. So much of his time was tied up in these soft manila folders. It was almost like viewing his life in the classroom through a series of mini movie reels, with each folder that he flipped through conjuring images of some of the more memorable moments that had occurred in room 117. There was the great slavery debate during *Huckleberry Finn*, the mock trial he presided over after finishing *To Kill A Mockingbird*, and the launching of the Baldridge Chronicle, a weekly 1920's newspaper that came out regularly during the duration of their reading of *The Great Gatsby*. With each folder he found, another warming reminiscence rose to the surface.

It had been a great three years.

There were other things that he had saved, most of which he had long since forgotten. He found a picture of his very first class, taken in front of the classroom window. He scrutinized each face, smiled as if he had just attended some private reunion, but shook his head when he discovered, much to his displeasure, that he had forgotten the names of more than a few. He was also stunned by the tiny stature of the little maple standing in the background. A look in a different drawer yielded more treasures from the recent past. He chuckled mildly when he came across the deck of famous American author playing cards he had received one year as a Secret Santa gift. Everyone teased him about it, and tried to make him believe that he had been snubbed, until he found the second half of his present and unwrapped it – a bottle of Chivas Regal.

"Okay," he said, holding up both gifts for all to see. "Party at my place."

He laughed even harder at the sight of the little stuffed birthday bear a couple of his students gave him to help him celebrate his special day.

"What in the world is this?" he asked them, laughing.

They were just standing in front of his desk, smiling.

"Squeeze his paw Mr. B.," they told him. "He will sing for you."

It was the most ridiculous, yet somehow touching thing he had ever heard. He turned the bear over and examined it whimsically, remembering the day he had received it. Good times. Then he found the paw and the tiny little patch that said "press here" and he was treated, one again, to a most curious rendition of "Happy Birthday."

One of the last drawers that still needed to be cleaned was the one that sat in the top left corner of his desk. For some reason, it had assumed the role of "junk drawer," which meant it housed everything ranging from staples and extra handouts to a rubber snake, three foam dice, a wooden football peg game and a handful of unopened Halloween candy.

What a mess, he thought to himself and he sifted through the all of the paraphernalia.

He lingered longer than he had planned. The darkening outside his window reminded him just how late the hour had become. Determined to wrap things up, he began taking handfuls of junk from the drawer and just throwing them into the nearest box. He was working frantically now, and once or twice he missed his mark, and wound up having to drop to his hands and knees in order to gather the wayward items. It was during one of these closer inspections that he discovered something he thought he had lost.

It was a white greeting card, whose edges were now dog eared. The front featured three vertical cartoon frames, chronicling the heroic exploits of a tiny red plane with a hook attached to its rear. The top frame showed the little plane streaking toward a large white cloud. In the middle shot, the plane had successfully hooked the cloud, and the bottom image showed the little red plane speeding by, cloud in tow, and the sun shining brightly in its wake. It was the perfect buildup to the pre-printed message inside:

THANKS FOR MAKING MY LIFE A WHOLE LOT BRIGHTER.

He smiled when he read the words, and despite the lengthening hour, stopped what he was doing to read the handwritten ones as well.

Dear Mr. B.,

I decided to get this card so that I could show my appreciation. I could never really thank you enough for everything you have done for me the past two years. You always make sure things are okay with me, no matter how busy you are. It was nice to know that I could count on you and talk to you when I needed to. There aren't many teachers like that. You could always make me laugh when I was having a bad day. Whether it was joking about the Mets or Jets or making fun of all those little things about Hillcrest that we both hate, you always knew just what to say. Little things like that really made it easier to wake up so early for school. I want you to know that you will always have an everlasting effect on me as an English student and as a person. I hope that we can still talk again in the future. Thank you again, so much.

Sincerely,
Derrick Patterson

The card touched him more now than the first time he read it. He recalled fondly the young man who had written it. Derrick

Patterson was a student of Cam's for two years. When Cam first met Derrick, the boy was an awkward, self-conscious, introverted young man with a history of struggling in school. He would rarely do homework, and often zoned out during class discussions. He was bright enough, Cam always thought. But there was just something missing. Cam tried on so many occasions, in such a variety of ways, to engage the boy. When Derrick would come to school with his Met cap, Cam would ask him about the last game the team played, or how he felt about their playoff chances. The conversation never went too far. The Aerosmith concert T-shirt the boy wore from time to time always engendered some talk about how it was that someone his age was into Aerosmith. Derrick mentioned once that it was his Dad's favorite band, and that he had heard a bunch of songs that way. Cam always enjoyed talking about the different songs, and would often push Derrick to share his favorite. The boy was typically reluctant, and the conversation would wane, usually concluding with Cam singing a few verses of either *Amazing* or *Walk This Way*. Derrick never knew what to say, but always smiled. Then he covered his mouth with the back of his hand and just became the same old Derrick again.

It wasn't until the morning of the English Regents that Cam finally broke through to Derrick. The boy had been struggling most of the year to maintain a passing average. Cam had worked with him after school on several different occasions, fine tuning Derrick's reading comprehension skills and essay writing. The boy understood the importance of the exam – if he did not pass, he would fail the course as well, and have to repeat it again in summer school or as a senior the following year. Around fifteen minutes before the exam was to begin, Cam discovered that Derrick was not there. He raced to the office, pulled the student directory and dialed the boy's home. The voice on the other end was weak and fading.

"Hello?"

"Derrick, this is Mr. B. Where are you? The test starts in ten minutes!"

"I'm, I'm not coming today," the boy said, struggling. "I can't."

"What do you mean you're not coming," Cam screamed. "You have to Derrick. You need to take the test."

216

All Cam could hear now was the sound of low, unsteady breathing.

"Derrick, Derrick, are you still there?"

"Something happened, Mr. B.," the boy finally said. "I can't get there. It's alright. It doesn't matter. I'll take the test another time."

A sudden, unexpected click prevented Cam from saying anything else. Despite the unspoken taboo associated with such an action, Cam jumped in his car, and with the boy's address in his hand, went to go try and save the day. As his car sped through town, and eventually down the boy's street, Cam examined each house carefully, looking for the right one. He noticed that there was an interesting mix of large, well-maintained properties and smaller ones which bore the signs of economic struggle. He was uncomfortably aware of the clock, was not really certain where he was going, and almost drove his car right off the road when the sequence of numbers jumped out of order.

"Fuck!" he screamed, pounding the steering wheel. "Where is number three?"

He drove some more, out of his mind with panic, until finally it appeared that the numbers had reset. He thought about rolling the dice and driving further, but another glance at the clock told him he did not have that luxury. He had just begun dialing the boy from his cell phone when he saw a small brick cape surrounded by a rusty chain link fence. He had a hunch he had found what he was looking for. He closed his phone and tossed it on the seat next to him.

As he rolled closer, he could see that the house was in alarming disrepair. The roof was stained and worn and missing several shingles. He could see from the road that the blacktop driveway was faded and cracked, and the front of the place was mostly hidden by bushes that were both overgrown and misshapen.

He sat in his car, looking for something that would corroborate his notion. He was fairly certain that this was the place, but did not want to make an ass out of himself. He thought about driving a little further, and again about calling Derrick, but abandoned both ideas when he finally saw, hanging loosely just to the right of a tarnished brass mailbox, a weather beaten number three.

He stepped across the broken concrete walk. He frowned at the large patches of brown crabgrass on either side, littered with sticks, leaves and an assortment of rusty car and bicycle parts. When he got to the front steps, he paused for a minute, just long enough to rehearse, one last time, what he was going to say. He certainly did not want to upset the kid, or creep him out, but someone had to do something. Someone had to pay attention.

Two pushes of the doorbell, and five knocks later, Derrick came to the door. He was wearing a faded Nike T-shirt and gray sweatpants. His hair was messed and his eyes sat in his head like two sunken pools.

"Mr. B? What are you doing here?"

"I'm here for you Derrick," he answered. "Can I come in?"

The boy turned his head nervously to one side, then to the other. In the bright light spilling into the house from the street, all of his uncertainty was now exposed.

"Uh, yeah," he said. "I guess so."

The house was dark and austere. The two rooms visible to his eye were decorated with the same mahogany paneling and a series of wrought iron shelves that housed a bizarre collection of tiny stone sculptures with peculiar faces. In the living room, where the two of them sat, the coffee table was cluttered with old newspapers and an assortment of other things that did not belong. It made both of them uncomfortable.

"What do you want?" Derrick asked, removing an empty Chinese food container from the table and placing it out of sight on the floor.

The two sat there talking for several minutes. Cam told Derrick how much he wanted him to take the exam. How he was proud of all the work that he had done, and how he really felt like the boy was on the verge of something really great.

"This is your time," he said to him. "You have come so far. And you are ready for this test."

Derrick wanted to smile, and thank his teacher for his kind words, but he had other things to say. His father had been in prison for much of the boy's life. He was in and out of several different correctional facilities for years, mostly for petty crimes. It bothered him more than he ever let anyone know. Then, just before Christmas, he was paroled, and returned home, with the promise that he would straighten himself out for good this time. For months, Derrick and his father spent a lot of time together, listening to music, watching ballgames, and working on the '69 Camaro his father had stored out in the garage. It was great. For the first time in his life, Derrick was beginning to feel like he was just another kid, like everyone else.

"Part of the reason why, aside from you Mr. B., that I was able to do so well this year so far was because of my dad," he explained. "It really helped."

Cam watched curiously as the boy's mood seemed to shift.

"I don't understand Derrick," Cam said. "So what has changed? What is going on?"

Derrick's eyes welled up. Large tears began rolling down the boy's face.

"He was taken away again last night," he said. "I don't know when I'll see him again."

The announcement hit Cam hard. He wanted desperately to say something soothing, even awe-inspiring, but all at once his tongue felt too thick for his mouth. He watched in uncomfortable silence as the boy began to crumble in front of him.

"What about your mom?" he finally managed to ask.

The disquiet prolonged itself interminably.

"She's sick," he said, wiping his face on his shirt sleeve. "She's in and out of the hospital all the time, getting tests and things like that. Something with her blood I think."

With each minute that passed, Cam could see the noose tightening around Derrick's neck. In a short time, the boy would not be able to sit for the exam. Cam struggled with pangs of helplessness, but somehow, he converted his panic into wisdom, and began illustrating all the ways that he could become the master of his fate – ways in which he could feel more in control. Later on, when thought about it, he wasn't sure if it was what he said, how he said it, or just the emotionally charged moment, but somehow, someway, Derrick Patterson picked himself up that morning, got into Cam's car, and scored an 86 on his English exam. Everything changed for Derrick after that day.

Sitting at his desk, with a cluster of boxes on either side of him brimming with papers and mementos that collectively told the story of his life at Hillcrest, he looked out into the courtyard, card in hand, and saw himself, one with his tree, as if he could see the future, and he thought, with more than just casual consideration and a lone tear in his eye, that perhaps there was the answer – that maybe at this point, with all that had happened, there could be no better ending than such a union.

TWENTY-NINE

A steady, painful vibration began somewhere deep inside Cam after Hayley formally called off the wedding the next day. He thought again about the tree, and how he just wanted to die, but felt as though even that was out of his grasp. Could he really bring himself to such an ignominious end? What would everyone say then?

His betrayal of Hayley haunted him, for he knew that she would never get over it. She spent the better part of her morning at work surrounded by a few close friends, typing tearful emails and making all the necessary phone calls.

"Do you want us to help you Hayley?" they asked. "Why don't you let us take of some of this for you?"

She appreciated the gesture, but needed to do it all herself – to restore her former independence and resiliency. These qualities were born long ago, as she listened to her mother suffer at the hands of an abusive ogre. She would sit in her room on the floor, with the lights low, surrounded by her dolls, listening to the horror. These inanimate friends shielded her from the harshness that lived just on the other side of her door, and transported her to other worlds. They were true, and would only play the roles that she assigned them; she was careful to wield her power judiciously. In these worlds she created, she was in charge, and she made certain that things were fair and that nobody got hurt or was forced to cry. Although she was young, and could scarcely attach words to the feeling she had fermenting in her heart, she knew that she would never play the odious part that her mother did.

As time passed, others began to see it as well. In her high school yearbook, she was recognized by her peers as a force to be reckoned with when the entire senior class voted her most likely to change the world. Her strength and resolve only grew stronger with the passage of time, something that she used in college to become president of her sorority. It was the same inner force that had her pursue Cam rather than wait for him, because she saw something that she believed she wanted; it was that same force that prompted her boss to promote her to head of marketing in just two short months with her firm. She could not forgive him. The little girl inside would just not allow it.

"I tried Cam," she told him that morning. "Tried to put it all behind me. Tried to forget. But I just can't."

"What does that mean Hay?" he said, choking back the swell of emotion.

"I can't marry you Cameron. I just can't. Some things are just not forgivable."

While Hayley was busy telling the world that the wedding was off, Cam was busy making an announcement of his own. He had staggered away from his exchange with Hayley the same way a defeated boxer retreats to his corner. He knew it was only a matter of time before his unknown assailant began scrolling down the list of names. He was powerless to stop it, but as he did with Hayley, at least he could be the one who decided when it happened. It was all he had.

"John," he said, closing the door to his mentor's classroom before sitting down at the desk in front of him. "I want to tell you something."

John looked at Cam with eyes that fell just short of him. He knew this day had been coming. He removed his glasses, folded his hands on his desk, and offered himself, as he had so many times before.

"What's going on Cam?" he asked. "I saw the boxes in your room."

Looking at him, John saw many things. A talented young teacher, a good friend, a man with limitless possibilities. He also saw a man who looked like a ghost.

"I want to apologize for the other night. I was out of line. I'm sorry."

John's eyes were warm, his heart forgiving.

"It's okay Cam, he said. "Don't give it another thought."

That was John. Always was. He would miss him the most.

"I'm leaving Hillcrest John," he said. "I'm not coming back. I just didn't want you to hear it from anyone else first."

"Leaving? What for? What is going on Cam?"

"It's far too involved to get into it now John," he said. "Just promise me that you won't believe everything you are probably going to hear."

The two just stared at each other blankly.

"Look, this is crazy Cam," John said. "You don't have to do this. Just talk to me. I can help you. Whatever it is Cam, I can help you."

A sense of self-determination welled up inside the broken man.

"I know you want to help John," Cam said. "I do. But you just don't understand. This is the only way. Don't look so morose. I'm not dying or anything."

John saw the grievous, pained look in Cam's eyes.

"Don't worry," Cam said quickly enough to move the moment along. "It will all work out."

John was again without words. His stomach burned with concern.

"What will you do?" he asked. "What about your career? Where will you go? How will you pay your bills?"

He thought a while before answering. Work was all he had left. His only hope was to get out of there before everything blew up. Even if the talk went around once he left, and the pictures surfaced, there was nothing tying him to any real crime. Sure, it was embarrassing, and perhaps something that would end his career in the classroom, but nothing that a change in vocation and scenery couldn't cure.

"I have a cousin in Scottsdale," he replied. "I think I'm going to take a break from the classroom. Maybe get something in publishing. Something like that."

"And Hayley is okay with this? I mean, this is a little drastic."

Cam licked his lips and sighed. Behind his vague manner was a sort of eerie resignation, looming quietly.

"Hayley will be fine," he said. "Whatever happens, she will be okay."

Cam spent his remaining time at school that afternoon in his room by himself, gathering what was left of his belongings. There were only a few odds and ends left to pack, like picture frames, a set of mini metal balance balls, his Mr. Met bobblehead, and the pewter bust of Shakespeare that sat atop his filing cabinet. The walls still needed to be stripped of his personal effects as well, including the series of Great American Novelists posters he purchased his first year and some of the artwork his students had created for him over the last few semesters. Although these were the last things to go, and by some accounts the least significant, they were the tiny touches that made his room the special place it had always been. Standing at the doorway, he took one last look at his space, the universe which he had ruled so well, stripped now completely of every visible trace that he had once been there. It was an odd sight, one that caused him to consider both his familiar past and secret weavings before closing the door behind him.

THIRTY

With a tear-stained face, and a steady stream of disjointed thoughts and echoing voices, Cam arrived home to an apartment which was dark and noticeably empty. When he flipped the light switch by the front door, he was shocked to see that most of the decorative items throughout their home were gone. For a brief moment, he thought they had been robbed. He considered calling the police until he remembered the state of things with Hayley. Then his heart sank.

In the lull of the battle between fear and disbelief, he walked around the place, making mental notes of all that was missing. *Is this really happening*? he kept asking himself. It did not seem possible, but every inch of the apartment screamed otherwise.

The more he explored, the more dire the emerging circumstance became. Cabinets were bare, shelves were empty, and the contents of most drawers were no longer there. Even the cat was missing. He checked around, visiting all of Othello's usual haunts, but he was nowhere to be found. He had all but given up when he remembered the cat's predilection for closets, especially the ones in their bedroom. He loved nothing more than to curl up under the warm cover of hanging clothes.

When he walked in, Cam was disheartened immediately; both closet doors were already closed. This was not a good sign. Usually, the quirky feline would wait for one of them to leave the door open, then in opportunistic fashion, slip right in and set up for the day. Then one of them would make the discovery, chastise him, and send him scrambling for cover elsewhere. It was not that often that he was already there when the door was shut properly. Still, there was hope. He checked his half first. He jostled the pants and shirts that hung to the floor, but found nothing. He even got on one knee and looked behind the mess of shoes and some of the sweaters that had fallen below, but there was no sign of him. He moved quickly to *her* side, opening up the doors with desperate angst. The sight blew him like a stiff wind against a ship's sail. The vacant bars and shelves assaulted him like nothing had ever done before. It was a vast emptiness matched only by the one housed secretly in his soul. She had taken everything, including the hangers. All that she left behind were a few dry cleaning bags and a note taped to one of the clothes bars.

Cam,

Sorry you had to find out this way, but I can't live here anymore. I thought it would be best if you weren't here when I took the first bunch of things. Believe it or not, this is hard on both of us. I will be back for the rest tomorrow, around dinner time. I want you to be there. I've been doing a lot of thinking. We will talk. See you then.

Hay

The advance of their dissolution was sudden and to his fragile mind unexpected. He took a T-shirt from the pile of laundry on the floor and wiped his forehead and the back of his neck. It was official. He had now destroyed everything that had ever held any meaning for him. The thought was overwhelming. The commotion inside of him was lawless and indescribable, and banged around riotously, stealing his breath until he could no longer remain upright. He crashed to the carpet; then, in a posture resembling one reserved strictly for prayer, he leaned forward and slipped out of consciousness. Moments later he came to and crawled into bed. His sleep was fitful, punctuated by several bouts of crying and restless, almost violent movements, but he did drift off, although most of his slumber was marred by a series of fragmented dreams that left him anxious and sweat soaked.

When he awoke the following day, the sun was bright; it flooded the room so that it appeared much less ominous than the night before. Maybe he still had one last shot with Hayley. He loved her. That had to mean something. And Christ, she loved him once too. Surely he could find a way to make her listen, to see him the way she always had and not as she did now. He clung only to the words that would support his fantasy – *I've been doing a lot of thinking. We will talk.*

He spent the morning looking through his dresser drawers for the picture he had taken of the white sheet with the heartfelt message for Hayley he had tied to the fence above the LIE underpass some years ago. Shit, it worked before. Why not now? He was pleased with the romantic gesture, certain that it was just the thing to help recapture that magic from the past, but his mood soon shifted when he could not locate the photograph. He found everything else but that damn photograph. Old ticket stubs, greeting cards, random keys and a bunch of pencils and pens. No photograph. He continued searching frantically, sifting through piles of assorted junk, until he came upon an envelope that contained some snapshots he had not seen in some time. He flipped through the contents of the envelope rapidly, marveling at how young he looked in all the photos. Confirmation. Freshman baseball. The Junior Prom and high school graduation. He shook his head. He found a few more pictures of friends from grammar school, and a couple of his grandparents' house and Belmont Racetrack. He wanted to linger longer, but after checking his watch he swallowed the urge and continued the search, stopping only when, out from between snapshots of their trip to Montauk, another image cascaded gently to the floor.

He swallowed hard and with sweaty hands, reached down to retrieve it. Maleigha. He had not seen the photograph in years. There she was. Young, beautiful Maleigha. Just as young and beautiful as the last time he saw her. She was standing in the driveway of his parents' house, her legs crossed, head tilted playfully to one side. She was smiling. He smiled now too, and thought that he would lapse, as he always did, into a montage of memories from their past together, but he felt old somehow and uncomfortably removed from that sweet memory he had carried with him all these years. It depressed him. He would have liked to have ruminated long enough to figure it all out, but to his surprise, all he could think about was Hayley, and making things right. It was this feeling that was most prominent when he closed his eyes, sighed, and put his lips to the picture of his young love one last time before crossing into the other room. It was there that he held the photograph over a lit candle and watched, almost hypnotically, as the haunting image melted slowly into nothingness.

He never did find the other photo for Hayley, but he had did not belabor his misfortune. There was much to do. This time, *he* was the one who stopped at A & S Pork Store, to purchase all of *her* favorites. Caesar salad, Sicilian rice balls, vegetable lasagna, and chocolate cannolis. He was also thrilled to have purchased the last bottle of Falling Star at the liquor store, although cursed the absurdity of his luck once again when he discovered that she had taken all the wine glasses. At precisely five thirty, the stage was set. Van Morrison in the background, candles, and fresh flowers created what was truly a welcoming scene. The place was perfect. He had even gone to the trouble of laying out the three photo albums which chronicled the heartwarming course of their lives together, from their first date at Lucky's to their engagement just a short time ago. It was all there, a pictorial history of their courtship; it was quite a compelling case.

He had been so methodical that he actually did not have time to worry; he surprised even himself at how calmly he had executed everything. But then there came a knock on the door twenty minutes later, shocking his heart into unbridled arrhythmia.

His steps were light and deliberate, like one who is negotiating the treacherous face of an icy lake that had just begun to thaw. He was ready, although he remained a curious mixture of fear and uncertainty. Just on the other side of the door was either salvation, a chance to begin anew, or the final blow, the parting shot that would complete his demise.

"Hay, I'm so glad you-"

He hadn't even opened the door halfway before halting his advance.

"Hello Mr. B." The voice was raspy and monotone.

"Melanie? What are you doing here?"

The girl was wearing a long, black wool coat and an expression Cam had never before seen.

"Is it true?" the girl asked.

"Is what true Melanie?" he replied.

She rocked back and forth a little in the doorway, as if weighing the gravity of the situation at hand. Her eyes were glassy, and strained past him to see what was happening inside.

"That you're leaving Hillcrest?"

He was tapping his foot wildly; his eyes were fixed above her shoulder off in the distance, to the place in the street where Hayley always parked her car.

"Look Melanie, I really don't have time for this right now," he said, inching the door closed.

"It's okay. You will be fine."

She hated when he was dismissive. It was the one thing she had grown to hate most about him.

"Nobody has to know, right Mr. B.?"

His face morphed into a quizzical mask.

"What did you say?"

"You heard me," she said, smiling oddly. Then she pushed the door open and slipped inside.

Outside, the sun had slipped below the distant tree line, signaling the approach of night. The street was oddly still. He felt suddenly like he was standing outside himself. The inside of his throat burned, like he had just swallowed a tumbler of whiskey, and his head began to throb.

"What are you doing here Melanie?" he asked again.

She did not answer, but nodded in a manner that suggested he knew very well the answer.

"It's okay." she said. "What I have to say should not take long. If it makes you feel better, nobody will have to know this either."

She circled the floor with curious agitation, disrupting the harmony of the room with her deliberate gait. His mouth grew chalky and the hairs on the back of his shot straight up under the wave of chills that flowed beneath. He watched her, like he was viewing her image through a lens, as she stood still momentarily, evaluating the surroundings and smiling before finally settling on the end of the sofa.

"There are some things you should know," she said, grabbing one of the throw pillows and clutching it against her chest. "You really should have listened."

He sat next to her, driven by a morbid curiosity that seemed to grow with every passing second. She began by telling him about the day in gym class, when she and Nikki had the argument, and Nikki showed her the text he had sent.

"She did *what*?" he asked.

"Don't be mad at her," Melanie said, reading the lines on his forehead. "She suffered enough. I was pretty rough on her."

She went on to explain how she waited outside the Comfort Inn, behind a tree, watching to see if what she had learned was true. She saw Nikki arrive, walk to the office, and return after a short time with a key. He pulled in moments later, carrying a bag. She saw he was nervous, perhaps even contemplating abandoning the plan, but he knocked on the door. Nikki answered, and they both disappeared inside.

"I suppose I should have just gone home," Melanie explained. "But I was so shocked, and bothered by what I had just seen. You know? It really didn't make sense to me. How could you? You were my favorite teacher. I loved you, Mr. B., and never thought that you would do something like that."

He sat numbly, the girl's words echoing in his head like the clashing of cymbals. He was convinced, now more than ever, that nothing in his world would ever make sense again.

Melanie got up for a moment; she walked over to the table he had prepared, lifted one of the candles and brought it back with her. She sat holding it, staring into the flickering flame while she continued to recount the events of that night. She told him how she was just about to leave when to her surprise, the door of the room opened, and she saw him, trying to sneak away. He was shaken, and rattled, so upset that he left without closing the door the entire way. That was when she moved in for a closer look.

"I was so happy that you left when you did," Melanie said. "I figured you guys had had a fight, or that you had come to your senses and realized how wrong what you were doing was. I don't know. I guess I was just looking to rub Nikki's nose in it."

She went on to explain that things changed a little after she opened the door, and saw something she had not expected; Nikki's lifeless body. She was covered to her waist, and her eyes were still open. Melanie described her confusion, how she could not imagine what had happened. She thought at first that Cam had killed her. A lover's quarrel perhaps, or some other contentious exchange. But there were no signs of a struggle, and her body was far too beautiful, far too perfect, to have been the object of any violence. So if it wasn't murder, then what was it? She did not know what to think.

"I just sort of stood there," she explained. "I don't know why. Maybe it's because we fought the last time I saw her. I don't know. But she looked so beautiful, so peaceful, like she was sleeping. And I wanted to do something for her. Maybe you'll think it's creepy, but I picked up her phone – I guess you didn't see it on the floor -- and snapped a few pictures of her. I just did not want her lying there, alone, without anyone paying attention."

As she continued to relay the details of her involvement that night, Cam began to catch a glimpse of the dynamic that had formed shortly thereafter. Now it made sense. All this time he had been fighting not one enemy but two. Melanie and Samantha. The unlikely duo had conspired against him, and continued their torture of him, until of course Samantha was killed. He began beating himself up over how he had not seen any of it before. Shit, it was so obvious now. Watching her, in her moment of twisted glory, he could not fathom how the undeviating course of the calculated plot had escaped him. He stood inanimate, with a quiet sense of defeat, but struggled still with why the two girls, who had nothing at all in common, had joined forces, and were so bent on destroying him.

"Why Melanie?" he asked her. "Why did you give those photos to Sammy?"

She sat up straight, almost at attention, like she had been waiting for him to ask the question. There was a strange luminosity now behind her eyes, as if the thoughts she was formulating would finally throw a light on the dim misery of her past.

"Do you know what it's like to be the outsider?" she asked. "The one who everyone else laughs at? To be the freak, the loser. The misfit. All my life I have been trying to fit in. But it never happened. Do you know what it's like to be the one who is always picked last for things? Or the one who never gets the invitation to the birthday party, or movie theater? It sucks. Just like it sucks to be the smart one, instead of the cheerleader, so that no boys give you a second look. I was tired of it."

His face still wore the mark of confusion.

"I still don't understand Melanie?" he repeated. "Why? Why did you give Sammy the photos?"

He watched as her eyes rolled a little while she summoned a scene from her not so distant past.

"After that night, I felt bad about having been at the motel, and I saw how upset you were. I was still angry with you, but I felt bad. I did. I wanted to help you. That's why I came to you that day, in your classroom. You probably don't remember."

He was recalling with alarming clarity exactly what she was talking about.

"And can you recall what you said to me?" she asked.

He nodded sadly. She was lost now in a wicked amalgam of recollections, of wrongdoings perpetrated against her by many. Somehow, they had all risen up at once, and took the form of the face before her.

"You treated me like some sort of freak. The way everyone treats me. All I'm good for is school work. Right? I'm the bookworm, the nerd, the geek who has no feelings. Right? I couldn't possibly help you, or offer you anything, right? That was a shitty thing to do Mr. B. So, I guess I wanted to hurt you, just like you had hurt me."

He sat, head slumped between his shoulders, as she railed on about the frustration that had commandeered her sensibilities.

"Besides, those photos gave me something that made me cool," she said. "For the first time. I liked it. They made me important. Sammy really wanted them, and I think she even thought I was pretty amazing for having gotten my hands on them. I know that because she was happy to introduce me to some of her friends in exchange for them."

There were still plenty of particulars he wanted answers to, but his mind wandered back to Hayley, and what he had originally planned for the night. He thought that perhaps Melanie being there would help him in his quest to win Hayley back. Once she heard that this twisted, misguided girl was responsible for so much of what occurred, maybe she would see things differently. The more he pondered the idea, the more plausible it seemed. He began probing further, trying to work out in his mind the logistics of things before Hayley arrived.

"So after Sammy was – after she disappeared, *you* took over?" he asked. "*You* are the one who has been torturing me, sending me those crazy notes? It was you? *You* have my money?"

She got up, returned the candle she had been holding to its original place, then fell back into the sofa. She sat now flippantly, lost in a peculiar sort of humor. Her roving eyes touched almost everything in the room, before finally becoming fixed magnetically on his.

Her behavior unnerved him. He motioned to her with his hand to speak the words on her lips, and she was just about to comply with his request when another knock came at the door. The shadow that had fallen across his heart lifted a bit. She was finally there. He could not wait to show Hayley just how it all happened. Surely she would see things differently now. His hand was damp, and slipped as he turned the silver knob on the door. Instantly, his knees buckled, his bowels twisted, and in the deepening twilight that only added to the improbability of the ghost that stood before him, she spoke.

"May I come in please?"

His heart beat now at painful and irregular intervals. The bleak darkness outside the door spilled into the room with hypnotic stealth, leaving him numb, silent. At that very moment, he thought of very little, yet somehow he found his mind tangled in the tendrils of every last detail of his ordeal. Each recollection collided into the next, rendering him weak and spastic, until at last, the heart sickening silence released its grip, and with eyes that were now flat and glassy in the pale moonlight, he finally spoke.

"Sammy?" he whispered. His lips were quivering. "How? How did you – I, I don't understand."

"May I come in please?" she asked again.

She was wearing a purple sweater, and a distinct sense of purpose. Her impatience emerged steadily as she marveled at the incredulity pasted to Cam's face.

"I really can't believe you're gonna just leave me standing out here," she said, taking the initiative to inch her way through the door. "This is no way to treat a dead girl."

Her entrance was one steeped in pure sorcery. With jaw agape and eyes dilated to the size of saucers, he followed her like one who was observing the flight of an apparition, terrified yet curiously charmed. She flitted around a bit, commenting about the apartment and how hurt she was that she had never been invited, and with her eyes burning at the sight of the candlelight and fresh flowers, she made a terribly awkward scene over all the trouble Cam had gone to for Hayley.

"So this is what it looks like when you really care about someone?" she gushed. "You know, I like flowers *too* Mr. B."

When she had seen enough of the room, she joined Melanie on the sofa, and together, they continued to unravel the patchwork of their scheme.

"So, after Melanie came to me with those photos of poor Nikki, I could not stop myself from thinking all these wild thoughts," Samantha began. "I was really into you Mr. B. I needed you, really needed you. More than you bothered to find out."

Samantha confessed that although she had gotten the idea of blackmail from a movie she had seen, her feelings for him were very real. She never had any intention, not at first anyway, of ever hurting him. All she wanted was to experience the thrill of being with her teacher, the way Nikki had. The only trouble was that she soon discovered that once was just not enough. She found her position of power over him to be alluring. It was like a drug, and she was shocked even herself at her dependency. So she did what every addict does – whatever it would take to get the fix.

"I really did not mean anything by all the emails and notes," she explained to him. "I just wanted you. That's all."

There was a brief moment of tenderness in her voice, one that yielded instantly to the emotion pushing from behind. "But then you started acting like a dick. You just kept blowing me off, making me feel cheap and dirty, had no time for me. And guess what – it really pissed me off. That's when I started fucking with Hayley."

Samantha detailed every last episode in the series of her methodical harassment, beginning with the crank calls to Hayley's office and culminating with that final trip to the gym, where she watched and waited for her outside. Although he heard every word she had spoken, and possessed no desire to add to the discourse, he felt compelled to speak.

"Wait, this doesn't make any sense," he said, trying desperately to fit the pieces together. "You attacked Hayley, and she shoved you against the car door. You hit your head, and Hayley dumped your body on the side of the road. She showed me where. The two of us stood there, that night, and looked for you. So I don't understand. What happened? How did you fool her? How are you even here?"

Her wicked laugh caught him off guard. She talked a little more about that night, and how she and Hayley had exchanged words. Then she just stopped. It flashed in his mind what may have occurred after the two scuffled, but he was still at a loss and continued to look at her through a mask of confusion.

"Wow, you still don't get it, do you?" she said, shaking her head.

Minutes later, another knock came. When she entered, his heart began beating again for the first time in days. He wanted to grab her, squeeze her tight and kiss her face and lips. He wanted to break down in her arms, cry on her shoulder and beg her to come back. He wanted to convince her that he was nothing without her. But the longer he looked at her, and she at him, he began to feel as if he were seeing her for the very first time. It had not been that long at all, but already she was not the woman he remembered.

"What's all this?" Hayley said, motioning to the elaborate set up he had intended for her. "Are you entertaining my friends?"

His mood was wavering with the feverishness of a leaf twisting in the wind.

"What is going on here Hay?" he asked.

His eyes darted from one to another; he saw the tacit smugness they shared and became enraged over the looks they exchanged. Then, in the charged silence that ensued, the clouds lifted.

"You're shitting me, right? I can't believe this. This cannot be happening. I can't believe you would do this. You asked them here, didn't you?"

She smiled oddly at him. Her eyes were emotionless.

"Yes Cam," she answered. "Seems that the three of us have a lot in common. We've grown close of late. Become sisters of sorts. Something you would not understand."

The moon shone silver through the window where Hayley stood.

"You treated each of us the same way -- very disrespectfully -- and that has sort of stuck with us. Yup, you were pretty shitty to all of us. You've been bad Cam, and we're all happy to hear that you're leaving. But, we didn't think it would be right to let you leave town without us saying the proper goodbyes."

She wasted no time. Her mood shifted instantly, as though it had suddenly broken loose from some prison deep within. She began her diatribe just the way she had rehearsed, lambasting him for his infidelity with Nikki and for all the lies that followed. She fired one rhetorical question at him after another.

"How long would this have gone on if Nikki had not died?" she screeched. "Or if Melanie here was not so good with a camera?"

She went on to speculate as to how long, if ever, it would had taken him to tell her about what happened at the motel that night if Melanie had not been there, and Samantha had not forced his hand. She demanded to know how much longer he would have left her in harm's way, knowing full well that Samantha was preying on her.

"Did you really think you were going to get away with all of this?" she asked.

He had no answers for her, only questions of his own.

"I don't know what to say Hay," he responded. "I'm sorry. I told you."

He was a little more composed now, drawing strength from a raging anger over the embarrassment he was suffering at the hands of this woman, this charlatan, who had chastised him for lying when she had done the very same, if not worse, to him.

"Yeah, I don't have anything else to say right now, but, I do have some questions for you. I'd like an explanation or two, like what happened that night outside the gym? The truth this time."

Hayley was very detailed in her recollection of that night. She described for him, just as she had done when she arrived home that night, how Samantha had been waiting for her by the gym. Only the exchange they had was not heated; it was more like a therapy session.

"Why have you been following me?" Hayley demanded, after forcing the girl into her car.

"Who are you, and what do you want?"

Samantha was stiff, and sneered at Hayley.

"You don't know me, but I came here tonight to kill you," the girl answered boldly. "To get you out of the way."

Hayley recoiled and looked intently at the girl. She was wearing blue jeans, and a black North Face jacket zipped all the way up to her chin. It seemed a little too warm for such a get-up. It made Hayley even more uneasy.

"Relax," the girl continued, mindful of Hayley's sudden alarm. "I've had some time to think. That's not what I want. I'm not going to hurt you."

The two women sat across from each other, in the vast emptiness between the tired buildings and the rush of people all around, saying nothing, suspended warily in an arrested state of silence. There they were, two sketchy figures scarcely visible in the dim twilight, each measuring the other's intent and resolve. The gap between the two seemed unbridgeable, widening with every second that passed until, in a voice that was both soft and somewhat tremulous, Hayley finally broke the silence.

"Why?" she asked. "Why would you want to kill *me*? What did I do to you?"

"*You* did not do anything," Samantha explained. "It's your future husband who is the issue."

Hayley leaned back, secure in the belief that she was no longer in any danger, and listened to the girl. Samantha explained how she had gotten ready to go out that night, with every intention of hurting Hayley, or at least threatening her. She was at her wits ends over Cam and his refusal to talk to her. The breakup with Bobby did not help either. She had just finished getting ready and was about to leave her house when her mother got in her face, accusing Samantha of being the reason why her stepfather had left them.

"You, you drove him out of the house, you lying little bitch!" she wailed. "You, and your ridiculous stories about him touching you. How could you do this to me!"

Her words smelled of gin, and her anger soon escalated into violence. She began punching Samantha and pulling at her shirt before finally grabbing her by the throat. The girl was stunned at first, but then a wave of unfathomable, untapped bitterness and hatred found the light, and all at once, she was crazed. In her mind was Bill's intrusive touch, and foul breath, and her mother's denial. She punched back wildly at first, with most of her advances missing their mark, but then remembered the surprise for Hayley that was resting in her pocket. She was swift and forceful. The tiny silver blade caught the lamplight just as Samantha pulled it from its cover; then she plunged it deep inside her mother's chest. The woman gasped and let go of her daughter instantly. Her eyes dimmed. She held up her hands in protest, but Samantha stabbed her again, and again, and again, each time more furious than the last, stopping only when the body crumpled over the back of the couch and onto the floor. As she continued to relay her tale to

Hayley, Samantha began to wilt a bit. Her voice was now small and fading, and her eyes filled with tears.

"I didn't mean to kill her," she said, the tears now streaming down her face. "It's been so long. I just wanted all of it to stop."

Hayley's head grew heavy as she listened to the young girl spill her pain. Something about her anguish, the dysfunction of her house, spoke to her. The two continued their discourse in Hayley's SUV, where, in the closeness of the car's cabin, Samantha went on to chronicle what happened next. After the bloody battle with her mother, she was desperate to leave the house for good; she placed her soiled clothes in a bag, showered, grabbed some odds and ends and a coat, and was off into the night. She headed toward the gym, with hatred still raging in her heart. She stopped only once, to dump the incriminating bag down the sewer. Then she waited for Hayley.

She explained to Hayley again how at first she thought about killing her as well, but then thoughts of a better way of destroying the man she now hated filled her head.

"I still don't understand," Hayley interrupted. "You said that you hate Cam. I get that. But I still don't really know why."

Samantha shook her head and laughed. She went into her pocket and took out a piece of peppermint gum.

"Remember the girl, Nikki Dillinger? The one they found dead a while back?"

"Yes," Hayley answered. "The overdose in the motel room?"

Samantha nodded. She pinched her gum wrapper into a little ball and flicked it out the window.

"Well, I found out who was with Nikki that night. And after I did, I couldn't help but think how fun it would be to have a little adventure of my own."

Hayley's thoughts began to spread out like a fan.

"Are you telling me that-"

"Yes," she answered. "He was the one with Nikki."

Cam just sat with his head in his hands, as Hayley continued to unfold what had transpired between the two of them outside the gym.

"After she told me about Nikki," Hayley said, "she informed me about what happened with her. I didn't believe her at first. But she showed me everything. Told me everything. You took advantage as well, just like her mother and stepfather, instead of being an adult about everything. I felt sorry for her, so I gave her some money, and told her to just go. But not before I took her number."

Samantha got a room at a motel, and Hayley went home. She turned over in her head all that she had learned. She was sickened at the sight of Cam. All she could do was contemplate the best way to proceed. She called Samantha the next day, and the two met again. Samantha told her even more this time, again crying about how she did not mean to kill her mother, but that she was not sorry either.

"It's okay Samantha," Hayley said, comforting her. "Sometimes, it's the only way. I knew someone like your mom once. Sure, my mom threw him out, and we moved on, but he was always still there. My one regret was that I didn't just kill him. It's the only way you are ever rid of someone like that."

Samantha confessed that she was scared about what would happen to her. She also mentioned Cam, and how she hated him for what he had done to Nikki, and then to her. Hayley's rage only grew. Hayley, Samantha, and Melanie talked a lot over the course of the next few weeks, mostly about what they should do. Each had her own reasons for wanting to see him suffer. At first, Hayley wanted to just get him. Go right after the bastard and make him pay. But the more she thought about all that he had done, the more elaborate her plan became. She decided that she would take everything she could away from him. Slowly. His money, his career, and then finally, his peace of mind.

"So you see Cameron," she continued to explain, "after Samantha told me all of it, I did a lot of thinking. Afterwards, I knew we had to help each other. There were people, and not just you, who deserved to be punished. And I have to say, it worked out perfect. Neglectful mother dead, pedophile in prison, and now you, a lying, cheating, immoral backstabber reduced to a whining mess, running from your own lies and deceit."

He could not stop shaking his head.

"So you two never fought?" he asked. "There was never any body? You just played me the entire time, didn't you? That night by the parkway? The house you tried to buy? The romantic dinner. And all the time you knew exactly what you were doing. I can't believe you. You fucking manipulative bitch. How could you-"

"How could I what Cam? Lie? How could I pretend to be somebody else? Is that what you were going to say?"

He appeared to be bathing now in his own treachery. He could not believe that it had come to this, and wondered silently if they had ever really loved each other at all.

"Okay, enough of this shit," he said. "What's done is done, you psychotic bitch. But I want my fucking money Hayley," he said, his face stained by an unnatural color.

She suddenly felt beyond all of it, like everything was almost just as it should be. The feeling spread to the others. They all felt like the righting of this one wrong was somehow, in some small way, making up for all of the other injustices that each of them had faced their whole lives.

"You obviously have not been listening," she said. "The money is most definitely part of this. You're a lying piece of shit Cameron. Just like every guy. And you deserve everything you are about to get. Besides, I don't think it's even possible now to give it all back. I already spent some of it. Necessities. You know, new cell phone, hotel room for Samantha while the police were busy tracking down her mother's killer. Melanie here is in line for a makeover. Oh yeah, and I forgot to tell you. I will be moving to San Francisco. I got a transfer. A little extra cash in my pocket will really come in handy now."

Cam tightened his jaw and became feverish and wholly combative, like he suddenly had been thrown into a ring.

"So this is it, huh? he said, mockingly. "This is your big plot of revenge. Take my money, force me to leave my job, and then come here and tell me all about it. That's it? Please. You're not so bad Hay. I think I can live with that."

Hayley managed to squeeze out a smile. "No Cameron, that's not all," she said, motioning to Melanie. "I thought it was. I had every intention of just leaving you to wallow in your mess. But then I decided that would be too good for you. So, we have one last thing to share."

She waved to Melanie, who reached into a white plastic bag and pulled out a shiny black object. Then she smiled and handed it to Hayley.

When he first saw the gun, he could not help but laugh. Just to see her hold it was absurd. He knew that she would never have the guts to use it.

"Oh, I see now," he said, laughing even louder. "You're going to shoot me, is that it? Go to jail, the three of you, just for the pleasure of seeing me dead? Is that it?"

Hayley thought for a second how she and the two girls would look standing in front of a graying, wrinkled, red-faced judge. The vision was fleeting.

"Nobody's going to jail Cameron," she said, releasing the safety on the weapon. "Since when is self-defense a crime?"

"Self-defense? This isn't self-defense," he answered. "You have set this whole fucking thing up."

"Well, I don't know about that Cameron," she said. This is *your* gun. You purchased it with *your* credit card -- remember? And it will, in just a few moments, have *your* prints All over it. And with your secret lover here and another witness to your crazed outburst after I came home and caught the two of you, and threatened to expose you for what you have done, I can't see how anybody would argue that. I mean, the way you threatened to kill all of us. Yep. It all appears to be very neat and tidy."

"Fuck that. You know why the gun was purchased and I never threatened any of you. Fucking lies Hay – all of it. Who's going to believe that shit?"

"True," she said, shrugging her shoulders ever so slightly. "That is true. All lies. But the wonderful thing about it is that nobody has to know."

She raised her eyebrows, smiled, and pointed the .38 directly at his chest.

"Nobody's going to jail Cameron," she went on smiling, "because nobody *ever* has to know."

The flash was bright, and the noise loud. The three women winced, and grabbed at their ears, protesting against the buzzing that remained within. They watched, almost hypnotically, as a

241

swell of blood emerged from beneath the folds of his shirt and bloomed like a liquid rose. It was a peculiar moment, terrifying yet oddly exhilarating. As the twisted spiral of smoke continued to drift up from the gun's barrel, filling the air with the redolence of triumph and despair, each remained speechless, weighing with a modicum of difficulty the fruits of their efforts.

They each took short, accelerated breaths, struggling with the mysterious and incalculable reality before them, and stood ruddy and ragged under sweaty clothes until the dust of illusion began to settle. Then, in the artificial light coming from the frosted street lamps just outside the window, with the buzzing now detaching itself slowly, all three looked to the floor at the crimson pool, and began talking with toneless deliberation about the quiet truth that now bound them together forever.